EVAN'S GATE

A cozy Welsh village mystery

RHYS BOWEN

Constable Evan Evans Book 8

JOFFE BOOKS

Revised edition 2022
Joffe Books, London
www.joffebooks.com

First published by St Martin's Minotaur Books in 2004

This paperback edition was first published
in Great Britain in 2022

Cover art by Dee Dee Book Covers

ISBN: 978-1-80405-589-2

NOTE TO THE READER

Please note this book is set in the 1990s in Wales, a time before smartphones, and when social attitudes were very different.

PROLOGUE

The small girl moved over the springy turf of the mountainside, her light feet making so little impression on the grass beneath her that she appeared to be weightless, a bright spirit only barely connected to solid earth. Her long, blonde hair floated out behind her in the wind, and she hummed to herself as she climbed higher and higher.

At last she reached the high meadow with the world spread out at her feet and stood for a moment, catching her breath, looking around in anticipation. Then she gasped. There it was, exactly as she had pictured it. She gave a small squeak of delight and ran to meet her destiny.

CHAPTER 1

Suzanne Bosley-Thomas sat in her car, staring out at the bleak landscape. Snow had dusted the peaks of the Snowdon Horseshoe, and leaden clouds were heavy with the promise of more snow to come. *Bloody Wales*, she thought. *It's supposed to be the middle of bloody May and instead it's like the middle of bloody winter.*

"God, I hate it here," she said out loud to herself. "I wish I'd never come."

You don't have to go in, a voice whispered inside her head. You could start the engine and drive straight home. Nobody would ever know that you'd been here. The thought was so appealing that her hand strayed toward the car key. Then she snatched the key from its slot, dropped it into her purse, and zipped her anorak right up to her chin. She couldn't risk not going in, not being part of this whole farce. There was too much at stake.

The wind was so strong that it almost snatched the car door out of her hand as she opened it. It took her breath away and made her eyes water as she hurried across the car park toward the Everest Inn hotel. As she got her first good look at it, she started in surprise and wondered briefly whether she was hallucinating. The Everest Inn resembled a giant Swiss chalet, complete with carved wooden balconies and pots of geraniums, so different from the plain grey stone houses in the villages she had passed. The snow-dusted mountains behind it added to the Swiss fantasy.

"Surreal," she muttered. Surreal was a good word to describe how she was feeling at this moment. At the etched-glass front doors she hesitated again. Last chance, the voice in her head repeated. Back to the car, down the pass to the A55, and then only an hour before you're back in England.

She took a deep breath, pushed her hair out of her face, and stepped inside. Warmth and soft music greeted her. The hotel foyer was a large, cavernous area with a stone fireplace taking up most of one wall. Her gaze swept over the brass and polished wood reception counter, the broad, carpeted staircase. No expense spared here. Then she froze as she saw them. That group of three men seated at the round coffee table near the fire — it was them, wasn't it? Yes, she recognized her brother, Henry. He looked just like her father at the same age. In fact the resemblance was so remarkable that she shivered and glanced back at the front doors. It was raining now, a mixture of sleet and rain peppering the glass.

"Can I help you, madam?" the girl at the reception desk asked at the same moment that one of the men at the table looked up and said, "There she is now." He got to his feet. "Suzie!" he exclaimed, coming to meet her. "It has to be Suzie. You haven't changed one bit. God, your hands are freezing. Come over by the fire."

"Bloody Wales," she said, laughing in embarrassment as he took her hand. "It wasn't always this cold, was it?"

"We were always here in August and I don't think it snows in August, even in Wales. Come and get warm. We've a fresh pot of tea and would you like something to eat?"

"Tea would be lovely, thank you." She perched at the edge of the leather armchair he had pulled out for her. "And forgive me if I sound very rude, but I'm not sure which one you are."

The man laughed. He had the sort of attractive face usually seen in cologne commercials, with white, even teeth, a great tan, dark hair curling over his collar, cut just a little too long to be socially acceptable. He was wearing a designer sweater, knitted in vertical lines. Suzanne had seen one in a fashion magazine and knew they were horribly expensive.

"I'm your long-lost cousin Val, dearest," he said. "You'd make a rotten detective, old girl. You must know your brother, which makes only two of us to choose from, and one is a priest."

Suzanne blushed as she glanced at the third man and saw that he was, indeed, wearing a dog collar.

"I'm sorry," she said, as the third man rose to his feet also. "So you must be cousin Nick, then. I didn't realize you'd become a priest."

"Well, we haven't exactly stayed in touch, have we?" Nick extended his hand to her. He had a pleasant, open face, with a shy, boyish smile. "How nice to see you again, Suzanne."

"All I heard from Mummy was that you'd gone to Canada years ago."

"That's right," he said, and now she detected the Canadian accent. "I went to Toronto the moment I got out of university. I moved to Montreal a couple of years later and I decided to study for the priesthood. I've been a priest for about five years now."

"God knows this family needed someone holy," Val said, and laughed again.

Suzanne's eyes had gone to her brother, who had said nothing so far. He was not smiling. Now that she had a chance to study his face, she was horrified at how old he looked. He couldn't be more than thirty-seven or so, but his appearance was distinctly middle aged. His hair was greying at the sides, as their father's had done, and deep frown lines were etched into his forehead. He caught her staring at him and nodded gravely.

"Hello, Suzie. Good to see you again. How has life been treating you?"

"Can't complain, Henry."

"Still working for whatshisname?"

"Yes, I'm still with whathisname."

"What is his name then?" Val asked. "Why all the secrecy?"

"No reason at all. I seem to remember Henry always pretended he couldn't remember the name of any of my friends." *As if by not giving them a name he had proved that they didn't matter*, she thought.

"I know he's that archaeologist chappy, but I really can't remember his name. Sorry," Henry said. "Wrote those books about Tunisia, didn't he?"

"Toby Handwell. Sir Toby Handwell these days."

"Still married, is he?" Henry asked, leaning forward to pick up his teacup.

"Why, do you fancy him?"

The other two men laughed, and she realized with a rush of pleasure that she had thrown her brother off balance. He wasn't going to find her such an easy target as he remembered.

"Here, have your tea before it gets cold." Nick handed her the cup. "Milk and sugar?"

"No sugar, thank you. Bad for the waistline."

"I shouldn't think you'd have to worry about that," Val said. "You look terrific. Still like the teenager I remembered. Unlike old Henry here, who looks as if he's got the cares of the world on his shoulders."

"My law practice is quite demanding, you know," Henry said, "and I seem to have acquired the running of the family affairs since Dad abdicated the position. Grandfather's estate and the properties here have proved most complicated."

"He's made his will then, has he?" Suzanne tried to sound only mildly interested. "Is this what it's about?"

"His will was made years ago. Very straightforward. I get Maes Gwyn. Everything else is to be sold and you get equal shares."

"Exactly how much more is there, beside the farm, I mean?" Val asked. "I have no idea at all how much Grandfather is worth. To look at him, you'd think he didn't have two pennies to rub together. Does he still wear that awful cloth cap?"

"Absolutely." Henry laughed. "Look, I shouldn't really be telling you this. The old man's not dead yet, and he's not going to die for some time by the look of him."

"You've seen him, then?" Nick asked.

"Yes, I'm staying at the farm."

"You are? Then how come he didn't invite us?" Suzanne demanded.

"I invited myself. If I'm going to inherit one day, I felt that I needed to get acquainted with the running of it."

"Does he still farm it, at his age?" Nick asked.

"He's got a manager, but he gets about surprisingly well," Henry said. "Of course he lost most of his sheep in the foot-and-mouth epidemic, but he's enthusiastic about restocking."

"You're not seriously thinking of living at Maes Gwyn someday, are you?" Suzanne asked, staring at her brother.

"Grandfather doesn't want it sold, and it's a good property. I may want to take early retirement from the law and playing at country squire sounds like a nice notion."

"But could you do that, after what happened?" Nick asked. "I know I had to think long and hard about coming back here at all, just for this visit."

"So did I," Suzanne confessed. "I almost turned around and drove straight back home."

"Oh, come on you two. It happened so long ago," Val said. "It was awful, but there's nothing we can do about it now. It doesn't make sense to dwell on the past so much that you can't get on with the present. If Henry wants to live at Maes Gwyn, I say good luck to him."

"It's probably a moot point anyway. By the time Grandfather dies, I'll be walking around with one of those Zimmer frames myself," Henry said, and this time he attempted a dry laugh that came out more like a cough. "You wait until you see him. You'd never believe he was turning eighty."

"So that's what we're here for, is it?' Suzanne persisted. "He really wants a big eightieth birthday party?"

"So I'm to understand," Henry said. "We're having a marquee, and the whole thing's being catered."

"God — a marquee. It will probably collapse under the weight of the snow," Val said with a chuckle.

"So where are the rest of you staying?" Suzanne asked.

"Right here," Val said. "Seemed convenient and comfortable."

"But isn't it — awfully expensive?" Suzanne glanced around.

"Costs an arm and two legs, but hey, what the hell? You only live once and you'd not catch me staying in one of those dreary bed-and-breakfasts. So where are you staying, Suzie?"

"In one of those dreary bed-and-breakfasts," she said. "And you, Nick?"

"I'm sure Nick's found some spartan monastery to give him shelter," Val said, with a smirk at his brother.

"As a matter of fact I'm staying here too," Nick said, his face lighting up with that boyish grin again.

"Good God. Then they must pay the clergy in Canada more than they do in England."

"I live very frugally for the rest of the year." Nick blushed. "I see no reason why I shouldn't enjoy myself when I travel."

"Following the example of all those Borgia popes, no doubt," Henry said dryly. "And they didn't exactly stint on the Vatican, did they?"

"Built for the glory of God, Henry," Nick said. "You wouldn't want to stint on Him, would you?"

"If he exists, Nick." Henry reached forward and filled his empty teacup again. "Which I very much doubt. More tea for you, Suzie?"

"Please. I hadn't realized how cold I was. This place is so delightfully warm, isn't it?" She took the cup of hot liquid and cradled it with her hands. "So who's coming to this bash? Not Father?"

"Oh yes. He'll be here."

"With his current wife?"

"No wife, current or otherwise, since I'm sure Mother's not coming."

"Wild horses wouldn't drag her here; I think those were her words. And what about your wife, Henry?"

"Not coming either. She thought this should be an occasion just for family members, seeing that it might be a bit awkward. Camilla runs from anything awkward."

"No significant others then," Val said. "Just the four of us again. How cosy. You're not married at the moment, I take it, Suzie?"

She tried to stop herself from turning red, but didn't succeed. "No, Val. I haven't been married for the past sixteen years. Not since Carl and I split up."

"And the kid? There was a kid, wasn't there?"

"Charlie? He's in the army."

"What on earth made him go into the army? What a ridiculous idea," Henry said.

"No money for university," Suzanne said, looking directly at her brother. "Options are limited when there's no money, and he's keen on mechanical things."

Nick leaned forward in his seat. "You have a son in the army? I had no idea. Has it been that long?"

"She was very young when she had him, remember," Henry said, and this time there was a hint of a smile on his lips.

"No children of your own yet, Henry?" Suzanne responded. "You'd better get busy. It would be sad if there was no one to inherit all that lovely property."

She saw him wince as if she'd struck him. *I've scored a point*, she thought, pleased with herself.

"I notice that Val wants to know about everyone else but divulges nothing of his own personal life," Nick said, with a quizzical look at his brother. "Isn't it about time you got hitched, Val, old man? You won't be young and lovely for ever, you know."

"All the more reason to make the most of it while I can," Val said easily. "Shall we dine here tonight? I gather they have a fine wine cellar and I, for one, don't feel like braving the elements to find anywhere better."

"I'm not sure whether . . ." Suzanne began when Val patted her knee.

"It's on me, of course," he said.

"Good idea," Nick said. "It is something of a celebration, after all. The first time we're all together since — since we were kids. That's definitely worth celebrating. In fact let's order a bottle of bubbly right now." He waved for a hovering waiter.

Suzanne watched him with interest. Not exactly the humble priest, the way they were in England, riding around on bicycles and living on donated food. And Val wasn't exactly the starving artist, either. How come the rest of her family had done so well when she was still living in an upstairs flat in Clapham? How come they all seemed so at ease? They were debating the merits of the champagne list now, animated for the first time. Had they forgotten all about Sarah? *Why are we here*? she wanted to shout.

CHAPTER 2

The wind hit the two men full in the face as they reached the bluff halfway up the mountainside. One of them, a skinny fellow wearing a plastic poncho over his business clothes, was panting heavily.

"Quite a climb, isn't it, Mr Evans?" he managed between gasps. "Can't think why you'd want to live up here." He looked with distaste at the shell of an old cottage, now reduced to four stone walls with gaping holes where the front door and windows used to be.

"Ah, but look at the view, Mr Pilcher." Evan Evans turned his back on the cottage and surveyed the horizon of snow-clad peaks. "And you should see it at sunset. Quite spectacular on a fine day."

"You'll change your mind when you have to traipse up here with the groceries after the Saturday shop," the first man said, grinning.

"You forget, I'm used to it." Evan Evans smiled. He was younger, broader, fitter than the other man, with unruly dark hair and healthy, boyish good looks that women seemed to find attractive. He was clad in a navy jersey and corduroy trousers and seemed oblivious to the misty rain. "I was born and bred around here. We have mountains in our blood."

"Rather you than me, mate." Mr Pilcher pulled up the hood of his poncho.

"You're not from these parts, then?" Evan asked, although he could tell the man wasn't from the accent and from the fact that they were speaking to each other in English.

"I'm from Lancashire, mate. I was working in the Lake District National Park until I was transferred here. It's not too bad because I can still nip home to the parents at week-ends, but they're a funny lot the Welsh. Take some getting used to, don't they?"

Since he was clearly a Welshman himself, Evan thought this wasn't exactly a tactful remark, but he had come to the conclusion that National Parks personnel found politeness to be an unnecessary part of their job. He had to humour this pen-pusher or he wouldn't get anywhere.

"So it looks hopeful this time, does it?" he asked. "Planning permission's finally going to be granted? I've been waiting to hear for a year now."

"In theory, yes." Mr Pilcher sucked through his teeth. "Of course you'll have to have the listed buildings bloke take a look at it."

"Listed building? This?" Evan stared incredulously at the tumbledown ruin. "It was an old shepherd's cottage before some English people gentrified it."

"Ah, but look at those walls, lad," Mr Pilcher said. He made his way gingerly across to the cottage and gave a half-hearted kick at the stonework. "Look at the thickness. Look at the mortar they used. These have to be pre-eighteen-hundred, maybe even pre-seventeen-hundred, which would make it automatically listed. And who knows about the foundation? It may have been built on the original foundation of a hill fort."

"A hill fort?" This was becoming more ridiculous by the minute. Evan had had several encounters with the National Parks Authority now, and each time he'd ended up feeling that he'd stepped into a twilight zone of bureaucracy.

"Look, it's just a bloody shepherd's cottage, and all I want to do is put a roof on it again and live in it," he said.

"Hold your horses, mate," Mr Pilcher said. "I understand your frustration, but these things can't be rushed. It's up to us to make sure that the integrity of the National Park is preserved."

"I don't want to add a pagoda or a swimming pool or even put plastic flamingos around it." Evan could feel his temperature rising. "I just want to make it liveable again, the way it always was. Now what is so complicated about that?"

"Look, lad, I can turn you down flat if I've a mind to," Mr Pilcher said. "The Parks Authority is all for reducing the number of residences within the park."

Evan had been staring past him as he spoke, trying to stay calm. His gaze followed the road up the pass, through the village of Llanfair, nestled directly below them, and then on until — he locked onto the Everest Inn.

"Hang about," he said. "What about the hotel down there? It was only built five years ago. How come they got permission? Don't tell me that Swiss chalets were once part of the Welsh landscape."

"Ah well." Mr Pilcher cleared his throat. "From what I understand they made a generous donation to the CAE — the area development fund."

"If I'd known bribery would work, I'd have tried it last year, rather than waiting patiently to go through all these planning committees," Evan said. "I was joking," he added quickly.

One quick glance at the man revealed that he obviously had no sense of humour or not one that matched Evan's. Maybe a good chuckle when he had to turn down someone's application, but irony would be beyond him.

"Look, mate," Evan tried another tack, "I'm getting married this summer. She's set her heart on moving in here right after the honeymoon, and you know what women are like when they've made up their minds about something. This isn't Caernarfon Castle, is it? It's a little cottage that can't even be seen from the road, and all I want to do is fix up the roof and move in. Is that too difficult? If you do your inspection today and approve it in principle, then the listed buildings bloke takes his little look, and I can start work. I'm planning to do most of it myself, you know. And hiring out the skilled labour to local firms — boosting the economy, isn't that what your development fund is supposed to be doing?"

Mr Pilcher had begun a circumnavigation of the cottage. During the two years that it had lain desolate, brambles had sprung up in what used to be a garden and Mr Pilcher moved cautiously, stepping through the vegetation with distaste. "Nothing much to see at the moment," he said. "You submitted plans, did you?"

"In the file you're carrying."

"Oh. Right. Let's take a look then." He opened the file. "Oh, dear me no. That won't do."

"What?"

"You'll not be allowed a Calor Gas cylinder up here."

"The last people had one."

"Different planning board in those days. No more gas cylinders, unless you'd want to bury it. Eyesores, aren't they? We have to think of the integrity of the landscape and the tourists. They want to see adorable shepherds' cottages, not unsightly gas cylinders."

"Then how do you propose I heat the place?" Evan demanded. "Trek up to the high bogs and cut myself peat?"

"You could have a buried oil tank and oil-fired central heating. Why don't you get yourself an oil-fired Aga?"

"An Aga? They're bloody expensive."

"But they solve the cooking and heating problems in one go, don't they? And resurrecting a listed building is going to be expensive. You could always change your mind and apply for a nice council house, mate. They give priority to local police, don't they?"

Evan wondered how Mr Pilcher had managed to last this long on the job. Surely he must have stirred up equally violent thoughts in other applicants? He sensed that the bastard was goading him, waiting for Evan to lose his cool, so that he had an excuse to turn down the project. Evan wasn't going to let that happen.

"All right. We'll think about the heating alternatives," he said. "What else needs to be done? The place was already on mains water — we'd just have to get it reconnected. And there's a septic tank in place."

"That would need to be reinspected — the sewage line and the tank itself. You'd need a plumber to certify its integrity."

Obviously integrity was Pilcher's favourite word at the moment. Evan wondered if he had been given one of those New-Word-a-Day calendars for Christmas. "Right." Evan nodded. "That should be no problem. Now, how do we set about getting the inspector of listed buildings up here?"

Before Mr Pilcher could answer, a loud beep came from Evan's hip. He took out his pager. "Damn," he muttered. "I'm afraid I've got to get down to a phone. It's my boss. Feel free to look around as much as you want to up here, although as I've said there's nothing to see. Four walls and a floor. That's about it. Thanks for taking the time to come up here."

"We'll need your septic tank inspection certificate and your heating proposal before we can proceed any further," Mr Pilcher said.

"Right you are. I'll get both to you within the next few days. I want to make the most of any summer weather that we get, don't I?"

"Could be like this all summer," Pilcher said with a dry chuckle. "I understand it does nothing but rain in bloody Wales."

Evan had already started down the steep track.

"You want to get yourself a nice council house, mate," Pilcher shouted after him.

* * *

"Where the devil have you been?" Detective Inspector Watkins's voice boomed down the phone line. "I called you fifteen minutes ago."

"Ten," Evan said, "and I was up on the mountain. It took me awhile to get down."

"I tried your mobile phone number first. Why didn't you have it on you?"

"Sorry, Sarge — I mean Inspector," Evan said. "I suppose I'm not used to carrying it around yet."

"Then you'd better get used to it, pronto. You have a police-issued mobile so that we can get in touch with you at all times, Evans. At all times — do I make myself clear?"

"You're in a lovely mood this morning, sir," Evan said. "And it is my day off."

"You're in the plainclothes division now, boyo. There's no such thing as days off. You work when there's work to be done. And there's work to be done right now. Do you know the caravan park at Black Rock Sands, just outside Porthmadog?"

"I think so."

"Then get yourself down here as fast as possible. I'll meet you at the entrance. It should take you what — half an hour?"

"Twenty minutes if I break the speed limit," Evan said and hung up.

* * *

It was closer to half an hour by the time Evan slowed to a halt beside the gate that led to the caravan park at Black Rock Sands. Porthmadog had been clogged with traffic and pedestrians, all of whom had emerged at the same moment to do their shopping the moment the rain stopped. There were patches of blue in the sky now, and steam rose from the wet surface of the narrow road as Evan left the sleepy coastal village of Borth-y-Gest behind. After Borth the landscape became wilder with green meadows leading to sand dunes and a windswept stretch of beach on one side and the heather-clad slopes of Moel-y-Gest on the other, rising to a rocky summit that dominated the landscape. As Evan got out of the car, the sun shone through a break in the clouds, turning the whole landscape into glorious Technicolor. The sweet smell of hawthorn flowers and sea tang greeted him, along with the cries of seagulls overhead. He stood, breathing deeply and enjoying the sun on his face, looking up with satisfaction at Moel-y-Gest, rising on the other side of the road. It had been the first mountain he had climbed as a small boy, and he still remembered the triumph and the sense of wonder as he surveyed the scene below him.

Then he turned his eyes away, shoved his hands in his pockets, and headed for the wooden gate. A sign outside said, HOLIDAY HAVEN. ON-SITE CARAVANS FOR RENT. TENTS WELCOME. HOT SHOWERS.

On the other side of the hedge, he saw two white police vans parked. He spotted DI Watkins's familiar fawn raincoat. The inspector was leaning against one of the vans, consulting his notes.

"See, I told you thirty minutes, didn't I?" Watkins looked up and grinned as Evan approached.

"The traffic was horrible in Porthmadog. Sorry."

"Yeah. And I'm sorry too. I shouldn't have bawled you out like that on the phone. This job gets to me sometimes."

Evan thought Watkins looked tired and drawn. If that was what promotion did to you, maybe he should stay a constable for the rest of his career.

"So what have we got here?" Evan asked. He fell into step beside the inspector as they walked across a broad expanse of meadow around which there were rows of caravans, ranging from impressive mobile homes to little two-wheelers that could be towed behind the family car.

"Missing child. Little girl, five years old. Staying in one of the caravans. Last seen on the beach this morning."

"Isn't that a job for the uniform branch? I seem to remember that a large part of my job up in Llanfair was finding lost kiddies."

"The uniform branch have been searching all morning," Watkins said, striding out with purpose over the short grass, "and we're here because the mother suspects foul play."

CHAPTER 3

A thin woman with bleached blonde hair was leaning against a white caravan, smoking a cigarette and staring out toward the ocean. She looked up as she heard them approaching and hastily stubbed out the cigarette under her heel. She was wearing jeans and a black imitation leather jacket tied tightly at the waist. She had a pale, pinched face, made paler by the blackness of the jacket, and her eyes darted nervously.

"Mrs Sholokhov?" Watkins asked. He pronounced it cautiously, as Show-lock-off.

"Yeah? What do you want?"

"We're from the North Wales Police," Watkins began.

She grabbed at his sleeve, her eyes wild with fear. "Have you found her? Oh God, tell me she's all right. Tell me it's not bad news."

Watkins prized her hand from his sleeve and patted it. "No, it's not bad news. We haven't found her yet—"

"Then what the hell are you doing back here again, worrying me?" she shouted. "You should be out there looking for her before it's too late." She spoke with a North of England accent, clipping the consonants and broadening the vowels.

"Hang on a minute," DI Watkins raised his hand to calm her. "Our men are still out there looking. We're doing everything we can to find her quickly, so just calm down."

"Sorry," she said, pushing her straggly blonde hair back from her face, "but I'm going nearly out of my mind with worry."

"I'm sure she'll turn up safe and sound," Evan said. "They nearly always do, you know."

"I 'ope so." She was staring past them, out toward the sand dunes and the beach. Evan had now defined the accent as coming from east of the Pennines — Yorkshire not Lancashire.

"We're from the plainclothes division," Watkins said. "I'm Detective Inspector Watkins and this is Detective Constable Evans."

Evan still got a rush of excitement when he heard those words. They had been so long in coming he had begun to believe he'd be stuck in the Llanfair subpolice station forever. But he had finally finished his training course and been assigned to shadow his old friend DI Watkins, much to his satisfaction.

"We came because we were given to understand that you thought someone might have taken your daughter."

"I don't know how she could have disappeared so sudden otherwise." Her voice rose again. "I mean one minute she were there, next she were gone."

"Is this where you're staying?" Watkins asked, glancing up at the small caravan with peeling white paint. "Your van? Did you tow it here behind the car?"

"Not likely," she said. "Bloody dump, isn't it? But I wanted Ashley to get some sea air to strengthen her up again." She put her hand to her mouth to stifle a sob. "Bloody stupid of me. Always doing the wrong thing."

"Has your daughter been ill?" Evan asked gently.

"Didn't they tell you? She's had major heart surgery."

"No. We haven't been told anything much," Watkins said. "Can we come inside and you can fill us in?"

"Right-o." She opened the door and went up the steps ahead of them. The interior of the van was cramped with a pull-down table taking up most of the available space and the bed serving as the seat on the far side of it. Big enough for a woman and a little girl, maybe, but not for two large policemen. Evan stood at the doorway and waited to see where DI Watkins would position himself. Watkins motioned Mrs Sholokhov to the bed/bench on the far side and perched on a foldout chair. Evan continued to stand and took out his notebook.

"Now, why don't you tell us what happened?" Watkins said.

"It were all so sudden," the woman said. "The sun came out this morning so I took Ashley down to the beach for some fresh air. I'm trying to build her up again after being in hospital so long. She were playing nicely on the sand, so I just popped back to the van for a fag. She weren't even out of my sight for thirty seconds. I went into the van, grabbed the pack of cigarettes, and then I glanced out of this window at the beach and I couldn't see her. I ran back down to the beach and there was no sign of her. As I were running back through the dunes, I thought I heard a car engine start and take off. I ran back to the vans, but there was no sign of a car either."

"Then what did you do?" Watkins asked.

"What did I do? What the hell do you think I did? I ran around like a crazy thing, yelling her name, knocking on caravan doors, stopping anybody I met and asking if they'd seen her."

"When you left her on the beach this morning, was there anyone nearby?"

"The beach was almost empty," she said. "There was a man walking his little white dog. I've seen him several times. Ashley liked the dog, even though she's not supposed to get near pets on account of her allergies. Then there were a couple of boys throwing stones into the waves, but they were a good way off and there was someone fishing way down toward whatever that place is called — Criccieth. Oh, and an old couple walked past a few minutes before I left her, but that were about all, I think."

"And what about on the caravan site? Did you find many people?"

"It's almost empty at this time of year, isn't it? There's a couple of hippie types who live here year-round. One is an artist — or at least he calls himself an artist. He makes sculptures out of old junk. The site owner has warned him to clear them up. Bloody eyesore, that's what they are. He were outside, working, but he said he hadn't seen anybody. There was a foreign couple — German, I think, in the big yellow van at the end, and then the site owner was in her office. None of them had seen anything."

"What about heard anything?" Evan asked, wondering as soon as he'd spoken whether he was supposed to be butting in.

"Like what? Screams or something?" she asked.

"I meant the car engine you said you'd heard. None of them saw or heard a car go past?"

"I don't know if I asked about that. I was half out of my mind with worry. I probably didn't even make sense."

"Then you called the police?" Watkins asked.

"The park owner called for me. I have to say they got here really quickly, and they were very nice. A policewoman stayed with me and asked me questions while the men went door to door and searched the beach."

Watkins consulted his notes. "And came up with nothing."

She nodded. "It's like she was snatched from the sky. It just doesn't seem real."

"How old is your little girl, exactly, Mrs Sholokhov?" Evan asked.

"Just turned five."

"Has she ever hidden from you for fun?" Evan went on. "I know I used to do that when I was little — scared the daylights out of my mother a couple of times."

Watkins glanced up at him. "She wouldn't keep hiding for three hours, Evans."

"Not intentionally, but I was wondering if maybe she ran off and then got lost or fell asleep among the dunes or got caught on brambles under a hedge or even got caught under a caravan — there's all sorts of possibilities."

"Our men worked over the caravan park pretty well," Watkins said, "and I believe the dog units are still out, going along the dunes. But if you say you only left her for thirty seconds, she couldn't have run far in that time, could she? Five-year-old kids don't have very long legs."

"And she were quite happily playing on the sand when I left her, or I'd never have gone."

Watkins got to his feet. "Let's go down and take a look at the exact spot, shall we, Mrs Sholokhov?" he said.

"It all looks the same," she said angrily. "There's nothing to see, only bloody sand."

They climbed down the rickety steps and took the path through the dunes to the long expanse of flat, sandy beach. It was now completely deserted, although Evan could make out a chequered police cap further along the dunes. He stared up and down the beach. No waves to speak of, just a gentle lapping as the tide came in. Certainly nothing big enough to sweep a child out to sea.

Watkins must have been echoing his thoughts. "Was the tide further in this morning? Would she have gone near the waves, do you think?"

She shook her head vehemently. "She were scared of the water. Always was a timid little thing, and she's become much more clingy since her operation."

She picked her way in high heels across the soft sand until they reached the firmer, wet sand. "Round about here she were playing, I think."

"What happened to her sand toys?" Evan asked suddenly.

"What do you mean?" she asked.

"Did she leave them on the beach? Were they just lying there?"

"She didn't bring any toys down with her," Mrs Sholokhov said.

"What? No bucket and spade? What kiddy goes to the beach without a bucket and spade?"

"She didn't go for digging much," she said. "She liked to run around and pick up shells and seaweed and pretend she was a mermaid. Very into pretending our Ashley is. Always being a princess or a magic horse or something."

Evan's eyes scanned the beach, trying to see where a child might have started a collection of shells or played with seaweed.

"You don't remember what shells she was playing with?" he asked.

"How do I know one bloody shell from another?" she snapped.

Evan gave her a reassuring smile. "I was just thinking that if she had shells in her hand or her pocket and somebody grabbed her, they might have fallen somewhere."

Mrs Sholokhov put her hand to her mouth. "Oh, my God. You do believe she's been kidnapped then."

Watkins gave Evan a warning frown.

"Of course not," Evan said quickly. "There's usually a very ordinary explanation in these cases. Kiddies go missing all the time and turn up safe and sound."

"We'll do another search of the whole area, Mrs Sholokhov," Watkins said. "I'm going to see if we can bring in a bloodhound and maybe his nose can pick up a scent better than our police dogs. And in the meantime, do you have a picture of Ashley you can show us?"

"Of course," she said. "What mother doesn't carry pictures of her daughter around with her?"

She led them back to the caravan, opened her purse, and took out several snapshots. They showed a sweet little child with elfin features and long, blonde hair.

"She's lovely," Evan said. "Pretty little thing."

Mrs Sholokhov pressed her lips together and nodded. Then she mastered herself. "Everyone used to stop us when she went out in her pram," she said. "They used to say she was like a little doll. Of course, I used to have hair that colour once. Now it has to come out of a bottle." Her laugh turned into a smoker's cough.

"Can we take the pictures with us for now?" Watkins asked. "I'd like to have them ready to send out on the internet — just in case." He put the pictures into the folder he was carrying then glanced up at Evan. "Evans, why don't you do the tour of the caravan park. See if anyone noticed anything out of the ordinary, like vehicles coming and going this morning."

Evan nodded. "Right you are, sir."

"And I'm going to talk to the uniformed boys again. I want reinforcements brought in from Caernarfon and from Bangor if necessary. And I want a WPC to keep Mrs Sholokhov company again." He looked at her with compassion. "You don't want to be on your own at a time like this, love. Do you have anybody in the area?"

"Nobody at all. I'm Yorkshire born and bred. I'm living in Leeds at the moment. I just brought Ashley here because I wanted her to get some good sea air, and the Yorkshire coast is too bloody cold. Not that this is any warmer, but my neighbour at home said that she always comes to Wales and how lovely it is, so I took her advice. Last time I do that, stupid cow. It's been bloody freezing all week. I've hardly been able to let Ashley out and then when I do . . ." She put her hand to her mouth again. "What am I going to do if we don't find her?"

Inspector Watkins put a hand on her shoulder. "We will. You'll see."

"What about your husband, Mrs Sholokhov?" Evan asked. "Is he at home? Have you told him yet?"

"Ex-husband," she corrected. "We've been separated about a year now."

Evan noticed Watkins's quick glance. "And where is he now?"

"I've no idea. If he did what he said he was going to do, he's back in Russia by now — and good riddance, that's what I say."

"Your husband is Russian?"

"With a name like Sholokhov what did you think he was, bloody Welsh?"

"Is he a Russian national?"

"Do you mean does he have a British passport?" she said. "Not when he left me, he didn't. He was granted asylum, but he didn't like it here. He wanted to go home."

"Mrs Sholokhov," Evan said gently.

She looked up at him. "Call me Shirley. I can't stand that name. Bloody mouthful isn't it?"

"Shirley, then," Evan went on. "You don't suspect that your husband has anything to do with this, do you?"

"He'd never do anything to hurt Ashley," she said. "He adored Ashley."

"Adored her enough to want to take her to Russia with him?" Watkins asked.

She stared out past them, and Evan could tell that this thought had crossed her mind before, however hard she had tried to suppress it. "I don't want to think that," she said. "I can't believe he'd put her through something like this. He knows she's been ill. He knows she needs me."

"You got sole custody, I take it?" Watkins asked. "Did he have visitation rights?"

"Of course they gave me custody. I'm her mother, aren't I? And we haven't seen him in a while, so we thought he'd gone back to Russia."

"How long?" Watkins asked.

She sucked in air through her teeth. "Several months now it's been that we haven't heard a peep out of him. Of course, we've moved around a bit since then—"

Again Evan saw Inspector Watkins give him the briefest of glances.

"I'll want full particulars on him, Mrs Sholokhov. A photo too, if you've got one. I have to treat this as a missing child case at the moment, but I'm going to stick my neck out and have all the ports of exit notified — just in case he decides to skip the country in a hurry with her."

"All right." She nodded.

"You've thought this all along, haven't you?" Evan said quietly. "You didn't want to think it, but you have."

She nodded again. "I've been living in fear that he might come back and get her."

"So why didn't you tell the first policemen that came around this morning? They could have put out the word and maybe stopped him before he left the area."

"I thought I was just panicking over nothing," she said. "I'm not usually the type that gets het up. I stayed calm all the time Ashley had her operation. Tower of strength, that's what people called me, and now I'm going to pieces because—" She pressed her hands to her mouth again, but this time she couldn't stifle the sobs.

"It's not too late," Watkins said. "If he has got her, he can't have left the country yet. Now you make yourself a nice cup of tea, and I'll have a policewoman up here to keep you company in a jiffy. All right?"

She nodded mechanically again.

"And in the meantime, why don't you write down all the details about your husband —his last address, what kind of car he drives . . ."

"Car he drives? Last time I saw him he didn't even own a car. You don't need one in London, do you, and we lived in Shepherd's Bush."

"So you've no idea what kind of car we should be looking for?"

"I just told you — we never owned one. If he wanted to get his hands on a car, I'm sure he could have borrowed one from his Russian mates. Proper little clique, they were."

"If you have any phone numbers for any of his friends, you might want to give us those too," Watkins said. "You don't happen to have a photo of him in your wallet, do you?"

"Not bloody likely. I've no wish to remind myself about him, thank you."

"So the marriage didn't end amicably then?"

"I wouldn't say that. Let's just say we recognized it was a mistake for both of us. He didn't want to stay in Britain, and I had no desire to go to Russia. Pretty hopeless, really, except I got Ashley out of it."

"Right then. You put down anything you can think of that might help us, and I'll be back." He headed for the door. "We'll let you know as soon as we hear anything at all. At least you know that he loves her, so she's not likely to come to harm. That's a good thing, isn't it?"

"I hope so," she said.

"We'll send round the WPC to stay with you," Watkins said. "Do you have someone you could call to be with you in case this goes on a bit?"

She shook her head. "I've got a couple of mates in Leeds, but no real family anymore — just the one aunt in Yorkshire, and she's too old to travel. I'll be all right. I'm used to being on my own."

Watkins pushed open the caravan door and stepped down onto the grass with Evan close behind him.

"So what do you think?" he asked.

Evan stared toward the beach. The sun had come out fully now, and there were a couple of boys flying a kite and a man walking a little white dog.

"Sounds to me as if it could be the father," Evan said. "But why didn't she tell us that sooner, especially since she thought she heard the sound of a car driving off?"

"I know. I get the feeling that she's the kind of woman who doesn't want to look a fool. She prided herself on being the tower of strength, didn't she?"

"Yes, but where her child was concerned, who'd worry about whether they looked a fool or not?"

"I know," Watkins said. "I'd run naked down the street if I thought someone had taken our Tiffany."

"I'd like to see that," Evan commented, and got a smile from Watkins.

"In a way I hope it is the father," Watkins said. "Better than other alternatives."

"I'd like to take another look at the beach," Evan said. "It was strange how there was nothing to show where she had been, wasn't it? I remember when I was a kid — I'd always build forts and ditches and collect odd things, but there was nothing."

"The actual spot could be underwater by now. The tide's coming in."

"I know, but you'd think there might have been some signs of a scuffle if someone had snatched her, wouldn't you?"

"Not if it was her dad. She might have gone willingly with him."

"But he'd still have had to run to have cleared that beach before Mrs Show-whatsit came back. I didn't see any big, heavy footprints, did you?"

"I'm not an expert on sand," Watkins said. "That stuff was pretty wet. I'd imagine footprints wouldn't last long on the wet stuff and don't make any impression at all on the softer sand."

"So you still want me to do a thorough search of the caravan park?" Evan asked.

"Yes, we'd better cover all bases. Find out who was here and what they might have seen or heard. Oh, and check around and under the vans too — any bins or outbuildings."

"Right."

Watkins got out his mobile phone. "I'm getting on the blower to HQ so that they can notify the ports right away. Pity she didn't know what kind of car he'd be driving. That's going to make it tough. And I'd better have the search widened around here too. We'll have our lads question people along the road to Criccieth and Borth-y-Gest. Someone might just have spotted a little girl in a passing car, especially if she didn't want to be in it. She can't just have disappeared, Evans. Somebody somewhere must have seen her."

CHAPTER 4

Henry Bosley-Thomas came out of the back door of the farmhouse and stood on the flagstone path, looking around him. The house was a solid square building of grey stone with white-trimmed windows, set amid lush meadows on the valley floor. In Henry's memory the meadows had been full of sheep. Now they stood empty, apart from a small group of new lambs in a paddock near the house. Foot-and-mouth disease had all but wiped out the Welsh flocks — the Ministry of Agriculture extermination process had seen to that. Not that it concerned Henry too much. He'd always been a town boy, living in comfortable suburbia until he went to boarding school, and farm animals were just something picturesque to be observed from car windows. But he could see that his grandfather had been very cut up about it. He'd talked a lot about it the previous night, after they'd downed half a bottle of Glenfiddich together. This farm was his grandfather's life —always had been.

Henry had been brought up to despise his grandfather. "Don't say that Grandpa is a farmer, for goodness' sake" — his parents' voices echoed through his head — "say that he's a country squire, if you like. Say he has a manor house in Wales, which he does, but not that he's a sheep farmer."

Both of old Tomos's sons were ashamed of him, which was ironic when it was the prosperity of the sheep farm that had paid for their expensive educations. At public school they erased any trace of a Welsh accent and never mentioned family. Henry's own father, Hugh, even hyphenated his last name to hint at a more distinguished ancestry. And they had raised their children with the same attitude. There had always been the yearly visit, which had been fun because of the cousins and the freedom, but his grandfather had always seemed a cold, remote figure, more interested in his farm than his grandchildren, never going in for hugs or games. Even when the tragedy had struck, he had shown no emotion, muttering something about sheep needing his attention and then stomping off in the direction of the hillside. It occurred to Henry that perhaps his grandfather had cared too much and didn't want to let himself down by showing his feelings.

Henry realized also that this was probably a family trait. They hadn't seen each other in — how many years was it now? All had gone their separate ways, all keeping to their own private grief and suspicions and fears. And now Grandpa had brought them back — issued a summons that couldn't be refused.

Henry stood and scanned that hillside now. He remembered it full of dark blue uniforms, the barking of dogs, flashlights bobbing around in the dark. All that sitting and waiting — the empty, scared feeling and a throat so tight that food could not be swallowed. Even as he thought this, that same gnawing fear returned to eat at his stomach. He'd been suffering from ulcers recently, which he'd put down to job stress, but he remembered that the stomach pains had started long before he'd held any job.

"This is ridiculous," he muttered to himself and deliberately set off over the stile and up the hillside track.

* * *

Evan left DI Watkins and was making for the nearest caravan when he glanced down at the beach again. That beach was worrying him. Maybe the mother had got the wrong spot. It would be easy enough, if she was in a panic. He decided to take one more look for himself. He couldn't believe that Ashley had vanished without leaving one single clue, even if it was only a couple of shells or a mound of seaweed. As he made his way back through the dunes, he saw the man with the little white dog and remembered that Mrs Sholokhov had mentioned seeing him earlier. She'd also mentioned that Ashley was fond of the dog. It wouldn't do any harm to question the man.

Before he could go in pursuit, however, the man spotted him, and came toward him.

"Are you with the police?" he asked, panting slightly with the exertion of walking over the soft sand. He was a genial-looking elderly man with the red face of one who enjoys his Scotch, dressed for the country in tweed jacket and tweedy trilby hat over white hair.

"Detective Constable Evans, sir."

"Have they found her yet?" he asked. The voice was not Welsh, but it had the flat vowels of the south of England. "I heard that the little girl had gone missing."

"Not yet, but we've got lots of people looking for her."

"I hope they find her. Nice little thing." He smiled. "I chatted with her a few times. Her mother said she'd been ill. She loved Trixie and she wanted to play with her, and her mother said it was okay in the open air."

"Her mother said you were on the beach earlier this morning around the time Ashley vanished," Evan said. "I wonder if you saw or heard anything unusual?"

"It wasn't me." The man shook his head vehemently. "This is my first time on the beach today. It was raining earlier and Trixie hates getting wet feet, so we stayed indoors until things had dried out a bit."

"You weren't on the beach at all this morning?"

"No, it couldn't have been me she saw. Like I said, Trixie doesn't like wet feet, do you, my love?"

The dog looked up with a silly grin and wagged her tail.

"Oh, I see. Well, that's a pity," Evan said. "We were hoping to find someone who might have seen Ashley."

"I don't imagine there would have been many people out on the beach this morning — it was blowing a gale out here. You should have seen the flag on my flagpole flapping. And this part of the coast is always quite deserted until the school holidays in August."

"You live here year-round, do you, sir?"

The man shook his head. "No, I live in Essex. I come here occasionally to get away. I'm retired now so I can do pretty much what I like. I've rented one of the holiday bungalows about a mile down the road." He looked back in the direction he had come and noticed two policemen crossing the dunes. "Look, if there's anything I can do to help find her — anything at all — I'd be more than willing to be part of a search party. Trixie's not a bloodhound but I'm sure she'd be willing to do her part too, wouldn't you, old girl?"

The white dog wagged her stump of a tail. The old man raised his hat politely and went on his way, leaving Evan surveying the empty beach. He wandered around a few minutes longer but saw nothing but a long strand of seaweed, high above the waterline, that could have been trailed and then dropped there by a child, but how long ago he couldn't say.

He stared back at the tops of the caravans, poking over the dunes, and shook his head. If someone had kidnapped Ashley, where had he hidden to watch for the moment when Shirley Sholokhov left her alone? The dunes were only gentle curves of sand and grasses here, none of them big enough to hide a man. How could Shirley not have noticed someone darting out across the beach as she made for the van? He tried an experiment, setting his stopwatch then running from the dunes to the water's edge and back again. It took over a minute, and that was without the time necessary to grab a child. Could Shirley have been wrong about the amount of time she took? Evan wondered if she had not told the exact truth to them because she was feeling guilty. Maybe she had paused at the caravan to light that cigarette and take a few puffs before heading down to the beach again. Maybe she hadn't looked through the van window at all to notice that Ashley had gone. Satisfied that this made more sense, Evan stomped back through the dunes toward the caravans.

He started with the closest caravans, knocking on doors and then searching around them thoroughly. Most were still locked and uninhabited, with curtains drawn and dustbins empty. He stepped over gas cylinders that formed boundaries between each of the vans. The National Parks bloke had been right, he had to concede. They were a bloody eyesore. He wondered when he'd get time to do anything more about his cottage. He should get in touch with the listed buildings inspector right away and find a plumber to certify the sewage line and the septic tank. He decided that it would be sensible to cut costs by clearing the line to the tank himself. No sense in paying someone else to do the digging. If he ever got a day off, that would be the first thing he'd tackle.

Evan glanced at his watch. Three o'clock. That meant school would be over for the day. Bronwen knew he was meeting with the National Parks inspector today. She'd be waiting to hear the results. He took out his mobile phone and dialled her number.

"Finally," she said, when she heard his voice. "I thought you might have stopped by at lunchtime to give me the news. I've been on the edge of my seat all afternoon. I found it so hard to concentrate that I said 'Very good' to Alud Davies when he told me that Peru was a football player. So what did the inspector say?"

"Still more hurdles ahead, I'm afraid, but not insurmountable ones. But listen, *cariad*, I can't talk now. I was called out on a case while we were up at the cottage. I'm down near Porthmadog. Little girl's gone missing."

"Oh, dear. Wandered off or what?"

"Not sure yet. Could be a case of abduction. It's all rather strange and rather vague. I'll tell you later. I just wanted to warn you in case I'm not back until late this evening."

"All right. I'll see you when I see you then, and you can give me all the news. Take care of yourself."

Evan smiled as he pressed the off button. That was what he liked about Bronwen — never a fuss, always understanding. She was going to make a great policeman's wife. He reacted as the words passed through his brain. It was still rather amazing to him that anybody was about to become his wife, that he was about to settle down with one woman for the rest of his life. At times he still went through momentary panic at the thought. But on the whole he couldn't think of anything he wanted more than to spend the rest of his life with Bronwen. He shoved the phone back in its holder and went back to his task.

CHAPTER 5

Evan had just taken the lid off a dustbin and was peering inside when a hand grabbed his shoulder.

"All right then. Let's take a look at you!" a voice said in his ear.

Evan spun to defend himself and found himself staring at Constable Roberts. The latter's face fell when he saw whom he had nabbed.

"Oh, it's only you, Evans. I thought I'd got him. Suspicious-looking character and all that." Then a grin spread across his face. "They've got you on dustbin patrol then, is it?"

Evan was only too aware that Roberts had never liked him and always been jealous of him, even more so now that he had made the plainclothes squad.

"You never know where a little kid could decide to hide, do you?" he answered evenly. "And I've just checked all this area, so there's nothing much more for you to do around here. Especially not when they've got dog teams out who've got better noses." And he gave Roberts a friendly grin.

He felt decidedly better as Roberts stomped off.

To reach the next caravan he had to climb over piles of rusty pipes and dustbin lids.

There was music coming from this one — *Worker's Playtime* on the radio, by the sound of it. He tapped on the door, then rapped louder. The door was flung open by a big fellow wearing a spattered undershirt and torn jeans.

"Yeah, what do you want?" he demanded aggressively.

"North Wales Police, sir," Evan said. "Just asking a few questions about a missing child."

"I already spoke to one of your blokes and to the kid's mother," he said, about to close the door in Evan's face.

"Well, I'm sorry to trouble you again, but I'd just like to go over what you told them," Evan said. "I'm Detective Constable Evans and you are?"

"Richard Gwynne," he said.

Evan remembered what Shirley Sholokhov had said about aged hippies. Richard Gwynne must have been in his forties or fifties and wore his grey hair tied back in a long ponytail. He had tattoos on both massive forearms and a peace symbol on a leather thong around his neck.

"You live here year-round, do you?" Evan asked.

"Have done for the past couple of years, but I may be moving on if that old cow won't let me do my artwork anymore."

"What kind of artwork do you do?" Evan asked, although he glanced back at the pile of rusty pipes and remembered what Shirley Sholokhov had said about the junk sculptures.

"I combine art with recycling," Gwynne said. "Too much stuff goes into landfills, doesn't it? I rescue it and turn it into art. I've got pieces displayed at all the major art galleries, you know."

Evan tried to picture mounds of rusty pipes lying next to Rembrandts at the National Gallery. "Good for you," he said.

"Yeah. I'm making quite a name for myself," the man went on, "only the park owner doesn't have an eye for modern art. She had the nerve to call it an eyesore. Told me I'd be evicted if I left my sculptures outside. So I imagine I'll be looking for a new place to park myself. Pity, because this suits me well. Quiet most of the year and close enough to home so that I can visit my old mum from time to time."

Evan was surprised that he was the type who visited his old mum and thought more highly of him. "She lives nearby, does she?"

"In the council estate just outside Caernarfon."

"Oh, right." Evan nodded. "So you're a local?"

Gwynne laughed. "Don't sound so surprised. Locals are supposed to go to chapel and work in slate mines, is it? I've done my share of working for a wage, boyo. Fifteen years with the bloody County Council. One day I said sod it. I'm not wasting another second of my life, so I chucked it in and came here. Paradise — or would be if that old cow would quit nagging."

"I won't keep you long, Mr Gwynne. I just wanted to ask you a couple of questions about this morning. You heard that the little girl disappeared about eleven o'clock. I wondered if there was anything you saw or heard about that time that might help us in any way."

"So they still haven't found her then?" He frowned. "Nice little thing, wasn't she? She came to watch me work a couple of times. Of course, I had to be careful, on account that I use a blowtorch, but she seemed fascinated. And she recognized that the figure I was making was a soldier, which is more than most people have done."

"I take it you have to work outside if you're using a blowtorch?"

"Oh yes. The whole thing would go up in smoke if I tried working in there — and if it did, the old cow would kill me."

"So were you working outside this morning?"

Gwynne scratched his stomach. "Only a short while. It rained, you see, until about half past ten, and the wind was bad too. The sand blows up when there's a wind, and it makes using a blowtorch impossible."

"So you came outside to work after half past ten. Did you see anyone around?"

"That foreign couple in the end van — she was hanging out some washing, and he was cleaning hiking boots."

"What about the little girl? Did you see her go to the beach with her mother?"

"No, I can't say I noticed her this morning, but I was concentrating on getting as much work done as possible."

"You didn't notice any strange men? Foreign looking?"

"What kind of foreign?"

"Russian."

The man laughed. "I've no idea what a Russian looks like, apart from athletes and ballerinas and Gorbachev and Yeltsin." Then the smile faded. "In answer to your question, like I told your bloke before, I didn't see or hear anything out of the ordinary."

"No car engines starting up?"

"Ah well, I wouldn't have noticed that — unless there was something odd about the engine."

"But you didn't see a car drive past?"

"I think the German couple went past at some stage. They've got one of those Volkswagen Beetles — looks like a big kid's toy, doesn't it?"

"No other vehicles?"

He thought, then shook his head. "Not that I can remember. It's usually pretty quiet around here, which is why I like it. I don't recall anything much until the mother came running up, screaming like a madwoman."

"What time was that, would you say?"

"After eleven, that's all I can tell you."

Evan held out his hand. "Thanks for your help and sorry to have troubled you."

"If you want any help looking for the little girl, I'll be glad to volunteer," he said. "They'll be sending out search parties, won't they? They haven't searched the mountain yet."

"Thank you, Mr Gwynne. I'll bear that in mind," Evan said.

The second man today to have volunteered to look for the little girl — she must have made quite an impression during the short time she'd stayed here. Evan worked down the line of caravans until he came to the yellow van at the end of the row. The line of washing was still flapping outside. Before he could rap on the door, it opened and a young man came out. He was tall and lean, with close-cropped hair like a European football player, and he wore cords and big hiking boots. He was carrying sleeping bags.

"Good afternoon, sir," Evan said, stepping out to block him. "I'm from the North Wales Police. Do you mind answering a couple of questions?"

"More questions?" the young man demanded. "We are supposed to be on holiday here, and all they do is hound us." He spoke with a strong German accent, but his English was grammatically correct.

"I'm sure nobody is hounding you, sir. You've been bothered today because a little girl has vanished from this caravan park and we're just hoping that somebody here saw or heard something that could help us with our inquiries."

"I told your man before that we saw and heard nothing. Now please, I need to put these things into the car." He tried to pass Evan.

Evan focused on the sleeping bags. "Are you leaving, sir?"

"Ya. My girlfriend does not like it here anymore. She does not feel safe."

Evan looked at the line of washing, flapping in the strong wind, and sensed this was a recent decision.

"Is she inside the caravan? I'd like to talk to both of you," he said.

"She does not speak good English like I do," the man said.

"All the same, you can translate for me if necessary," Evan insisted. When the man opened his mouth to protest, Evan went on. "A little girl is missing, sir. Don't you want to do everything you can to help us find her before it's too late?"

The man shrugged. "I suppose so." He dumped the sleeping bags on a picnic table, then opened the van door. "Marlis, *komm 'raus*," he called. A lean and fit-looking girl came to the door and looked down at Evan suspiciously.

"I'm sorry to trouble you again," Evan said. "I'm a detective constable, North Wales Police. You've heard about this missing girl, haven't you? Do you know the little girl we're looking for? Did you ever see her?"

The young woman glanced at her boyfriend, then nodded. "Ya. We see her. But not today. This morning we go for a short climb up that mountain."

"What time was that?"

She shrugged. "Maybe after ten o'clock? And we are returning maybe twelve o'clock? We go into the town to have a cup of coffee."

"But the English do not know how to make coffee," the man said. "We order coffee and we get instant coffee made with milk. Pah!"

Evan was not forming a favourable picture of the couple. "We're not English here, we're Welsh, sir," he couldn't help pointing out.

"When it comes to making coffee, there is no difference," the German said.

Evan tried to keep the pleasant expression on his face. "So you left the caravan site around ten. Were you back when the girl's mother was running around in a panic?"

"Oh yes. She came here, making a big fuss," the German said.

"Then you were back before noon. That would have been around eleven-thirty."

The man shrugged again. "Very well, if you say so. When we are on holiday, we don't observe the time so much."

Evan got the feeling that they couldn't care less about the missing child. She was an inconvenience.

"So you've decided to head out today, have you? Where would you be going?"

"We don't know yet. Maybe up to Scotland."

"How long do you plan to stay in the country?"

"Another week, maybe two. It depends on how we like it and how much it rains." He glanced at his girlfriend, who nodded agreement.

"We think this is springtime, no? But it is more like winter. Look at that snow! We can't believe this."

"You never know in Wales," Evan said. "One day it's bad, the next it's glorious. The only thing we can guarantee is that nothing lasts more than a couple of days." He opened his pad. "Now if I could just have your names, addresses, and phone numbers — just in case we need to contact you again."

"What for?"

"I have no idea, sir, but it's routine to get contact numbers for anybody who was around at the time of a crime."

"A crime?" The young woman registered surprise. "The little girl is missing, no? She has not been — how do you say it? — taken away by somebody bad?"

"We don't know yet. That's why we're asking all these questions. The whole beach area has already been searched, and there's not a trace of her so far. So if you can think carefully — when you returned from your outing this morning — did you look at the beach at all? Did you happen to notice the little girl playing? Did you see anybody else — anyone you hadn't seen before in the caravan park, any strange cars parked?"

The couple stood silent. The girl was staring down toward the beach as if trying to jog her memory. "I looked at the beach," she said. "It was empty. Nobody on it at all when I looked."

"But you didn't look at your watch?"

"We don't wear watches when we are on holiday," the man said. "At work it is always hurry, faster, and too much stress. This is why we come to walk in the mountains."

Another thought occurred to Evan. "You say you climbed Moel-y-Gest this morning." He looked across to the mountain, its heather-covered slopes now glowing in bright sunlight. "You must have had a good view of the whole area then. Was the little girl out on the beach at that stage?"

"I think not," the German woman said. "The wind was very strong, and there was some rain, too. Not a good weather for beach playing."

"Right. Thanks very much then," Evan said. "Now, if you'd just write your names and addresses for me, and if you've got a mobile phone with you — that would be very helpful."

The man took the pad and pen and wrote, handing the book back with a curt nod.

"Thanks very much." Evan took the pad. "Let's hope we won't need to be in touch with you and that it all ends happily. And I hope you enjoy the rest of your holiday."

"Thank you," the German said.

The young woman had already gone to the clothesline and was yanking down the washing with great force and speed. Evan watched with interest. If they seemed so disinterested in the missing girl, why were they so anxious to get away?

CHAPTER 6

As Evan made his way along the second row of caravans, he fought with growing unease. A couple of times he paused and glanced back at the Germans' car. Should he have taken a look inside the boot? Should he have asked to see inside the caravan? But then what reason had he got to suspect the Germans, other than that they were in a hurry to leave? They weren't even around when the child went missing. The grumpy sculptor had seen their car going out during the morning to back up their story. And the child's own mother suspected her ex-husband had snatched the little girl. Perhaps the Germans had heard bad rumours about the British police or simply didn't want to be involved in any kind of incident over here. Or, more simply, they were overstressed from their jobs and wanted a hassle-free holiday. That had to be it. Evan breathed easier and climbed over another gas cylinder.

The whole of this second row of caravans was untenanted and locked. Evan decided he should visit the site owner, rather than waste more time poking into empty rubbish bins and storage lockers. He headed for the white bungalow close to the gate. There was smoke coming from the chimney, and a hand-painted sign directed him to OFFICE, REGISTER HERE.

He let himself into a registration area with a high counter and sliding-glass panel, like that seen in any motel. There were voices coming from a room behind the glass. He rapped on the panel, heard the voices suddenly quiet as a TV set was switched off; then the panel slid open.

"Can I help you?" The speaker was a large woman, wearing an old-fashioned pinny over a flowery dress. It was hard to say how old she was, as her hair was bright orange, but Evan guessed at least fifty.

"North Wales Police, madam," he said, this time producing his warrant card for inspection. "I know you've already been questioned about the missing little girl, but we have some more information now and we'd like to get everything straight."

"So they haven't found her yet? Oh, that's too bad. Lovely little thing, weren't she? I watched her running over the grass — light as a fairy."

"No, we haven't found her yet, but we've got all our manpower out looking."

"That's good. About time you boys earned your wages. Never much crime around here, is there? I used to say to my husband when we drove to do the shopping in Porthmadog, 'All you ever see is policemen sitting on their backsides drinking coffee.'"

Evan ignored the insult and managed a smile. "Are you from these parts then, Mrs—"

"Paul," she finished for him. "Brenda Paul. And no, we're not from here, although we've been here almost twenty years now. From the Birmingham area originally. My husband, Jimmy, had a bad heart and had to take early retirement from work, so we looked around for a place on the coast and found this. He died ten years ago now, and I've been running the place alone ever since. Of course I take on extra help in the summer, but the rest of the year there's not much happening so I manage on my own — apart from the handyman who comes to cut the grass and that sort of thing." She paused suddenly as if the idea had just come to her. "Look, do you want a cup of tea? I've got the kettle on."

"Thanks. I could use one." He rubbed his hands together. "That wind's still cold out there." He was finding that people often relaxed when they went back to their regular routine and told him things they might not otherwise have done.

"I know, it's been a terrible spring so far. I've got people come here regular in April and May called to cancel this year. And drop-ins are way down too." She went on speaking as she moved out of Evan's view and then opened a door to his left. "Come on through, love," she said.

Evan followed her into a warm, comfortable room with both bars of an electric fire going and bright, crocheted rugs thrown over the backs of two easy chairs. A cat was sitting in one of them. Mrs Paul motioned for Evan to take the other.

"Won't be a jiffy," she said, and true to her word she returned with a tray containing a bone china tea service and a plate of chocolate biscuits. "Here, take one." She offered them to Evan as soon as she put the tray on a coffee table. "Keep you going until the tea is brewed properly. I can't stand weak tea, can you? My husband, Jimmy, always said you could stand a spoon up in a cup of my tea. They say tea drinking is good for the heart, don't they? Didn't do much for poor Jimmy though. He went just the same. That's why I was so interested in the little girl."

"Oh right. Her mother said she'd had an operation." Evan paused with the chocolate biscuit in front of his mouth.

"Heart transplant." The woman leaned confidentially forward. "Didn't you know that? One of the youngest recipients ever in Britain. Poor little mite was born with a badly deformed heart. They didn't think she'd live long enough to attempt the transplant, but she came through just fine."

She broke off long enough to pop into the kitchen and come back with a teapot sitting under an equally bright crocheted cosy.

"That should have brewed enough by now," she said, and started to pour into the teacups. "I reckon a heart transplant might have saved my Jimmy," she continued, "but of course he was too old. If they have hearts, they give them to the young people first, don't they? And very right too. They've got their whole lives ahead of them."

She handed Evan a cup. "Milk and sugar's there on the tray, love. Help yourself."

Evan poured a generous amount of milk into the black liquid, still digesting what she had told him. "A heart transplant — are you sure? But wouldn't she need to be taking all kinds of drugs?"

The woman nodded. "I know she had to take some kind of antirejection drugs. Her mum told me."

"Then why didn't she mention that to us? I'd have thought that was very important."

Mrs Paul nodded. "She's a strange one, isn't she? I let her stay here cheap because I felt sorry for the little one, and between you and me, I thought we could have some nice chats. It gets lonely this time of year. But she's hardly said two words to me since she came here. Off and out all day — I don't know where she goes. It's not like she knows anybody around here."

"She goes out a lot?"

"Oh yes — sometimes she's gone all day. I see that little blue car going past early in the morning and doesn't come back before dinnertime."

"I thought she brought the little girl here to be out in the fresh air and play on the beach."

"Oh, she does that too, when the weather's nice enough. Maybe she just feels hemmed in — that van isn't big enough to swing a cat, but she asked for the very cheapest thing we'd got. I gather they've no money, since the husband walked out on them. Not that he was any use when they were married. Seems he wouldn't even look for a job, she said. He expected her to go out to work, even when she was pregnant and then after the baby was born. Of course, when they found the little girl was sickly and needed constant attention, then she had to stay home and they had to live on the public assistance cheque. So I think she's had it hard, and she's getting on her feet now, she says. Got a job and a good safe place to live and trying to get on with her life without that bastard."

"He was a bastard — did she say that? What, just because he wouldn't work?"

"And he had a terrible temper and bouts of depression. Never really took to living in England, she said. She thought he only married her because it guaranteed he wouldn't be sent back to Russia again, but then all he wanted to do was to go home."

Evan thought that for a person who hadn't said two words to the landlady, Shirley Sholokhov had divulged a lot. He decided to risk divulging a little himself.

"She thinks that her ex-husband might have snatched the child," he said. "You're in here most of the time, are you? I notice this window looks out on the gate. You didn't see any strange cars this morning, or any strange men?"

She shook her head. "I'd have noticed if a strange car came through that gate. Of course if he was on foot, and he parked the other side of the hedge, there are several places where he could have slipped in and out without me seeing him. So she thinks the husband came to get his kiddy, does she? She did tell me he was very fond of her and he wanted more visits, but she had said no. She's a tough lady, I'll say that for her, so maybe she pushed him too far."

"At the moment we have to keep all options open," Evan said. "We've got men scouring the area in case the child just wandered off. Kids do that, don't they? I know I gave my parents a fright several times." He smiled at her and she gave him a coy smile in return. "So who else might have been around this morning?"

"The park's almost empty," she said. "I've just got that Gwynne fellow, the one who makes those dreadful obscene sculptures."

"Obscene? He told me most people didn't know what they were supposed to be." Evan looked amused at the horror on her face.

"I know breasts when I see them — and other parts of the anatomy too, dangling down. And there was one of two of them together once, and you could see what they were doing right enough. I've told him it isn't wholesome, having those indecent things on view where kiddies can see them. He told me they were great art and I didn't appreciate them. I said they were junk as far as I was concerned, and if they appeared outside again, he could find somewhere else to park his van."

"Yes, I've spoken to Richard Gwynne," Evan said. "And the German couple. Tell me about them."

"Oh, they're the kind of people I like," she said. "No trouble. Clean-cut, healthy young people. No drugs or booze. Paid for a week up front, they did."

"And they've been here a week, have they?"

"No, only four days."

"Well, they're leaving early then," Evan said. "They were packing up when I left them."

"They are? That's strange. They didn't tell me. I hope nothing's wrong. Anyhow, they're not getting a refund. It says no refunds, clear as crystal over the desk."

Evan decided to pay the Germans another visit when he left Mrs Paul. "And who else is here?"

"That's the lot right now. There are those holiday bungalows a little further down the beach. They've got people staying in them because I passed there this morning and I saw several cars parked and some boys kicking a football around."

"So you went out this morning?"

"Only to get the paper at the newsagents. I do that every day, about nine o'clock. It was proper miserable then — drizzling and blowing hard. It's on days like this I wonder why I ever left Birmingham."

"Yeah, and then the sun comes out and makes you realize it's one of the loveliest places on God's earth," Evan finished for her.

She gave him a motherly smile. "You're from these parts, I can tell. Do you speak the language? I know all the police have to these days, but I mean really speak it?"

"Oh yes. It's my first language. We always spoke it at home."

"I never got the hang of it myself," she said. "I tried learning it once, but it was beyond me. I can say yacky da and dee-olch and that's about it."

Evan got the feeling that she'd keep him there all afternoon if he didn't make a move. He drained his teacup and got to his feet. "Thanks very much for the tea, Mrs Paul. That was just what I needed. Lovely. And thanks for all your help too. I expect you'll be seeing more of us if the little girl isn't found quickly, so if you see or hear anything strange, don't hesitate to call, will you?"

"I won't, love. I want that little girl found as much as you do. Poor little thing. What kind of father would put his child through something like this? They're all the same, foreigners, aren't they? You can't trust them an inch — like those Germans taking off early. I've a mind to slip down to my caravan and count the crockery and blankets."

"You do that, Mrs Paul. And you'd better do it in a hurry because they were rushing to make their getaway."

"Right." She got to her feet also and grabbed a cardigan from the back of another chair.

Evan smiled to himself in satisfaction. He couldn't look at their car or the caravan without a search warrant, but a nosy landlady could do both.

As they came out of Mrs Paul's bungalow, they were just in time to see a green Volkswagen Beetle bouncing over the springy turf and out through the gate.

CHAPTER 7

Fr Nicholas Thomas stood at the doorway to the bar at the Everest Inn and looked around with distaste. Even at this hour of the afternoon, a smoky haze curled around the oak beams. Having lived in Canada for so long, he had forgotten how much the British smoked. Then he spotted his brother at the far end of the bar at the same time that Val looked up and waved.

"What can I get you?" Val Thomas asked.

"It's a little early for me, thanks," Nick said.

"Aw, go on, we're on holiday," Val insisted.

"Okay. A white wine then please. A chardonnay."

Val threw back his head and laughed. "Do real men in Canada drink wine? I'm surprised you weren't chased out of town."

A momentary spasm crossed Nick's face, then he smiled too. "You forget, I'm not a real man. I'm a priest. We're supposed to be different, aren't we? And Canada has become very European these days."

"Funny, isn't it?" Val said. "You and I — what very different lives we lead. Who would have thought it when we were kids? You a priest! You were never particularly holy, were you? — I seem to remember you sneaked out of chapel at school as often as I did. And our parents certainly didn't encourage any more observance of our religion than church on Christmas Day."

"And who would have expected you to be an artist?" Nick countered. "I always thought you'd take over the family business and be the driven CEO type."

"I discovered I don't like being tied down to one thing," Val said. "I get bored easily, and I seem to have a knack for painting pictures for which people pay large sums of money. Suits me just fine. I don't think I could ever have been the proverbial starving artist, any more than you could have been the humble, starving priest. We were obviously brought up to expect the good life."

"After boarding school? The food was abysmal, and we had to have cold showers."

"Ah, but that made men of us, didn't it?" Val laughed and tossed across some pound coins to the young woman who had put a glass of wine in front of Nick. "Between you and me, I was damned glad to go away to school. I don't think I'd have survived if we'd been stuck at home."

"Me too. I couldn't wait to get away. That was why I went to Canada, I suppose. The further, the better."

"You can't go far enough though, can you? I don't think even Australia would work." There was no longer a smile on Val's attractive face.

Nick nodded agreement. "No, it sort of follows you, doesn't it?"

* * *

After leaving Mrs Paul, Evan visited holiday bungalows further down the beach. Two of them were occupied by families who recalled seeing the little girl on the beach on several occasions but had only been on the beach briefly that morning. They had seen no strange men or cars parked along the road. But then they wouldn't, would they? Evan reasoned as he walked back toward the caravan park. When he'd been on holiday as a boy, he'd been so intent on having fun and making the most of his time on the beach that a spaceship could have landed nearby and he wouldn't have noticed it. And parents on the beach watch their own children, not other people's.

He was walking toward his car, when he remembered what Mrs Paul had told him about the heart transplant. It was just possible that she had got it wrong, but if not . . . he was sure that transplant patients had to take antirejection medication on a regular basis. And it could be fatal if they stopped taking it. Mrs Sholokhov had been clearly distraught when she'd spoken to them, but how could she have forgotten to mention such an important factor for the child's survival? Evan almost broke into a run as he crossed the caravan park. The small blue car Mrs Paul had mentioned was parked in front of Shirley Sholokhov's caravan, but when he tapped on the door, he got no answer. He knocked louder, wondering if she'd fallen asleep, then clambered up on the wheel to peep in the window. The caravan was empty.

He turned and hurried back across the field. Did that mean the child had been found? Had he missed all the action while he was out here, doing useless legwork, repeating what had been done before? He sprinted the last few yards and jumped into the car.

As he drove back along the road, the wind got up and sand peppered the seaward side of his car. Evan glanced down at the beach where there was a gap between the dunes, then pulled over abruptly. A man was standing on the beach, looking up at a flight of gulls through binoculars. A birdwatcher with binoculars might be just the break they needed. He might not even know a little girl was missing and might have witnessed something he hadn't understood that morning.

Evan crossed a field and waded through the soft sand of the dunes. The man continued to stare through his binoculars. Evan didn't want to startle him, so he yelled out, "Hello there!"

The man put down the glasses and turned toward the sound of Evan's voice.

"Could I have a word with you, sir?" Evan asked.

"Am I going to get in trouble?" the man asked in Welsh. As Evan came closer, he saw a small, skinny man whose clothes seemed to be one size too big for him and a head that seemed too big for the rest of his body. He was looking at Evan with an innocent, boyish face, but his greying hair and the creases at the sides of his eyes indicated that he was probably a lot older than Evan. There was something familiar about him, and Evan tried to place him. "Have you come to take me away?"

"Why, what have you done?" Evan asked.

"I don't know, but I've been arrested before. They gave me nice tea and buns and they showed me how the car radio worked. I thought the police had come to arrest me when I saw all the cars this morning. Are you with the police?"

Now the penny finally dropped. Daft Dai. He almost said the words out loud, then checked himself at the last moment. He was well-known in the area around Llanfair, up in the mountains where Evan lived. He had turned himself in for a murder he hadn't committed when Evan was first a constable in Llanfair. He was a few sandwiches short of a picnic was the general consensus. Crazy but harmless.

"Dai, isn't it?" Evan asked.

"I know you." The man's face broke into a boyish smile. "You used to wear a uniform. Did they take it away from you?"

"No. I've moved to what they call the plainclothes branch now. I'm a real detective."

"Oh, I see." Dai looked impressed. "Do you drive a police car?"

"What are you doing down here, Dai?" Evan asked. "Do you live down here now?"

"I live at the home. Do you know it? It's very nice."

Evan remembered there was some sort of sheltered accommodation for people like Dai in Porthmadog. He'd had to visit it once when one of the residents had started exposing himself on the beach.

"Yes, I know it, Dai. In Porthmadog, isn't it? How long have you lived there?"

"Since my mam died. Don't know how long that is. A long time now. They said she didn't suffer, so that's good, isn't it?"

Evan nodded. "Yes. That's good. So what are you doing out on the beach? Birdwatching, is it? Is that your hobby?" A thought swiftly crossed his mind before he dismissed it. Crazy but harmless, remember.

"It's all right at the home," Dai said, "but they have the telly on all day. I can't hear myself think, and I don't like being cooped up inside. I'm not used to it, see."

"Of course you're not. So now you go out birdwatching, is it?"

Dai nodded. "Mrs Presli lends me her binoculars if I'm very careful with them. They're very good. You can watch birds flying."

"What kind of birds do you like?"

"The white ones," Dai said, pointing up at the wheeling seagulls. "They're pretty, aren't they?"

Evan composed the sentence carefully in his head before he asked it. "I bet you can see a lot of things through those binoculars, right, Dai?"

"Oh yes. All kinds of things." Dai beamed.

"You weren't out on the beach this morning, were you? Because if you were, you might be able to help the police."

Dai nodded, his big head bobbing up and down on the scrawny neck. "All right."

"Listen, Dai. A little girl was playing on the beach further along at the caravan park. You didn't happen to see her, did you?"

"Her name's Ashley."

Evan started. "You know the little girl I'm talking about?"

"Oh yes. I've seen her on the beach before. I spoke to her once and she told me her name."

Evan felt his pulse quickening. "What about this morning, Dai? Were you out here this morning?"

"I think so. After the rain they said I could go out, but I didn't get far before it was lunchtime."

"Were you on the beach here?"

Dai mused about this. "Somewhere along here."

"But did you see Ashley this morning? Did you see the little girl?" Evan insisted.

Dai shook his head. "The beach was empty, except for the birds."

"Did you walk? Along the road and through Borth? You didn't see Ashley going for a ride in a car, did you?"

Dai shook his head again, then he said thoughtfully, "She might have gone up the mountain, though. I saw some people going up the mountain."

The German couple, Evan thought. "How many, Dai?"

"I don't know. They were far off. Two or three, maybe?"

"And as you walked along the road, you didn't notice any strange cars parked, maybe with a man sitting inside, did you?"

Dai nodded. "There was one strange car parked near here."

"There was?"

Dai nodded again, his head going up and down like one of those animals that nod in the back of cars.

"Really? What did it look like, Dai?"

"It was white and it had a word painted on the front."

"Oh," Evan said in disappointment. "Did that word say 'Heddlu, Police,' Dai?"

"Might have done," Dai said.

"Right. Thanks for your help then, Dai." Evan held out his hand. "Listen, Dai. The little girl has gone missing. If you find her, you'll come and tell us, won't you? Or if you find any toys that she might have left on the beach?"

"She's lost?" Dai asked, his eyes looking surprised and sad. "Ashley's lost. Is that why all the policemen were here?"

"That's right. So anything you can do to help find her . . ."

"I'll help find her," Dai said. "She had pretty hair, didn't she?"

"Yes, she did. Bye then, Dai. *Hwyl.*"

Dai stared at Evan like a dog that is about to be abandoned. Evan had to smile. "Do you want a ride back in my car, Dai?" he asked. "I'll take you home."

Dai's face lit up. "Then I won't miss tea," he said, and trotted along beside Evan like an obedient pet. On his way into town Evan radioed to HQ that he was on his way in and was told that the DI was expecting him at the Porthmadog police station.

"No news about the little girl then?" he asked. "I gather Mrs Sholokhov went somewhere in a police car, so I hoped that . . ."

"No, I expect WPC Howells took her out for a cup of tea, poor thing," the dispatcher said.

"Oh, right. Tell the DI I'll be there in five minutes then."

He dropped off Dai at the home and arrived a few minutes later to find the room full of blue uniforms. DI Watkins was addressing them, perched on the edge of a table at the front. Evan was dismayed to see that DCI Hughes, the senior detective in their division, was also there, looking dapper as usual in a well-cut, dark grey suit with a white silk handkerchief protruding from the pocket.

"Ah, here's Evans at last," Hughes said, managing to imply that he was somehow late and they'd all been waiting for him.

"Sorry, sir. I didn't know there was to be a meeting," Evan said. "I was out interviewing the people at the caravan park."

"I don't suppose you came up with anything, did you?" Again he made it sound as if Evan wasn't capable of coming up with anything. Evan was conscious of those uniformed coppers staring at him.

"Not much," he said. "The caravan park is almost empty. Nobody saw anything of the little girl at all this morning. The only thing that seemed strange to me was a German couple. They were leaving three days early, and they couldn't wait to get out either."

"Did you let them go?" Hughes demanded.

"Yes, sir. I had no reason to detain them. But I did take their car's number plate, and I have all their particulars, including mobile phone number."

"Ah. Good man," Hughes said, at last handing out a small morsel of praise.

"And they did have an alibi for this morning," Evan said. "They climbed a mountain and then went for coffee in town. That should be easy enough to verify."

"I don't suppose their departure had anything to do with this, anyway," Watkins said. "And we can always find them again if we need them."

DCI Hughes stood up. "Well, I'll leave you to it then, Watkins. You've got someone working on tracking down the father, have you?"

"We've sent out a message to all the ports of exit to be on the lookout for him and the little girl," Watkins said, "but as of now it's still a missing child report, not an abduction."

"If I were you, I'd proceed as if this were an abduction and track down the father right away. It's just possible that he paid someone to snatch the child and have her delivered to him. I'd have him tailed right away, Watkins."

"Very good, sir. Thanks for the suggestion." His face was expressionless.

The moment Hughes made his grand exit, Watkins muttered under his breath to Evan, "What the hell does he think we're doing — waiting for him to tell us when to breathe? Sanctimonious git." He looked up at the officers in the room. "Sorry about the interruption. Now where were we?"

"Roberts was just about to give you his report, sir."

"Ah yes. Roberts — beach area?"

"Nothing, sir. I only saw one suspicious person, and he turned out to be Constable Evans." This got a good laugh.

Watkins consulted his notes. "So everything has turned up negative. No possible sightings in Criccieth or Borth or Porthmadog. Nothing found on the beach or the dunes. And all the adjacent homes have been contacted, have they?"

"Yes, sir. Jones and I did that. No one's seen her."

"And Evans, you had another go around the caravan park. What was this about the German couple?"

"They were rushing to get away, sir. The man said something about his girlfriend being upset by the whole thing and just wanting to get out of there."

"And you thought there was more to it than that?"

"I really don't know. I'd like to have searched their caravan. I did take a look inside the car, it was one of those Beetles and easy enough to look inside, and I didn't see anything suspicious there."

"You don't think they could have taken the child? They really were German and not Russian, I suppose?"

"They sounded German to me," Evan said. "And they had a German number plate."

"We should keep an eye on them," Watkins said. "Where were they heading, did they say?"

"Maybe up to Scotland, they thought."

"Okay. Give me the car number. We'll get it to the ports in case they decide to do a bunk on us. The port authority police are going to be fed up of hearing from us." He adjusted the papers in front of him. "Right. So what have we got? Searches of the area negative. Dogs turned up nothing. Did they manage to bring in the bloodhound?"

"Yes, sir, but he couldn't pick up a trail on the beach. We thought the original area where she'd been playing was probably underwater by the time the dog got there."

"That's a lot of bloody use then. So the only thing we've got to go on, apart from Evans's Germans, is the mother's suspicion that the father is responsible. I've already got someone working on contacting the father. And just in case it wasn't him, but a stranger abduction, we've got someone printing up posters for us to put up around the area. Any other suggestions?"

"Has anyone searched the mountain yet?" Evan asked.

"You mean the hill behind the site?"

"I know it's not over one thousand feet, but I've always thought of it as a mountain myself," Evan insisted. "I've just spoken to someone who says he saw two or three people up there this morning. By the way, you'll never guess who it was. Remember Daft Dai?"

"The one who claimed he'd killed those men on the mountain?" Watkins grinned.

"Daft Dai? Oh, we all know him," Roberts said. "He's always coming into the station and asking to be arrested. I think he likes the tea and buns we give him."

"Excuse me, sir," a young policewoman raised her hand, "but shouldn't we be checking him out? I mean it has been known before that someone who is mentally unbalanced goes after a little girl."

"This one's harmless, I think, Gwen," Watkins said.

"And he was genuinely startled when he heard that the little girl was lost," Evan said. "Given his desire to be arrested, I think we have to take it that he had nothing to do with her disappearance."

"And yet you still think we should search your bloody mountain, Evans?"

"Just a thought, sir. To make sure we've covered all bases."

"Yes, I suppose you're right. It would be easy enough to hide a child up there among the rocks and heather. How do you boys feel? Are you up to another search party before it gets dark?"

"Of course, sir." One of the constables got to his feet. "Anything we can do to find the little girl. You'll want the dogs, won't you?"

"Absolutely. Then let's get back there. We've got four hours before it gets dark. That should be long enough to give it a thorough going-over."

"There's one more thing I thought I should mention," Evan said, as the meeting dispersed and they walked to Watkins's vehicle together. "You know Mrs S said that Ashley had had an operation? Well, the park owner says that it was a heart transplant."

"A heart transplant? Bloody hell," Watkins said.

Evan opened the passenger side door and got in. "So she'd be on all kinds of drugs, wouldn't she? So how could her mother have forgotten to mention them to us?"

"We'd better pay her another visit on the way over," Watkins said, as they pulled out of the car park.

"I tried to as soon as I found out, but apparently the WPC had taken her to get a cup of tea."

"She should be back by now. Did the park owner say anything else interesting?"

"She said that Mrs S went out a lot, always coming and going."

"Bit of a nosy parker, this park owner, would you say?"

"Definitely. She's miffed with Shirley Sholokhov because she thought they could have some good chats, and then Shirley kept herself to herself."

Watkins chuckled. "But if she notices when Shirley comes and goes, you'd have thought she'd have spotted a strange car or a strange man, wouldn't you?"

"That's what I thought, but she says there are several places where someone could slip through the hedge to a car parked in the lane."

Evan shook his head as they left the town behind. "You'd have thought someone would have seen something, wouldn't you? It's so exposed here. If someone grabbed Ashley from the beach, he'd have had to sprint across a couple of fields with the child in his arms. Don't tell me that nobody would have noticed."

"It is pretty empty at this time of year," Watkins said. "Even so, he would have been taking a terrible risk."

"If it were Ashley's father, he was obviously willing to risk anything to get her. You'd risk anything to get your daughter back, wouldn't you?"

"Yep. I suppose I would," Watkins agreed.

And yet Mrs Paul had described him as a bastard, moody, violent.

They drove into the meadow and parked beside the blue car. This time the door was opened by WPC Howells. "Oh, hello, Inspector, hello, Constable Evans," she said. "Any news yet?"

"Not yet. How's Mrs Sholokhov holding up?"

"Not too well. The doctor's given her a sedative," she said in a low voice, glancing back into the van.

"Is she still awake because we have to ask her something," Watkins said.

"You can try, but don't upset her again if you can help it, will you? She was in a terrible state earlier, threatening to kill herself if anything happened to Ashley."

"It won't take a minute." Watkins stepped past her into the caravan. Evan followed. Mrs Sholokhov was lying on the bed, looking pale and haggard. She opened tired eyes as Watkins sat down beside her, then struggled to sit up.

"Any news?" she asked.

Watkins put a hand on her shoulder and eased her back down. "We're doing everything we can, but don't worry. We've alerted all the ports. Your husband won't be able to leave the country with her. It's only a matter of time before we find them."

She nodded, pressing her lips together.

Watkins looked up at Evan, who stepped forward. "There was one thing, Mrs Sholokhov," Evan said. "I understand that your little girl had a heart transplant. Is that right?"

She nodded again. "One of the youngest recipients the hospital had ever done," she said.

"So she's presumably on medication?"

"Of course she is."

"But you didn't think it was important to mention it to us this afternoon?" Watkins asked.

"I should have done, shouldn't I?" She brought one hand up clumsily toward her face. "I just can't think straight. But don't worry, if she's with Johnny, he'll make sure she takes it. He was always fanatical about her taking her pills. And he has copies of her prescriptions for the times she stayed overnight with him. So she'll be fine, unless he takes her to Russia." A sob rose in her throat. "Oh, God. Who knows what kind of primitive medicines they have over there?"

WPC Howells sat on the bed beside her and patted her reassuringly. "They'll find him before he gets to Russia. Now you just try and have a little sleep." Her look told Watkins and Evan to leave.

"She's pretty much convinced that Ashley's father took her, isn't she?" Evan said, as they walked back to the car.

Watkins stared up at the mountain. "I hope to God she's right."

CHAPTER 8

The sun was sinking as a red ball into the layer of sea fog on the horizon as the tired search party finally picked its way down the mountain. They had found nothing but a child's hair slide with a teddy bear on it, which could have been lying there for ages. Evan and Watkins had taken the main path up to the summit while the crew fanned out, moving up through the rocks and heather from the road. After all the rain, the path was extremely muddy.

"We might just get lucky and pick up footprints if anyone brought the kid up here," Watkins said. "Of course, if anyone brought her up here, he was probably carrying her, but then his prints would be heavier than usual."

Evan stared at the path ahead. "That's interesting," he said. "Those Germans said they hiked the mountain this morning, but they certainly didn't take this path. Look at this — a herd of sheep came across here and there were no sheep on the mountain today — and there are no prints on top of the sheep, are there?"

"They could have chosen not to take the path," Watkins agreed. He glanced up at Evan. "You suspect those Germans of something, don't you?"

"Let's say they made me a trifle uneasy."

"I think you've got good instincts, boyo. When we come down, I'll have their car stopped and searched, and we'll get in touch with the German police too — just in case."

* * *

Pink twilight was glowing on the mountainsides and highlighting the last of the snow as Evan finally drove up the pass to Llanfair. Rivulets of water cascaded down the steep green slopes and danced along the side of the road. The bleating of new lambs floated on the evening breeze. Evan felt the tension melting away. Now he knew why it was so important to live in the cottage. It was remote, removed from all the tensions and tragedies going on in the world. Once he got home, he'd be in a haven of peace.

For now, of course, home was not a haven of peace on the mountainside, but a dreary two-up-two-down terraced miner's cottage in the village. Evan had been living there since he moved away from Mrs Williams's tender care to prove that he could fend for himself. In truth, he hadn't been doing too well at the fending. He had learned to boil eggs and cook spaghetti, but that was about the limit of his culinary skills. When he got home, he was usually so tired and hungry that it was easier to fry up eggs and bacon than learn a new cooking skill. And at the back of his mind was the thought that someday soon Bronwen would be doing the cooking.

The place felt cold and damp as he let himself into the front hall, this being one of the few homes that had never had central heating installed. It had never really warmed up after the winter, and he was usually home too late to think about making a fire. Instead he put on the kettle to make some tea, then opened the fridge to see what he might eat. The choice was egg or cheese, and he didn't fancy either. He turned off the gas under the kettle again and did something he'd promised he'd never do. He went across the road to the pub.

The RED DRAGON sign was swinging in the stiff breeze, each swing being accompanied by a loud squeak. Evan pushed open the outer door, then ducked under the oak beam that led to the main bar. He was greeted by warmth, voices, and Frank Sinatra in the background — the village's taste in music being a little behind the times. A fire was burning in the fireplace at the far end of the bar. A group stood around it, silhouetted against the firelight. Another group stood around the bar, in the centre of which was a tall young man wearing a turtleneck and smart sports coat. Evan took a moment to register that the man was Barry-the-Bucket, the local bulldozer driver who had never been seen in anything but dirty overalls until recently. He was leaning on the polished wood bar, his face inches from barmaid Betsy's as he whispered something to her and she responded by blushing and slapping him playfully.

A minor miracle had taken place in the village when Betsy and Barry fell for each other, Evan decided. He welcomed it as it meant Betsy had stopped her relentless pursuit of him. She was no longer wearing sexy sweaters and exposed midriffs, but a demure white blouse. As she moved away from Barry, she spotted Evan making his way through the crowd to the bar.

"Well, here he is at last, then," she said loudly. "We thought you'd got lost, Evan *bach*. What will it be? The usual?"

Her hand had already moved to draw a pint of Guinness.

"Lovely, thanks. And what have you got to eat tonight then, Betsy? What delicacies to tempt a hungry man?"

"Ooh, listen to him," one of the men chuckled. "You want to watch it, Evan, boyo. Barry's standing right here and he gets awfully jealous."

"I thought you were supposed to be learning to cook." Betsy gave him a stern frown. "I'll have to tell Bronwen if you keep popping in here for your dinner."

"I don't keep popping in. I've been looking for a missing girl since this morning, and I'm starving."

"Missing girl, eh? Oh, that's bad. Did you find her?" Old Charlie Hopkins turned to Evan from where he had been propping up the bar, his hands nursing a half-empty glass.

"Not yet. It seems she might have been taken by her father."

"That's what always happens when people get divorced, isn't it?" Betsy said. "They do it to spite each other and don't think about how it might upset the children. They should make sure they're marrying the right person before they start bringing children into the world, that's what I say."

"Quite right, you tell 'em, *cariad*," Barry said, patting her hand. "But not everyone can be as lucky as you, meeting a spectacular bloke like me."

"Anyone would think you were Irish, the amount of blarney you talk, Barry," she said, pushing his hand away. "I hope you find her, Evan *bach*. Now what were you wanting to eat? I've got a nice toad in the hole or I can do you some plaice and chips."

"Toad in the hole will do nicely, thanks, Betsy."

"I'll just pop it in the microwave. It won't take a second," Betsy said, darting away from the bar.

"Are you going out tonight then, Barry?" he asked the bulldozer driver. "I've never seen you all tarted up on a weeknight."

Barry actually blushed. "Betsy took me shopping in Bangor and helped me pick out some things."

"Ooh, you want to watch it, boy," Charlie Hopkins chuckled. "Next it will be picking out home furnishings, and then you're done for."

"He could do worse," Evan said, reaching across to pick up his glass of Guinness. "Everyone has to settle down sometime, you know."

"There speaks the voice of experience," Barry said. "Just because you've been caught, you want every other poor bloke to suffer too — and don't you dare tell Betsy I said that!"

Evan smiled and was just taking a long, appreciative sip of his Guinness when a hand slapped him on the shoulder.

"Well, look who's here."

Evan managed to move his glass away without spilling stout down his front, and turned to see Evans-the-Meat, local butcher, standing behind him.

"Careful, man. You nearly made me spill my drink," he said. "And why shouldn't I be here? I'm here most nights."

"I just thought you'd be wise to stay away, on account of how Mr Owens-the-Sheep wants your head."

"Owens-the-Sheep? He's not still mad about what happened during the foot-and-mouth epidemic, is he? I thought we'd patched that up long ago."

"Not that, boyo. Today. That man you took to see the cottage today — that's what's upset him."

"Why would that upset him?" Evan frowned. "We only walked up the track and back again. We didn't go over Bill Owens's land. Oh, don't tell me he left the gate open when he came down."

"No, worse than that. You left the bugger up there, didn't you? Left him to make his own way down."

"I had to. I was paged by my boss."

"I dare say you had to," Evans-the-Meat said, "but you should have brought him down with you, not left him on his own to do more mischief."

"He couldn't keep up with me," Evan said. "I was in a hurry. Why, what happened?"

"Let Bill Owens tell you himself," Evans-the-Meat said. "He's over by the fire and he's on his third whisky chaser."

Evan took a deep breath and followed the butcher to the group by the fire. "I understand that you had an unpleasant encounter, Mr Owens," he said.

"I did. Thanks to you, young man," the farmer muttered, his face red and his consonants slurred. "You brought trouble to me today."

"I did? What kind of trouble?"

The old man stared down at the empty glass in his hand. "That bloke was a National Parks inspector, wasn't he?"

"That's right. He had to inspect the cottage I want to rebuild. Did he do any damage to your property?"

"He damaged his wallet, that's what," Roberts-the-Pump, owner of the local petrol station, exclaimed with a loud laugh.

"You wouldn't find it funny if it happened to you," Owens said. "Trouble was, Evan *bach*, he didn't go straight down the mountain, he starts snooping around where he's no right to, and he finds my new barn." He sucked through his teeth in disgust. "You know that compensation I got for losing my flock last year. Well, the wife says why put it all back into sheep at our age? You've kept saying you were going to rebuild that old barn. Now's the time to do it before it falls on someone's head and kills them."

"Oh," Evan said, realizing where this conversation could be going. "And you didn't get planning permission."

"What do I need permission for? That barn's been up there since before that little squirt was born. I don't need permission to rebuild something on my own land."

"That's probably not how he saw it."

"It wasn't. He tells me I could be in a lot of trouble. He says I have to submit plans for approval before the committee, and the structure has to comply with National Park standards and be built of local materials, just like everything else."

"That's what he told me too," Evan agreed.

"Bloody daft, if you ask me," Roberts commented. "Next they'll be telling me that my petrol pumps have to be chiselled from local slate."

"They probably will, boyo. You'd better watch out." There was general laughter.

"But you need a barn on your farm, Mr Owens," Evan said. "Tell them that. Tell them the old one was falling down, and you have to take your lambs inside if the weather turns nasty like yesterday. I'm sure they'll understand."

"I'm not at all sure," the farmer said. "None of them are locals, are they? This bloke comes from Lancashire so he tells me. Speaks no Welsh. What would he know about sheep farming? I've already had to deal with one lot of bureaucracy within the last year; I'm not standing for another. I told him the barn's going up and if he wants to tear it down again, he'll have me and my shotgun to deal with."

"That probably wasn't a good idea," Evan said, thinking of the officious Mr Pilcher.

"No, I don't think he took it too kindly," Mr Owens said. "He stomped off, not looking very pleased, and I told the dogs to follow him, just in case he felt like more snooping. You've never seen anyone get down the mountain so fast in your life as when he saw those dogs coming after him. As if they'd hurt a fly!"

His old body shook with silent laughter.

"All the same, Mr Owens, I think you'd better go down to National Park headquarters and convince them that you're just rebuilding the barn the way it always was."

"Maybe you're right, young man," Owens said. "You don't seem to be able to fight authority these days, do you? Not like the old days when a man's farm was his own property and people had to ask permission to walk across it."

"So did he give you your permission then, Evan *bach*?" Roberts asked.

"Not exactly. He thought it might qualify as a listed building."

"What does that mean?" someone asked.

"You know, of historical value, worth preserving."

"That old shepherd's cottage? Historical value?" There was a loud outburst of laughter. Evan smiled too.

"That's what I told him, but he thinks the walls and foundation might have been there long enough to make it qualify."

"And what would that mean for you, trying to build it up again?" Roberts asked.

"I don't know. I haven't met the listed buildings bloke yet," Evan said.

"You should ask him if you need to re-create the smell," Mr Owens said.

"The smell?" Evan asked.

"Yes, old Rhodri, last shepherd up there, always kept a lamb or two inside the place. Well, it wasn't very big and it always smelled like a zoo in there — cross between a zoo and wet wool. You'd need to re-create that, I'd imagine."

"Evan, do you want this toad in the hole or not? It's sitting here getting cold," came Betsy's high, clear voice toward him.

"Excuse me, gentlemen. Dinner calls." Evan made his way back toward the bar.

"Make the most of this. You won't be allowed in here anymore when you're married," Evans-the-Meat called after him. "The little woman will expect you to spend your evenings at home with her."

"As if your wife ever sees you in the evenings, Gareth," Roberts-the-Pump said.

"Ah, but it's different when you're newlywed. You have to break wives in slowly, over the years, don't you?"

Evan picked up his plate, suddenly not so hungry. They were right. He should have gone straight to see Bronwen. She'd been waiting all day for news about the cottage. He carried the plate through to the lounge, set it down on the nearest table, and ate it as quickly as possible. Then he drained his glass, put the plate back on the counter, and went to leave.

"Where are you off to now in such a hurry?" Charlie asked him.

"I haven't told Bronwen about that damned inspector yet."

"See, what did I tell you?" Evans-the-Meat called triumphantly from the fire. "Once they get you hooked, they have you dancing like a bloody puppet. You'll be next, Barry, boyo."

"Don't you listen to him," Betsy said. "Just because his wife doesn't want him at home because he's a pain in the you-know-what."

Evan heard the laughter as he pushed open the door into the cold night air. He walked briskly up the village street, past the shops and the row of cottages, until he came to the low wall of the school playground. Like many old-fashioned village schools, the Llanfair schoolteacher's residence was at one end of the school building. This practice was dying out as children were bused to newer schools in the towns.

There was talk that the Llanfair school would be closed as soon as the new steel-and-glass building was finished outside Porthmadog.

Evan almost broke into a run as he crossed the playground and tapped on Bronwen's door. She opened it looking like a long-ago figure from folklore, her ash blonde hair loose over her shoulders and wearing a floor-length robe of deep blue.

"Oh, Evan, I'd almost given up on you. I was about to go to bed and read." She raised her face for his kiss. "Come on in, you poor thing. Have you been out all this time looking for the little girl? You must be starving."

"Actually, *cariad*, I've already had a bite to eat."

"What was it — bread and cheese?"

"Toad in the hole."

"My, but your cooking skills are improving. I'm impressed."

Unfortunately it was just not possible to lie to Bronwen. Evan gave her a guilty smile. "I popped into the pub and grabbed a quick bite to eat. There was nothing in my fridge, and you're right, I was starving."

"Then why on earth didn't you come up here? I could have fixed you something."

"You were the one who told me I had to learn to fend for myself."

"That doesn't mean that I don't understand that there are times when you're too tired to want to cook, you daftie. I'm sure the food they serve down at the pub is taken straight from a package and microwaved — full of stuff that's not good for you."

"It filled the spot, but now I've got the most awful indigestion because I gulped it down as quickly as possible, knowing that you'd be waiting for me."

"I don't know." Bronwen smiled, shaking her head. "You men. I'll be glad when I can finally look after you and make sure you eat properly. Sit down. I'll pour you a brandy to settle your stomach."

Evan sat by the fire that Bronwen always lit on cold days and watched her moving around the kitchen, her hair and her robe floating out around her as she moved, as if she was a magical creature of no substance. Again he was overcome by the wonder that she had chosen him. She brought back a brandy snifter with a generous amount of cognac in it. "Here. Get that down you." She pulled up another chair beside him. "Now, tell me all about everything — first the cottage."

She listened patiently as he went through the whole encounter.

"Well, I think it sounds positive, don't you?"

"I hope so — if the listed buildings man isn't even more officious than Mr Pilcher. Anyway, I'm going to get busy myself. As soon as I've got a moment of free time, I'll start digging out the sewer line and have a plumber come to check it."

"I wish they'd hurry up," Bronwen said. "I can't wait to get in there and start painting and putting up curtains and making it look like home."

Funny things women look forward to, Evan thought. He reached across and stroked her hair.

"And what about the little girl? You didn't find her yet?"

Evan shook his head. "No trace of her. I kept hoping that she'd just wandered off and got lost, but that doesn't seem likely now. We've had our blokes combing the whole area and asking at all the houses nearby."

"So you think she was kidnapped?"

Evan sighed. "It was most likely her own father who took her. He's a Russian and was planning to go back to Russia."

"Well, that's better than other options, isn't it?" Bronwen said, staring thoughtfully into her own glass. "At least she's still alive, and he'll look after her and there's a chance of getting her back."

"When you put it that way, you're right," Evan agreed. "We'll know more when he's been traced. The ports have been alerted so he can't flee the country with her."

"Well, that's good then."

Evan leaned back in his chair, feeling the cognac flowing through his system. "I'm so whacked, I don't think I've got the energy to go home," he said.

"Who is telling you to?" Bronwen gave him a teasing smile as she got to her feet and ruffled his hair.

CHAPTER 9

On a level area of paddock outside the house, a large tent was being erected. Shouts of men and the sound of guy ropes being hammered into the soil echoed back from the valley walls and made sheep look up and trot off in alarm. Old Tomos Thomas stood on his doorstep, scratching his head.

"You didn't have to go to all this trouble," he said to the men standing beside him. One of the men was his grandson, Henry Bosley-Thomas. The other, managing to look like an advertisement out of *Hare and Hound* for the elegant country squire in well-cut slacks and a checked Viyella shirt, was Henry's father, Hugh Bosley-Thomas, creator of their hyphenated surname.

"You asked the family to help you arrange a party for your birthday, Father," Hugh said, in a voice that betrayed time at an expensive public school and then Oxford.

"I didn't think you counted yourself as family any longer. Haven't exactly been coming to visit too often, have you?" old Tomos said.

"Let's not spoil today with talk of the past, Father. I was happy to do it."

"Yes, but I didn't mean a bloody great circus tent. What are you planning to put in there — a lot of bloody elephants and a wire walker?" The old man, in contrast, spoke with a soft Welsh lilt. He looked like any other sheep farmer from the area — his face weathered from a life in the outdoors, his high boots caked with mud, his flat workman's cap on his head.

Hugh gave him a tense smile and glanced swiftly at Henry. "We had to invite all the neighbours, Father. You know what bad feeling it would create if anyone was left out."

"So what's wrong with passing around a few beers and packets of crisps at the pub?"

Hugh glanced at his father and realized he was being baited. Old Tomos always had liked to tease. He had always made sure that he put his boys in their place, didn't want them to get above themselves, no fancy ideas. Luckily he hadn't succeeded, Hugh thought. He and his brother, Robert, had both done extremely well at Oxford. They had gone into business together, marketing farm products, and had prospered. Now he lived in the stockbroker belt near Guildford in Surrey and had conveniently forgotten he had started life on a Welsh farm. Until now, of course — summoned back here by the old man and his eightieth birthday party.

"I told you nothing fancy," old Tomos repeated. "I don't want none of your posh foreign eats."

"We know that, Grandpa," Henry said, stepping up on the other side of the old man as he made his way toward the marquee. "It's going to be a simple cold buffet — ham, beef, prawns — all the things you like, and then they're going to have a spit outside, barbecuing lambs."

Tomos turned and smiled at him. "You're a good lad, Henry. You've done well for yourself in spite of everything."

"In spite of everything?" Hugh demanded. "He was brought up to nothing but the best. He damned well should have done well for himself." He looked across at Henry. "So what's wrong with your wife?"

"Nothing, why?"

"I mean why is she not here?"

"The same reason our current dear stepmama is not here, I'd imagine." He glanced across at his father, went to say something more, and caught his grandfather staring at him. "She thought it was a family thing and she'd feel left out," he added quickly.

"Still no children?" Hugh asked.

"Not yet."

"What's wrong with that wife of yours, or aren't you trying?"

Henry flushed. "Really, Dad, that's none of your business."

"It is my business. I need someone to take over the bloody firm someday. You won't do it. Val and Nick won't do it. God knows Suzanne can't do it."

"Why — have you asked her?"

"Look at her, as if she could run a multimillion-pound company," Hugh said, his voice laden with contempt. "Poor Suzie. What she needs is someone to take care of her. Is she still with old whatshisname?"

"So I gather."

"He won't ever marry her, will he? She's wasting her time."

"Obviously she doesn't think so. She's a grown woman, Father. Let her run her own life."

"Yes, but look what a mess she's made of it so far," Hugh said. "Is she here?"

"Yes, she's working away, decorating the marquee with Val and Nick."

"Decorating?" Tomos demanded.

"You can't expect people to sit down to dinner in a plain tent, Grandpa," Henry said. "They're covering the poles with flowers, so they tell me."

"Bloody 'ell," Tomos said, pushing his cap back on his head. "I hope my neighbours won't think that any of this poncing up was my idea. A simple get-together was what I said."

"It's good for everyone to be busy, Grandpa," Henry said. "No time to think."

His grandfather looked at him long and hard. "Maybe you're right, boy," he said.

* * *

"Right, everyone, thanks for coming in so bright and early on a Saturday morning." DI Watkins surveyed the faces around him. Apart from Evan and Glynis there were two sergeants in uniform, one from Porthmadog and one from Caernarfon, who had been responsible for coordinating the searches.

"No problem. We want to do everything we can to find this little girl and bring her home, don't we?" Evan said, and was rewarded with a dazzling smile from Glynis Davies, the other detective constable at the table and Evan's senior in the department. As always he found himself thinking that those looks were wasted in the police force, as were her brains. She had it all — and she was dating the chief constable's nephew — on a career track straight to the top, so it would seem. It would be easy to envy her, except that she was also genuinely nice — and a feast for the eyes.

He wrenched his thoughts away from her in time to hear Watkins saying, "And that seems like the only thing we can do right now, eh, Evans?"

"What was that again, sir?" Evan felt Glynis's amused gaze on him, as if she'd been reading his mind. "Sorry, my brain's still fuzzy this morning. Working too long without a day off," he added.

"I was saying there is no point in any additional searches of the area until we've located the father. Rough night was it, last night?" he added, with a grin.

"Not particularly." Evan managed a smile of his own. "And about not searching the area — one thing we haven't done is to arrange for a search of the bay by boat. I know the waves were small and harmless and the beach stays shallow there, but there's always the off chance of a rogue wave, isn't there? We can't completely rule out the possibility that she was swept out to sea. That would certainly explain how she vanished with no trace at all."

"Good point," Watkins said. "Can your boys arrange for that, Jones?" He turned to one of the two uniformed sergeants at the table. He was round and jolly looking, like an off-duty Father Christmas, while the other was small and dour, with the rugged square jaw of the typical Welshman.

"No problem," the jolly one said. "It's worth doing, although if she's drowned, her body will be washed up somewhere around the coast in a couple of days anyway."

Glynis shuddered. "Don't let's think that way. Let's stay positive and assume that she was snatched by her father. One good thing we know is that he hasn't left the country yet, unless he's using false identity documents and a disguise for himself and the child."

"So he could be hiding out anywhere," Watkins said. "You've been looking into his whereabouts for us, Glynis. Have you come up with anything positive to go on yet?"

"Based on the last address his wife gave us of a flat in Shepherd's Bush, I've been in touch with the Met. They've checked the address, and the landlord says he moved out about a month ago. He left no forwarding address." She looked around the group. "Then I've also been in contact with the Home Office, and I've got all the details on him from when he applied for asylum. The name on his application is Ivan Sholokhov, but I understand he goes by Johnny these days. Comes from just outside Moscow. Applied for asylum at our embassy in Berlin. Apparently he was on a Russian Mafia hit list because he was a lorry driver and he refused to carry their drug shipments among his cargo."

"A good guy, then," Evan said thoughtfully. "One with a conscience because you can bet they would have paid him well to do it."

"Who now has no conscience about stealing his daughter?" Glynis asked.

"Perhaps that is different in his mind. Who knows how the Russian mentality works?" Watkins said. "As her father maybe he thinks she rightfully belongs to him, and he's outraged by the British system of justice that gave custody to the mother."

"The mother was awarded custody — do we know that?" Glynis asked.

"You're suggesting she might have been the one who took the kid in the first place?" Watkins looked impressed. "A caravan on a deserted beach is certainly a good place to hide out, isn't it? Can you check into that for us, computer whiz?"

Glynis grinned. "You men would be lost without me, wouldn't you? It's not that hard to learn how to use computers, you know."

"Not for you, maybe," Watkins said. "I took the course and I'm still in the dark. So you'll check into the mother and the custody for us. Now what else should we be doing?" He looked around the room again.

"It's now almost twenty-four hours she's been missing, so I think it's time to get the word out," Sergeant Howell Jones said. "We've made up the posters for local distribution, and I'll have my blokes putting them out as soon as we get the go-ahead from you, but what about going national?"

"We've sent out a general alert to the other police forces in the UK to be on the lookout for Sholokhov and the child," Watkins said, "but we didn't have a photo of him, just a description. Do we have a photo now, Glynis?"

"Right here." Glynis held up a sheet showing a picture of a light-haired man with high Slavic cheekbones. "Shall I send this around now then, and the little girl's photo with it again?"

"Good idea." Watkins said. "Now what else should we be doing?"

"Alert the media," Evan said. "Send them the photos and ask anyone who thinks they've spotted them to call us."

"Right, Evans, do you think you can do that?"

"I'll give it a try, sir," he said, with what he hoped was conviction, while really having no clue about how one contacted media.

"Good man."

"And what about Interpol?" Evan asked. "If he has managed to smuggle the child out of the country, maybe using a false identity, we should alert the Russian police and have them be on the lookout for them."

"So how do we contact Interpol, sir?" Glynis asked. "That's something I haven't had to do yet."

"I thought you were the only one in the department who knew how to deal with foreigners," Watkins quipped. "Well, this is something I do happen to know about because there was that case involving the Greek family and the father who was prosecuted for taking his child back to Greece without the mother's permission."

"Oh, right," Evan said. "I remember that one. Under British law he wasn't allowed to take his child out of the country without permission of the other parent. But that wasn't in Wales, was it?"

"No, but it came up in discussion at a training session, and the bloke who was doing the training was from the National Criminal Intelligence Service. He talked us through the various steps. So if this now counts as a criminal abduction, then the next step is to contact the NCIS. Then they get in touch with the Foreign Office, and they are our liaison with Interpol."

"Liaison with Interpol. Well, doesn't that sound exciting?" Sergeant Howell Jones joked. "What an exciting life you blokes lead. Much better than recovering stolen cars."

"Do we have a last known address for him in Russia?" Watkins asked, ignoring the comment.

"I've got an address of next of kin and a place of birth," Glynis said. "They would be a good place to start, wouldn't they? I doubt he'd go back to his last known address before he defected, especially not if the Mafia are still after him."

"Don't you think all this may be a bloody waste of time and money?" The other sergeant spoke for the first time, a heavily accented Welsh voice. "I mean, if the father gets as far as Moscow with her, we haven't a hope in hell of getting her back."

"Don't be such a pessimist, Bill," Watkins said.

"Well, can you see the Moscow police sending him back to us to be prosecuted? Or making him give up his own kid when he's the rightful father?" the sergeant asked.

"That doesn't mean we don't try." Glynis frowned at him. "And even if he's the father, that doesn't mean he has the right to take her out of the country without his spouse's permission, unless he has been granted sole custody, which we don't know yet."

"I'm just saying they might not see the law the same way we do," the sergeant said. "In many societies the father is the only one with rights, isn't it? They keep their women in their place at home, not running around like they do here." He shot a glance at Howell Jones, the other sergeant, and it was obvious that the barb was aimed directly at Glynis.

"Not in Russia," she said evenly. "In Russia women drive tanks and bulldozers, remember."

Evan grinned to himself.

"I don't think it's up to us to make any decision." Watkins cut short the discussion before it turned ugly. "Once we hand the information over to NCIS and the Foreign Office, it's their headache, isn't it? We've done our bit. Glynis?"

"Don't say it — you want me to contact the NCIS for you. All right." She picked up her pen and added another item to the list in front of her, then looked up as another thought struck her. "And isn't there some kind of missing child database? We should definitely get her on that."

"On the computer, you mean?" Watkins asked.

"All right. Me again." Glynis laughed. "I don't know whether to feel flattered or like the general dogsbody."

"But you're so quick at these things. It would take Evan and me half a day to turn the bloody thing on." He got to his feet, nodding in satisfaction. "That should give us enough to get on with, shouldn't it? Let's meet back here at four this afternoon. That gives us all plenty of time to do what we have to."

"And what exactly will you be doing, sir?" Evan asked.

"Me? I'm supervising, coordinating, and I might pay Mrs Sholokhov another visit too. Just in case there is something she's remembered or hasn't told us. And I'm bearing responsibility on my shoulders, so none of your cheek. Got it?"

"Oh, yes sir, absolutely." Evan and Glynis exchanged a grin as they left the room.

"Glynis, do you know how one goes about contacting media?" Evan asked as they came out into the hallway. "I haven't a clue how to start."

"Don't ask me, I'm already doing nine-tenths of the work," she said. "Check the Yellow Pages. Look up newspapers, call the radio and TV companies. That should do it."

"Right." Evan went to find a telephone with a sinking feeling in his stomach. He had never had a good relationship with phones — probably a phobia inherited from his mother, who still held a phone six inches from her head and yelled into it. He started off with the news desk at BBC Wales. The person who took the information spoke Welsh and seemed so interested and concerned that Evan then felt confident enough to tackle the English television channels and major newspapers. All promised to run something on their regional news and on national if they could fit it in. It was a good start, and Evan felt rather pleased with himself. This was such new territory for him.

He located the DI in the cafeteria, finishing up a cheese-and-tomato roll and a cup of what might have been either tea or coffee. It was hard to tell in the cafeteria. Evan was tempted to make a quip about relaxing on the job but decided against it. He and Watkins had developed a good working relationship and even a friendship when Watkins had been a sergeant. Now he was an inspector, and Evan had to remind himself that the dynamics had changed. He got himself a cup of tea and a beef-and-pickle sandwich and brought them to Watkins's table.

"If you say anything about me slacking off while you're run off your feet, you're fired," Watkins said cheerfully.

"The thought never crossed my mind," Evan said, pulling out a chair beside the inspector. "I just wanted to tell you that I've pretty much covered the media. Channel S Pedwar C is going to do a piece on it tonight. They're sending up a cameraman and a reporter, and they'd like you to call them and let them know when they can meet you at the caravan park."

"Excellent," Watkins said. "Local television exposure. Couldn't be better."

"And I've got promises from all the big boys in London that they'll try and squeeze it into their newscasts — at least the regional ones."

"Well done. We'll have you as our media consultant before you know it."

"If I'm your media consultant, do you want me to come along for your TV spot today?"

"To coach me on what to say?"

"To check your makeup." Evan grinned.

"Cheeky bugger. I'll have you search that mountain again if you're not careful."

"So what would you like me to do now?" Evan asked.

"I don't suppose you can give Glynis a hand, can you?"

Evan made a face as he took a sip of his tea. "You know my computer skills are about as good as yours. I'd be more of a hindrance than a help, I think."

"You're going to have to learn how to do it sometime," Watkins said, "but I agree this isn't the moment. Speed is of the essence, isn't it? We want this bloke found and brought in before he finds a way to skip the country."

"Remember to ask the mother for details of Ashley's medication when you see her today," Evan said.

Watkins nodded. "Good point. And that's something else you can ask them to mention on the TV broadcasts, isn't it? They like the human drama angle, don't they? Little transplant victim's life could be in danger unless she's found straightaway. Makes it more newsworthy somehow. You can give the media that titbit when I've got the facts straight from the mother."

"Right," Evan said, not relishing the prospect of repeating all those phone calls.

Watkins took a last bite of roll, scattering grated cheese over his plate, then got to his feet, brushing crumbs from his raincoat. "I'm off then for my TV spot and my next grilling of Mrs S." He paused and looked back at Evan. "Was this supposed to be one of your days off, too?"

Evan nodded.

"Why don't you take a couple of hours to yourself then? I won't need you before four, only take your mobile along this time, just in case something comes up, okay?"

"Okay. Thanks. As it happens, I've got something I'm dying to do."

"Take a nap?"

"No, dig out a sewer line," Evan said, with a smile.

* * *

The weather was fast deteriorating again as Evan made his way up the mountain track, clutching a spade. For the first time he reconsidered Mr Pilcher's thoughts on not finding the view so thrilling when he had to stagger home with groceries. Of course they'd have a car, wouldn't they? Bronwen wouldn't have to carry the shopping up from the road on foot. But they only had one car, and he'd need it to drive to work. Possible complication ahead. He brushed it from his mind and set about attacking the task in hand.

There was a low stone wall around the cottage, and the previous occupants had made some attempt at starting a garden. It hadn't been too successful, given the exposed setting and the fact that it had been a holiday cottage and they had only shown up sporadically. There were a couple of good-sized bushes growing by the front gate. There had been roses along the house walls, but the fire had wiped them out. Still, the beds had been dug and it was a start. He stood at the gate, picturing the finished product — the beds a mass of blooms, a small kitchen garden at the rear, new roses climbing over the front door. He had never done much gardening himself, having lived in a terraced house in a city for most of his life, but Bronwen loved to garden and possessed a green thumb. If anyone could make a go of this, she could.

The first spatters of rain in his face reminded him that he'd better get on if he wanted to dig out the sewer line today. He had seen the septic tank on the plans, and he knew that the sewer and water lines pretty much followed the front path. That involved taking out flagstones before he started. He put his spade under the first of them and prized it up. Then the next. He was red faced and soaked in sweat by the time the front path was only dark earth and the flagstones were stacked in a neat pile beside the gate. In spite of the rain, which was falling quite steadily now, he took off his jacket and placed it under the large bush. Then he picked up the spade and started to dig. The soil was heavy and wet and each spadeful came away with a loud sucking sound. He realized that his plan to dig this whole thing out in one afternoon was maybe a little ambitious, but he had no idea when he'd get any more free time while the missing child case was ongoing. He dug down six inches, then another six, and still hadn't located any lines. At last he felt the chink of something solid as his spade cut through the earth and met resistance.

"Finally," he said, and dug more carefully. The last thing he wanted to do was damage either line. He bent to scrape away the earth from around what was probably the waterline. To his horror, what he took for the pipe moved and a piece of it came away in his hands. He found he was standing there, holding a long, thin bone.

More careful scraping revealed more bones. It could be anything, he decided — a sheep that had died, even a former shepherd's favourite sheepdog. Then he came upon the shoe.

CHAPTER 10

"Where's the fire then, Evan *bach*?" Charlie Hopkins shouted as Evan came running down the track and almost passed him without a word.

"Not a fire, Charlie," Evan paused, gasping for breath. "I've just found a skeleton outside my cottage. I've called my inspector and he's on his way, but he told me to tape off the area, just in case."

"A skeleton, outside Rhodri's old cottage, you say? A human skeleton, do you mean?"

"That's exactly what I mean, Charlie."

"*Escob annwyl!* Now who could that be, I wonder?"

"I've no idea. I didn't like to unearth any more, once I saw what had to be a shoe."

"I don't recall anybody dying and not getting a proper burial, and old Rhodri's wife died in the hospital so we know he didn't knock her off on the quiet, although I wouldn't have been surprised if he had, miserable old witch that she was."

"I think this might have been a child," Evan said. "It was only a little shoe."

"I only recall the one child up there — old Rhodri only had the one daughter on account of his wife dying young

— and she's still going strong, so it must have been before my time." Charlie slapped Evan on the back. "With your luck, boyo, you'll find that it's a listed skeleton — probably some ancient Celt, sacrificed by the Druids, and you'll have archaeologists digging up your entire front yard for ever more." He gave one of his wheezy laughs that turned into a cough.

"Don't say that!" Evan exclaimed. "Besides, it can't be that old because it's above the waterline, and I don't imagine the cottage has had running water that long, has it?"

"No, it was only put in about seventy-eight or seventy-nine, if I remember rightly. They got some kind of government money for rural water and electrification. My mother's family on Anglesey had been getting their water from the pump at the bottom of the hill all their lives. You'd have thought they'd have been happy to have the water laid on but my old *nain* said she didn't trust the tap water. At least she knew that her pump came from her own spring and not from water that somebody's sheep might have peed in."

Evan laughed. "Some people just don't like change," he said. "But I can't stand talking, Charlie. I've got to get the area taped before the boss shows up, or I'm in trouble."

In fact he was just tying off the last of the yellow tape across the gate when he saw a white incident van coming up the pass at a speed that was definitely exceeding the limit. It stopped outside the small police station, which had been closed since Evan went into plainclothes training.

Evan saw DI Watkins get out, plus a tall, red-haired man he recognized as a forensic tech.

"Up here!" he shouted, indicating the track, and watched them struggling up the slick, steep surface.

"You want to actually live up here?" Watkins gasped, as he reached Evan on the bluff. "You want to walk up and down this bloody mountain every time you run out of milk?"

"It will keep me fit, Sarge — I mean sir," Evan said.

"All right, show me what you've got, and it better be good, boyo." Watkins looked around him. "Because I've had to postpone my television appearance thanks to you. If you hadn't been so bloody insistent, I'd never have come, not when we're in the middle of an important case like this."

"It's over here, just inside the gate." Evan led the way. "I didn't like to dig it out, without permission, but I think it's another child. That could be significant, don't you think?"

He pointed down at the trench he had dug. "See — right there. That's a child's foot, isn't it?"

Watkins squatted and poked the object gingerly. "Certainly looks that way," Watkins said. "What do you think, Lloyd?"

"Looks that way to me, too," the tech replied.

Watkins stood up again and looked at Evan. "So are you suggesting there might be a connection with our missing child?"

"I'm suggesting we find out who this was and how long he or she's been here," Evan said.

"If the body's already down to a skeleton, then some time, I'd imagine," Watkins said. "What do you think, Lloyd?"

"No way of knowing." The young man gave an unconcerned shrug as if the object in the trench had been nothing more than a discarded cigarette packet. "Could be two years, could be twenty-two or forty-two," Lloyd said. "I'd prefer not to touch it, myself. I'm trained in crime-scene techniques, but you really need a forensic anthropologist for something this old. He'd know what to look for. I'd be scared of disturbing evidence."

"Where do we find a forensic anthropologist?" Evan asked. "Do the North Wales Police have one?"

"What do you think we are, the bloody Met?" Watkins demanded. "But I seem to remember that there is one on call from the university in Bangor."

Lloyd nodded. "Some bloke from the university came out a couple of years ago when we found some bones down an old well. It's wonderful what they can do. He'll probably be able to tell you exactly how old this body is and how the kid died — all that sort of stuff."

"However old it is, we've definitely got a crime scene, haven't we?" Evan asked, staring down at the little foot with growing unease. "And I think we should act quickly, sir. It's just possible that it wasn't Ashley's father who snatched her, but someone who's taken a child before."

"But this could have lain here for years. It could have been a child who died from natural causes, and they were too poor to pay for a funeral. They did that kind of thing in the old days, didn't they?"

"In the old days, yes." Evan continued to stare at the foot. "But I've been digging out this trench to locate the waterline and I haven't reached it yet, so apparently this child was put here after the line was connected, which makes it less than twenty-five years ago."

"You're suggesting that someone stole a little kid, killed him or her, and then buried the body inside this cottage gate? Why would anyone do that when there are miles of wild mountains he could have chosen? Look up there. Mile after mile of opportunity to dig a grave where nobody would see it. No, there has to be a reason for the skeleton being here. Who owned the cottage before those yuppie English people?"

"An old man called Rhodri was still living here when I came to the area, and I got the feeling he'd been the shepherd up here for most of his life."

"Is he still alive?"

"As far as I know. He went to live with his daughter in Bangor. That would be easy enough to check out."

"Right. You can do that, then." Watkins stood up and brushed off his hands. "Only, let's hold back until we've got some kind of accurate dating from our university bloke. If the bones are more than a few years old, they won't have anything to do with our current investigation, so we can put them on hold for a while. Our number one task is to find a missing child."

He turned to the forensic tech, who was fishing in his anorak pocket for a cigarette. "Lloyd, can you get me in touch with the anthropologist chap? Tell him I'd like him up here as soon as possible — could be important."

"Right, sir," Lloyd shoved the cigarette packet back into the pocket. "And you presumably want the site protected from the elements until it's been gone over?"

"Yes, we'd better. And I've still got to get myself down to the caravan park to meet the mother and the reporter before our team meeting at four. I'll be interested to see what Constable Davies has come up with in the meantime."

"Probably solved the whole case single-handed," Evan quipped.

"I suspect you're jealous because she can work the computer and you can't," Watkins said with a grin. "Well, don't just stand there, Lloyd. Get cracking. I want that anthropologist up here ASAP."

He set off down the mountain at a great rate. Evan watched his back with interest. When Watkins had been a sergeant, he'd been easy-going and matey. Now that he was an inspector and running the show, he was metamorphosizing before Evan's eyes into another DCI Hughes. Evan put on a spurt to catch up with him. "That skeleton. It's not anyone from around here, at least during living memory. Old Charlie Hopkins — you remember Charlie from the pub, don't you? The one with the missing teeth — he says he can't think of anybody from the village who died and wasn't given a proper burial."

"Could be donkey's years old."

"But what about the water pipe?"

"Maybe you just missed it. It's easy enough to do — a couple of inches too far to the right or left."

"So you really think I should wait to check out the former shepherd until the anthropologist has had a chance to date the bones?" Evan asked.

"Seems like a lot of extra work for nothing if we find the remains are fifty years old."

"It looked like a modern shoe, didn't it? Like a trainer?"

"Hard to tell until they've washed all the mud and muck away. It wasn't a Victorian boot or anything, that's for sure, but I don't think kid's shoes have changed that much during my lifetime."

Evan stood and watched as DI Watkins prepared to get back into the police van. "So you don't need me until the meeting at four?" he asked. "Then maybe I should keep an eye on the site until someone shows up."

"Yes, you could do that," Watkins agreed. "And if we can get the anthropologist up here, you can give him a hand. You might learn something." He opened the van door. "Come on, Lloyd. I haven't got all day."

"Hang on, sir. They've just gone to look up the anthropologist's number for me," Lloyd called back, maintaining his balance with one outstretched arm as he came down the mountain with the mobile phone close to his cheek. "Right. Okay, go ahead." He had stopped and scribbled down a number. "Good. Got it then. Cheers, mate."

He came running down the rest of the way to the van. "I've got a number here. Do you want me to call or do you want to do it yourself?"

"You can do the calling while I drive," Watkins said. "I've got a lot to fit into a short time this afternoon. If anyone's caught speeding, it better be me."

The van took off, scattering gravel. Evan watched it go then made his way back up the hill to the grave site. He was glad that Watkins hadn't required him to do something else because he was feeling strangely protective about that little grave. Someone's poor child was buried there, maybe a child who had gone missing like Ashley — a child the police had never managed to find. But that was stupid, wasn't it? Inspector Watkins had to be right — nobody would have chosen to bury a child inside a cottage garden when there was a whole mountain range to do it in. He couldn't wait to talk to the old shepherd, and he couldn't rule out that English couple either. It would be worth checking whether any children had vanished from the region where they had their home in England.

An hour passed and no policeman appeared to guard the site, so Evan used the time to dig out more of the trench, well away from the little grave. He located where the water pipe emerged from the house and began to dig it out, hoping to find the sewer pipe beneath it. But he couldn't concentrate on the digging. That little foot and leg bone had strangely affected him. He couldn't shake off the sense of urgency that nagged at him and the fear that this could be happening to Ashley at this very moment somewhere in these mountains.

He squatted beside the open grave and stared down. That really was a little shoe he was looking at, wasn't it? He bent and carefully scraped away some of the mud.

"Hey, what are you doing?" A woman's voice behind him made him almost lose his balance and fall into the hole.

He righted himself and looked up to see a young woman in jeans and a Harvard sweatshirt staring at him. She had a fresh face, free of any makeup, freckles, and a light brown ponytail. *An American student, obviously*, he thought, and got to his feet. "I'm sorry, miss, but this area's off-limits at the moment. See the crime-scene tape? Now if you'd just move away."

"I can see the crime-scene tape," the girl said, "but I thought its purpose was to keep people out."

"It is."

"Then why were you messing around, touching things?"

"Because I'm a police officer, miss. A detective constable."

"Then didn't they teach you at detective school not to go messing up crime scenes?" she demanded.

"Hold on a minute — I can assure you I wasn't messing up any crime scene—"

"I saw you, digging around down there," she interrupted.

Evan had heard that American women were assertive, but this one was downright aggressive. He was longing to tell her it was none of her bloody business, but he suspected that she'd be on the phone to the chief constable at the first hint of rudeness on his part. So he managed what he hoped was a pleasant smile. "Well, you can rest assured that no harm is coming to any crime scene, so thank you for your concern and please move along."

"Please move along?" she demanded. "Didn't they tell you I was coming?" Then she added, in response to his blank face, "I'm the anthropologist."

"Oh. Oh, I see." Evan blushed, feeling stupid. "I'm sorry. I wasn't expecting the anthropologist to be a woman."

"Strangely enough, they do allow women to be things other than nurse, secretary, or teacher these days." She gave him a patronizing smile.

"What I meant was that I was told the anthropologist at the university was a man, and you look too young to be a professor."

"I age well," she said. "Clean living and all that. What were you doing down there?"

"Well, I was the one who dug it out in the first place," Evan said. "It's my property, look you. I stopped as soon as I came upon what I thought was a shoe. I was just scraping away a little more mud to make sure I hadn't got it wrong."

"I'm sorry. I shouldn't have jumped on you like that," she said. "I didn't see a uniform, and I thought you were some thrill seeker helping himself to a bone or two. It's so easy to disturb good evidence." She held out her hand. "Jan Telesky. Dr Jan Telesky, associate professor of forensic anthropology. I'm on sabbatical from Cal State, Chico."

Evan took her hand. "Constable Evans, North Wales Police," he said.

"Do you have a first name? I'm not big on formality."

"It's Evan."

"Evan Evans?" She started to laugh. "Did your parents lack imagination or what?"

Evan smiled too. "It's quite common around here to have two names the same — I can think of a Robert Roberts, Tomos Thomas—" He stopped, his mouth open. "Hang on a minute," he said, "that reminds me of something."

"What?" she asked.

"I think I might know who this child could be."

CHAPTER 11

Suzanne Bosley-Thomas moved around the tent like an automaton, putting baskets of primroses in the middle of each table. *Only a few more hours and it will be over*, she thought. *Then I can go home.* She glanced up at Val and Nick, laughing and shouting at each other as they strung fairy lights across the ceiling. They actually appeared to be enjoying themselves. But then Nick had always been a happy little boy, and Val had always been good at concealing things. Henry, as usual, was doing his duty, ordering the caterers about as if they were army recruits and he was the drill sergeant. And her father was conspicuous by his absence. He had popped in to say good job, looks splendid, and other such waffle and then gone again. To her he had hardly said a word, but then she knew how he felt about her. He had always disliked her and blamed her, and there wasn't a thing she could do about it. Tears welled up and she brushed them away. She was not going to crumble today. They were not going to feel sorry for poor, misguided Suzanne.

Henry appeared at her shoulder. "Why on earth are you putting out all these bloody flowers?"

"They're called table centres, Henry." She stared him down, conscious of how much she disliked him. Thirty years of bullying were enough. "They are quite usual among people who know how to entertain."

"But why go to all this trouble for the old man? You know what he thinks of flowers, and he doesn't want anything pretentious."

Suzanne stood, cradling one of the baskets of primroses in her hands. "But we all know that this isn't about Grandfather, don't we, Henry? This is a wake."

* * *

Evan watched with growing impatience as Dr Telesky worked at what seemed to be a snail's pace, using minute tools and sometimes even a small brush, until at last the whole skeleton was revealed. It lay there, staring up at Evan with its sightless eye sockets and grinning mouth. The front teeth were angled slightly forward. Evan remembered that she had sucked her thumb until she was five. The others had teased her about it. Could it really be her, so far from where she'd vanished? Could someone have brought her here, alive or dead? He shuddered and folded his arms to stop himself from shivering.

"Can you tell if it was a boy or a girl?" he asked.

"Not definitely at this stage. Probably a girl," she said.

"And can you tell how old it is?"

"PMI, you mean?"

"PMI?" Evan looked blank.

"Post-mortem interval. How long she's been there. Did you mean that or how old she was when she died?"

"Both."

"In answer to the second part, I'd estimate between four and six. Not older than six anyway. She still has her primary teeth. And as to the PMI — I'd say less than forty years."

"Why forty and not fifty?"

"Because of the clothing." She leaned forward and lifted a scrap of fibre with tweezers before dropping it into a plastic bag. "Cotton doesn't last long. This appears to be man-made fibre. Polyesters weren't common before the sixties. The soles of her shoes are man-made too."

"But you think she's been her for some time, do you — more than a year or so?"

"More than a year, yes," she said, looking up at him. "There's no adhering soft tissue, no odour of decomposition, and take a look at the surfaces of the bones — all those split lines and checking. Of course those things tend to happen more quickly on a younger victim, but we've got something else to go on here." She reached up and tugged at a branch that was drooping over her as she worked. "That's a good-sized bush growing beside the gate. More robust than any of the other bushes because it's had more nourishment."

Evan fought to keep his face expressionless as she went on. "If you want to know where a body's been buried, you only have to look at the plants above it. Go for the healthiest plants. Good fertilizer, you see."

Evan thought back to the lab tech and his apparent detachment. Coming from this fresh-faced young woman with her ponytail, it was even harder to take. But he supposed that they had to stay detached if they were constantly around crime scenes. He'd heard of surgeons making jokes throughout operations, and there were plenty of policemen who traded jokes over corpses. One way of coping, he supposed. He wondered if he'd ever get so used to death that it wouldn't affect him.

Dr Telesky was still talking, pointing now to the child's right foot. "And see how one of the roots has gone right through one foot and out the other side — right through the leather of the shoe. Amazing isn't it, what roots will do?"

Evan swallowed hard. He remembered that foot and how lightly it had danced over the springy turf, as if the body it supported weighed nothing at all.

"Now this is useful because it will help us to narrow down exactly when she was buried here. I'll take a cutting from the root. They have rings in them like trees do, you know. A competent botanist will be able to tell me how old the root is; then we'll know how long she's been here."

She looked up at Evan as she withdrew a pair of clippers from her backpack. He shut his eyes as she snipped at the root close to the foot.

"You said you might have some idea who she was?" she asked with interest. "You've got an unsolved missing child case on the books, have you?"

"Yes," he said. "Twenty-five years old. Little girl who vanished from the mountain above Llanrwst. That's on the other side of the Glyders from here."

"Twenty-five years ago?" She laughed. "You surely weren't in the police force then? Or are you another one who is much older than you look?"

"No," he said. "I was seven years old at the time. I was one of the kids she played with." He was going to add, "She was my friend," but he couldn't.

"Oh my. Then this can't be too easy for you, then. Not just any other case."

"No, it's pretty important for me to know for sure whether it's Sarah or not."

"Then I'll do my utmost to get you a definite answer. Her family will be glad to know too, I'm sure. It's the most unbearable thing in the world not knowing what happened, falling asleep every night with the faint hope that your child still might be alive somewhere. It destroys more lives than just this one."

Evan looked at her more favourably. So she was human after all. She had put the root clipping into another plastic bag and now produced a camera from her bag of tricks. "Did they ever have any suspects? Was foul play suspected in those days?"

Evan stepped back as she aimed the camera at the grave site. "I don't really know. Like I said, I was just a little kid at the time. I just remember helping to look for her, not finding her, and feeling scared."

"Of course. You would. It will be interesting to see the police files from the time and whether anyone was suspected."

"Can you tell if there was foul play?" Evan asked, as the flashbulb went off again and again from different angles. "She looks as if she was arranged very peacefully."

"Child molesters often give their victims a nice burial," she said, not looking up from her camera. "Instant remorse. But I can't tell you how she died. There's no obvious trauma to the skeleton, but a big hand over her face could have suffocated her easily enough."

A vivid image of Sarah came to him, the way her long, blonde hair floated out behind her as she ran, the way she was always laughing. Then he pictured that big hand, clamping itself over her face. What else had been done to her? He didn't want to ask.

"They have DNA testing these days to find out who she was, don't they?" he asked.

"That's the most expensive way of finding out," she said, "and it takes time. Dental records would be the simplest. But yes, it is possible to do a DNA match. Bone cortex or tooth pulp work well, and the match is made with the mother or siblings. It's always maternal DNA we use for the match."

"She had siblings," Evan said. "A brother and a sister. And I expect her mother's still alive too."

"They live around here?"

He shook his head. "No, they used to come on holiday once a year to stay with their grandfather." He straightened up. "Look, I really have to go. I've got a meeting with my boss at four. What will you do next?"

"I've taken photos of the site. Now it's a question of moving the skeleton down to the lab, taking soil and plant samples from around it. I'll need help getting this lot down the mountain."

"A police constable is on his way. So it's alright if I go, is it?"

"I guess I can't stop you," she said.

"You'll be all right, alone up here then?"

"I'm a big girl. I can take care of myself." She went back to lifting bones into a tray.

CHAPTER 12

As he ran down the mountain, Evan got the feeling that she was annoyed with him for leaving. Less than an hour ago she'd been shouting at him for mucking around with the site and a fat lot of use he'd been ever since, mostly standing and watching while she did things. The problem with women was that you never knew what they really wanted, he decided. They threw out hints and men were supposed to guess right. They said that you shouldn't go to the trouble and expense of buying them flowers or taking them to a restaurant, when they really wanted you to say that nothing was too good for them and they sulked when the flowers or the dinner out didn't happen. Why they could never come out and say exactly what they wanted was beyond Evan. Bronwen, thank goodness, was better than most, and she didn't sulk.

He called to check that the constable was on his way, then drove as fast as he dared down the mountain pass. It was ten to four. His driving kept pace with his mind, which was also in overdrive. Why had he kept all of this shut away, never thought of it for years when he had been so devastated by it at the time? The Thomas children had never returned to the valley again, and Evan's family had moved away soon afterward, down to the city of Swansea, where he'd had other things to occupy him, like learning how to hold his own with the bigger, tougher city boys.

He remembered now that he had helped to look for her, joining his father and grandfather and all the other men from the area as they combed the mountain, using torches as darkness fell. But all the time he had known that the search was a waste of time and she wouldn't be found. He knew exactly what had happened to her. She had been taken by the fairies.

* * *

"You live here, don't you?" Sarah had asked him, the first time they met in the meadow behind his grandfather's house. He had been five years old at the time and thought she might very well be a fairy herself. He had been busy putting back stones that had fallen from a drystone wall around his grandfather's property, and when he looked up, there she was. She had a little elfin face and long, almost white-blonde hair that was so fine it danced on its own as she walked. And her eyes were light blue. Evan had never seen light blue eyes before, nor blonde hair, except in films. Most of his neighbours and schoolmates in the Ogwen Valley of North Wales were dark haired, like he was. Furthermore, the other children in the valley wore sensible, long-lasting clothes in colours that wouldn't show the dirt. She was wearing a light filmy dress that floated out around her.

Evan had nodded, too overcome to speak.

"Good. So you can show me the fairies."

Evan had been at school for a whole year and considered himself as tough and worldly as any of the boys in the mixed infants. "There's no such thing as fairies," he'd said scornfully.

Her blue eyes opened even wider, like a doll's. "Oh, but there are. My grandfather says so. He says they're called the Tylwyth Teg *and that means the fair family in case you don't speak Welsh, and you can see them up in the mountains if you're lucky." She'd skipped ahead of him, lighter than air herself. "My grandfather says he saw them once when he was young. He says they were dancing in a fairy circle and they wanted him to dance with them, but he knew that they'd take him forever if he stepped into that circle so he ran away."*

She paused to look back at Evan with a pitying look. "So maybe you just haven't been lucky enough to see them yet. You have to go right up into the mountains. I don't suppose you're allowed up there alone because you're not old enough."

"I'm almost six years old," he said. "And I can go where I want."

"Then you can take me," she said. "You can show me the kind of places where we might see fairies."

"What kind of places?" He still didn't believe in them, he told himself, but he wasn't stupid enough to turn down an opportunity to be with her, and to show off how well he could walk and climb.

"My grandfather says the entrances to the kingdom of the Tylwyth Teg *are always underwater, like caves at the bottom of a lake. So if you see them, it's likely to be near a lake or a pond or a waterfall, and always on misty days." She gave him the sweetest smile that lit up her whole face. "So next misty day, you can take me and maybe we'll see them."*

"Sarah, where are you?" a voice called, and an older boy, dressed in khaki shorts and an open-necked shirt, came striding across the meadow toward them. "Oh, there you are, you naughty girl. You know you're not supposed to wander off. Now give me your hand and come along. Mother's waiting to take us on a picnic." His voice was loud and clear, with an annoying edge to it — the same kind of voice as the posh tourists who stopped their big cars to ask for directions and always shouted in case Evan couldn't understand them. He gave Evan the briefest of glances as he dragged Sarah away.

As Evan stood watching her go, skipping over the tussocks of grass in that remarkable weightless way, he heard the big boy say, "You know Mother wouldn't like you mixing with the local children."

Then Sarah had looked back at him with her sweet smile. He worried that he'd never see her again.

* * *

Evan found himself in the car park of the Caernarfon police station with no recollection of how he'd got there. DI Watkins and the rest of the team were already assembled in the incident room as he burst in.

"Sorry. I got held up," he gasped.

"It's all right; you're not late. It's only just four," Watkins said. "Did the anthropologist turn up?" he asked, as Evan took a seat at the table.

"Yes, and she's unearthed the skeleton, and what's more, I think I know who it is." The words came tumbling out, like rapid-fire bullets.

"Really? And who is it?" Watkins looked mildly interested, that's all.

"I didn't think of it at first because she went missing on the other side of the mountains, and I'd forgotten all about it, but her name's Sarah Bosley-Thomas. I was there when it happened. I knew her."

Now he had Watkins's undivided attention. "You were there — how long ago was this, then?"

"Almost twenty-five years. I was seven years old when she disappeared."

"I thought you grew up in the south, in Swansea."

"We moved down there when I was ten." Evan was conscious that he was still speaking quickly. "Up until then we lived outside Llanrwst, and my dad was with the North Wales Police in Colwyn Bay."

"I never knew that."

"We lived with my grandfather, actually, on his farm."

"Does he still live there?"

Evan shook his head. "No, he died some years ago, and my father's brothers sold the property. I wish I'd had a say in it — I'd have definitely wanted to keep it. Lovely spot it was, with a view right across the valley."

"So it was a local girl from that area — Ogwen Valley?"

"No, she was a visitor. She used to come and stay with her grandfather for the summers on the next-door farm. There were several grandchildren, and I used to play with them."

"And the little girl went missing?"

"Yes." Evan stared out of the window. Sparrows were twittering and fluttering in the hedge. "They were playing up on the mountain. Sarah was the youngest. She got tired and said she was going home. She never showed up. They had search parties all over the mountain, but they never found her."

"Up above Llanrwst?" Watkins asked. "Then how the hell did she wind up above Llanfair? If someone had grabbed her, he would have had to bring her over the top of the Glyders and down again, when there were a thousand spots on the other side he could have hidden her — lakes he could have thrown her in, caves, potholes — plenty of opportunity to hide a body."

Evan tried to control the shudder. "Unless he had some connection to the cottage, and he brought her back."

"Ah, right. You were going to check out who was living there at the time, weren't you?" Watkins said. "We'll need a positive identification on the skeleton first, just to make sure we are speaking about your missing girl — but it certainly sounds as if she could be the one."

"Can we get on with the matter in hand?" Bill Edwards, the grim-looking sergeant, interrupted. "I'm sure this skeleton of Evans's is most fascinating, but aren't we supposed to be tracking down a missing girl who might still be alive?"

"Yes, you're right, Bill," Watkins said. "Let's put this on hold until after our meeting, Evans."

"But I think it's important, sir," Evan said. "The two cases could possibly be connected."

"Come on, Evans," Bill Edwards said. "You're not trying to say that our missing girl is connected to a child who disappeared twenty-five years ago?"

"She could be."

Evan detected a patronizing grin. Bill Edwards obviously thought he was a new detective constable and thus too keen. He needed taking down a peg or two.

"So you're telling us that someone grabbed a little girl twenty-five years ago and has behaved himself ever since, until now, when it enters his fancy to grab another one?"

"Maybe not," Evan said. "Maybe he hasn't been in the area all that time. He might have just come back, and it's possible that Ashley is the latest in a long line."

"Do you think we might be barking up the wrong tree then?" Glynis Davies asked, her intent look letting Evan know that at least she was going to take him seriously. "You think Ashley wasn't taken by her father after all?"

"We won't know that until we find the father, will we?" Watkins interrupted. "And finding him has to be our number one priority at the moment. So let's put Evan's skeleton on hold until we've got some positive identification. We'll consider the child's father our prime suspect until we've located him, and it's been proved otherwise."

"Good idea," Bill Edwards muttered. "So would somebody like to brief us on what's been done so far? Our men have blanketed the entire area with posters. We've established a hotline number for tips. I understand that the boat search was negative. Now what about Interpol?"

"Constable Davies?" Watkins asked, turning to her.

"Right, sir. I've been in touch with NCIS and given them everything we have on the father. They're going to contact Interpol and have the Russian police try to locate Sholokhov."

"But we don't definitely know that he's skipped the country, do we?" the other uniformed branch sergeant, Howell Jones, asked.

"He hasn't, unless he was using false identity documents," Watkins said. "We've checked with the port authorities."

"The NCIS says that unfortunately false documents are too easy to come by these days, especially for those who mix in asylum circles. He could have bought himself a fake EU document, and then it would hardly have been checked."

"But we circulated a description, didn't we?" Evan asked. "And the fact that he was traveling with a little blonde girl. That should have made him easy enough to spot."

"Could he have got out before we notified the ports?" Glynis asked.

"Not very likely, is it?" Watkins said. "It was only two hours after Mrs Sholokhov reported the child missing that we spoke to her, and we notified the ports pretty soon after that. Say two and a half hours — where could he have taken the child in that time?"

"Manchester airport?" Bill Edwards suggested.

Watkins shook his head. "Not with all the time it takes to clear security these days. It's an hour and a half's drive, then he'd have to park, check in, go through security. It's just not possible in two hours."

"And do flights actually go from Manchester to Moscow?" Glynis asked. "Wouldn't he have to go down to London for that?"

"If he was smart, he'd be on a plane going somewhere else," Evan said. He picked up a pencil and doodled along the edge of the pad in front of him — fierce black rectangles that looked like graves. "Maybe he'd take her to Frankfurt or Berlin and then rent a car and drive the rest. It's easier to get through checkpoints with a car. In fact if I'd been him, I'd have taken her to Holyhead and across to Ireland."

"You're probably right," Watkins agreed. "But he hasn't attempted to fly out of Dublin or Belfast yet, as far as we can tell."

"Then he has to be lying low in this country," Glynis said. "We might have to wait until someone locates him."

"This all presupposes he has money," Evan said. "Didn't his wife say that he never held a job, and they lived in poverty? I'd imagine what he's doing now requires a hefty amount of cash."

"You're right there," Watkins said. "But you never know how these foreigners work, do you? He could have had a whip-round among the other Russians who wanted to help him prevent the mother from getting custody."

"In the meantime, what about Ashley's medicine?" Evan turned to Watkins. "Did you get the prescription?"

"Yes, I've got it." Watkins said.

"Might it be an idea then to contact chemists and warn them to be on the lookout for someone bringing in this particular prescription?" Glynis asked. "It's not the most ordinary medication in the world, is it?"

"We could do that, although if he's had copies of her prescriptions and he's been planning this for some time, he'd have filled them already, wouldn't he?"

"Yes, I suppose he would," Glynis agreed. "In which case, we could find out where the little girl's prescription has been filled recently. It might give us a clue as to where he is staying."

"That's a smart suggestion, Davies. Can I leave that to you, then?" Watkins said.

Glynis glanced at Evan and grinned. "I should learn to keep my mouth shut," she said. "It only seems to get me extra work."

"I think it's bloody brilliant," Evan said. "If we find out it's been filled somewhere else in the country, we'll know right away whether he's got her or not."

"Apart from that, any other suggestions?" Watkins asked.

There was silence. A million thoughts were flying around in Evan's head, but he couldn't put them in order before Watkins went on. "Then we'll just have to wait until someone contacts us — maybe tonight's newscasts will produce someone who's seen her. If the father's in the clear, he might well come forward himself."

"What about the missing child database?" Evan asked, remembering one of the things he'd been thinking about. "You were going to look into it, Glynis. Did you manage to get Ashley added to it?"

Glynis shook her head. "I inquired about it, but we can't enter her. They only take children who are missing. If Ashley's been abducted by her father, then she's not officially missing. She's a victim of a crime."

"I hate to think that we're wasting precious time," Evan said. "How did your interview with Mrs Sholokhov go, sir? Did she tell you anything else that could be useful?"

"Nothing really. It's quite clear that she's convinced her ex-husband has taken the child, and she knows he'll take good care of her — she's not worried about that, she says. But she's terrified he'll take the girl to Russia, and she'll never see her again. That was about it. I pumped her on anything she might remember about the beach and cars parked at the caravan park, but she stuck to the story exactly as she told us. In fact she was very tight-lipped, and she only perked up when the TV reporter spoke to her. Then she was a real ham for the camera — wringing her hands and doing the whole grieving mother bit."

"Is the piece going to air tonight?" Evan asked.

"That's right. Six o'clock news."

"We'll have to make sure we watch that, won't we?" the round-faced sergeant Jones said, with a wink to his mate. "Did they think you had star quality then, Inspector?"

"Give it a break, Howell. We're looking for a missing kid, for God's sake. I don't know what I'd do if my Tiffany were missing. I'd go bananas. I'd search nonstop until I found her. So I'm taking this one rather personally. Can't say I feel like laughing, if you know what I mean."

"Sorry, sir. Didn't mean to offend," the sergeant muttered.

Evan looked at his DI with approval. There was always an undercurrent of rivalry going on between the detective and uniformed branches, almost a resentment of the comparative freedom that the plainclothes boys enjoyed.

"And, sir, you wanted me to get back to the media about her heart transplant and the medication once you'd spoken to the mother," he said. "Shall I release that news to them now?"

"Good idea, Evans," Watkins said. "And apart from that, all we can do is wait. We've got our posters out, thanks to you boys," he nodded to the two sergeants. "We've the child's picture airing on newscasts across the country, and we've set the wheels in motion for the Russian police to start looking for him over there. I hope to God we find him quickly."

"And I hope that he's the one who took her," Evan said, "because the alternative is that a crazy person who takes little blonde girls has come back to the area."

"She was blonde too, the little girl you knew, was she?" Watkins looked up from his notes.

"She looked almost exactly like Ashley — same little elfin face; long, blonde hair; very dainty."

Watkins sucked air through his teeth. "Bloody hell. So maybe your hunch isn't so wrong after all."

CHAPTER 13

Watching Sarah being dragged away by her brother had seemed like the end of the world to five-year-old Evan. He had feared that he would never see her again. Then he had started patrolling the borders of the Thomas property and found a good vantage point on some rocks where the hillside rose steeply behind the farmhouse. Perched precariously on the very top of the tallest rock, he could look down on the back of the house. Sometimes, when the light was right, he could see into the kitchen and watch them eating a meal. Sometimes they came out to play badminton or croquet on what passed for a lawn, when they had chased off the sheep. Sarah was never allowed to play, of course. They made her hold the mallets, or pick up the badminton birds for them, but she did so willingly, darting out like a little bird herself.

There were five of them, Evan discovered: Two big boys, one of whom had come to fetch her that afternoon, a middle-sized girl who sulked a lot and made a fuss about the others cheating, and a boy slightly older than Evan who trotted around obediently after the others. Sarah was the youngest. There were also two women who called them in to meals or warned them not to get their clothes dirty and two men who came down only at weekends. One drove an E-Type Jaguar and the other an Aston Martin. Evan wasn't particularly interested in cars and too young to know about them, but some of the bigger boys in the village had seen them driving past and been impressed with the make and models.

When the Thomas children were out, which was most fine days, Evan wandered the hills above his house, looking for evidence of the Tylwyth Teg. *He was pretty sure that Sarah was wrong and fairies belonged with Father Christmas and the bogeyman — things you didn't believe in anymore when you started school. His parents said that there were no fairies in the world any longer, but his grandfather wasn't so sure. One never knew with the* Tylwyth Teg *when they'd show up again. They could stay in their kingdom underground for hundreds of years and then one day they'd pop up again, just like that. What nonsense you do tell the boy, his mother had said. You'll have him believing your silly stories.*

But when Evan went for a walk the next Sunday with his grandfather, the old man showed him a fairy ring. See how the grass is greener, and it makes a perfect circle? That's where they dance, his grandfather said.

Have you ever seen them? Evan asked.

Not I personally, but I've heard of people who have. There's a young chap roams up on the hills, a bit soft in the head, I suppose, but he swears he saw them once. Little lights bobbing in the mist, he said, and when he got closer, he could see they were fairies.

Evan couldn't wait to tell Sarah this. As it happened, he had to wait until the next summer. Their holiday ended, they packed up the cars and drove away without his having a chance to speak to her again.

* * *

Evan came out of the police station and stood breathing in the balmy evening air. A few days ago it had been snowing on the high peaks; now it felt as if summer had arrived. That was the local joke about Welsh weather — if you didn't like it, just wait, and in an hour it would have changed. He wondered if the American anthropologist was still working on the hillside and drove quickly up the pass, hoping to find out what she might have learned. The first tourists of the year were wandering through Llanberis, having just ridden the train down from Mount Snowdon and now looking for somewhere to eat. He honked his horn as an American couple stepped out into the street, looking the wrong way for traffic. They jumped back and gave him an apologetic wave.

As he approached Llanfair, he looked up and saw the shell of his cottage, but no sign of the American woman. No strange car was parked beside the road, and there wasn't even a police vehicle around anymore. That indicated that she had finished her work and taken everything of interest down to the lab. Quick worker, Evan decided. Quick tongued, too, the way she had leaped on him without waiting to find out who he was. Bronwen would be amused when he told her.

He parked the car outside the now closed police station and decided to take a look for himself at the grave site. Slanting rays of the setting sun bathed the hillside around him. As he paused for breath, he was conscious of the silence. Usually at this time of year, the mountain slopes would echo with the bleating of lambs and the deeper baas of sheep. Now he could hear a lark singing high in the air, the twitter of small birds, even the drone of a passing bee. He wondered how many years it would be before the flocks returned to the hills and whether something as terrible as foot-and-mouth disease was lying dormant, waiting to happen again.

The yellow tape was still across the entrance to his garden, where he had tied it, but the former grave was now empty, a little puddle of water pooling at the bottom, with no indication that a body had ever lain in it. When would they know that it was really Sarah? he wondered, and wished he had taken Dr Telesky's phone number. He had to know, one way or the other. He had to do what he could to speed this up. If it were a question of dental records or even of DNA testing, then they'd need to locate other family members. It occurred to Evan that this was something he could get a jump on at this moment, when he was too wound up to go home and relax. At least he could drive over to the Thomases' farm and see if the old man was still alive.

He ran down the steep slope, keeping his balance instinctively, as he had learned to do as a young child, climbed back into his car, and drove up the village street. He thought he saw the front door of the schoolhouse standing open, but he didn't slow down to make sure. The last buildings in the village, until you came to the Everest Inn at the top of the pass, were two chapels, Capel Bethel on the left of the street and Capel Beulah on the right. Evan looked across at the notice board outside Capel Bethel to see whether a biblical text had been chosen this week.

On the billboard outside Capel Bethel were the words: "Make a joyful noise unto the Lord. Praise him with cymbals and trumpets."

On the billboard opposite, outside Capel Beulah, there was also a text from the Bible: "If I have not love, my speech is no more than a sounding brass or a tinkling cymbal."

* * *

Evan smiled as he drove on. This war of the Bible quotes never ceased to amuse him, and no doubt all the villagers, too. It certainly kept the two preachers and their wives busy, when they were not finding other ways of attacking each other. At the top of the pass, where the road swung either right down Nant Gwynant toward Beddgelert and the ocean or left to Betws-y-Coed, he stopped to admire the sunset for a moment. A layer of sea fog had formed on the horizon, and the red ball was being swallowed into it. He stayed motionless, watching, until an impatient hoot from a car behind him reminded him that he was at a junction. He turned left and drove away from the ocean.

Something was going on at the old Thomas farm. A large tent had been erected in the meadow beside the farmhouse, and cars were parked all the way down the drive to the road. Some were even parked at dangerous angles along the hedgerow. Evan hesitated. Old Tomos Thomas had been a grumpy, introverted old man, with scarcely more than a curt "*Bore da*" if Evan's family had passed him. He had talked about sheep over the drystone wall to Evan's grandfather but had never come on a social visit that Evan could remember.

So this had to mean that the farm had been sold to new owners.

He was about to drive on when he changed his mind and turned into the lane leading up to the farmhouse. At least the current owners might know what had happened to the old man and where he might be found if he was still alive. The cars parked beside the house indicated that yuppies might have taken over. BMWs and a Saab and a Jag — no longer as long and sleek as the old E-Type that Evan had so admired — were parked in a row. Evan squeezed in beside them. There was music coming from the tent. Evan went toward it, following another couple, the woman clinging onto the man's arm as she picked her way in high heels over the grass.

The tantalizing smell of barbecuing meat wafted toward Evan, and he saw that a spit had been set up outside with two lambs on it. Inside the tent the atmosphere was smoky and loud, with shouted conversation competing with a band playing Beatles music. A young man in a dog collar came up to Evan.

"Hi," he said. "You haven't got a drink. Bar's over there against the wall."

His accent was transatlantic.

"Sorry," Evan said, "but I'm not really sure what's going on. Is it a charity event because I don't have a ticket or anything."

"Then you didn't get an invitation?" the priest said. "Do you live around here? We tried to make sure we included everybody."

"No, I live in Llanfair on the other side of the mountains," Evan said.

"Ah, a gate-crasher then." The man smiled. "Saw all the cars and decided to drop in?"

"Not exactly. I'm with the North Wales Police, making inquiries."

The smile faded instantly from the man's face. "Inquiries about what?"

"A little girl who vanished twenty-five years ago. She was staying at this place. I'm trying to contact her grandfather, who used to live here."

"Still does live here," the man said. "This is his eightieth birthday party, and I'm his grandson, Nick Thomas."

"Good heavens, Nick! I'd never have thought you'd have turned out . . ."

"To be a priest?" Nick smiled. "No. I don't think I was particularly saintly as a child. But then I'm not particularly saintly now. Do I know you?"

Evan extended his hand. "I'm Evan Evans — the obnoxious little kid from the next farm who used to follow you all around and beg to play with you."

"Good God." Nick laughed and shook his hand. "You've certainly changed, haven't you? You were a skinny little thing in those days, and small, too."

"I finally grew when I started playing rugby. It was a case of getting bigger or being squashed."

"And you're with the police force now?" The smile faded from Nick's eyes. "You said you were here about Sarah. Are there any new developments then?"

"There may well be," Evan said. The band had just finished "A Hard Day's Night" and Evan lowered his voice. "A child's skeleton has been found. We think it may be her."

* * *

Once outside the marquee, Evan took out his mobile phone. He stood among the parked cars in the gathering darkness, hearing the music and laughter spilling out of the tent. "Evans here, sir," he said, in response to the curt, "Watkins."

"I'm over at the Thomases' place near Llanrwst, and they're all here, sir."

"Who is all where?"

"The Thomas family — back for the old man's eightieth birthday."

"And? So you think they'll be able to help you identify the remains?"

"No, sir. More than that. Don't you see — none of them has been back here for twenty-five years. Now they're all back, and it's happened again."

CHAPTER 14

"So you've finally turned up, have you?" Bronwen stood at her front door looking at him with not exactly warmth in her eyes. Instead of her usual long skirts and baggy sweaters, she was smartly dressed in tailored black pants and a silky shirt. "I thought it was Saturday evening, and we were supposed to be going out."

"I'm sorry, *cariad*." Evan kissed her as he stepped into her living room. "A lot's been happening today."

"But I can tell you started partying without me," she said. "I can smell the booze on your breath. What did you do, pop into the Dragon for a quick one?"

"No, I had to go and interview some people who were celebrating an eightieth birthday, and someone shoved a glass of champagne into my hand. By that time I needed a drink, so I downed it."

"Eightieth birthday, eh? I hope they weren't being cited for drunk and disorderly. Were they having a rave up?" Her smile disappeared as she looked at Evan's face. "What is it, love?" She put her hand up and touched his cheek.

"It's all rather horrible actually," he said. He took her hand and held it against his cheek.

"Not that little girl? They haven't found her, have they?"

"Not that little girl, no. Another one."

"Another child was taken?"

He turned away, staring at the flames from a new log leaping up into the chimney. Bronwen liked a fire in the evenings, even in summer. "This one was long ago. A little girl disappeared and she was never found, in spite of extensive searches. Well, today I was digging out the sewer line at the cottage, like I told you I was going to, and I dug up a skeleton — a child's skeleton, Bronwen, and I'm pretty sure it's her."

She came up behind him and rested her hand gently on his shoulder. "Outside our cottage? Evan, how horrible for you."

"It's funny," he said, still staring at the flames, "but I'd put it out of my mind for all this time. Never thought about it once when we moved down to Swansea, and now I can't stop thinking about her. I want to know who the hell took her and what exactly he did to her before he buried her outside our cottage."

"Evan, you don't have to make this too personal," she began.

"Of course it's personal. It's too damned personal. Don't you understand, I knew her. I played with her. I should have been there to protect her."

"Now that's rubbish and you know it. How old were you when this happened?"

"Seven," he said. "She was six, a year younger. I thought she was the most lovely thing in the world — probably a lot like you as a child. I always took good care of her when we went up into the mountains, but that day I'd decided to go fishing with my dad. When we got back, the search parties were already out. We joined them. They had dogs and everything, but we never found her."

"How very sad."

He nodded. "It was more than sad; it was so bloody unfair. Who could have done that to such a beautiful child?"

"Did they ever have any suspects?"

"I don't know," he said. "I'm going into HQ in Colwyn Bay tomorrow to look up the old files. Whoever took her must have carried her right over the Glyders and down to our cottage. That's quite a feat."

"Unless he took her down to a car and drove her here."

Evan hadn't considered that possibility. "But to take her down to the road, he'd have had to come through the Thomases' farm or my *taid*'s farm. There were always farm dogs around, and she could have cried out."

"Unless she was already dead."

"Right." He looked away.

Bronwen went over to the kitchen table and poured a glass of red wine. "Here," she said, "drink this."

Evan sank into the chair in front of the fire. "Thanks," he said.

Bronwen came to sit on the arm.

"So you're going to get the case reopened, are you? If they didn't find anybody then, it will be darned near impossible now, I should have thought."

"We absolutely have to get the case reopened, Bron. Don't you see, it's just happened again. A sweet little blonde girl has disappeared — vanished without a trace."

"Oh, I do see. So you're suggesting that it might not have been the child's father who took her after all, but the same man who killed the first little girl."

"Sarah," he said. "Her name was Sarah. And do you know what I just found out this evening? They are celebrating her grandfather's eightieth birthday at this very moment. All the family members who were here twenty-five years ago and haven't been back since. They've all come back again."

"Evan, you're not suggesting that one of her family did it, are you?"

"I've been wondering about that. I remember how they couldn't wait to get away. How they'd closed ranks and wouldn't speak to anyone. And if it was a family member, she'd have gone willingly enough with him, or her."

"But you weren't talking about grown-ups, were you? She was playing with other children, surely?"

"Two of them were older boys, probably twelve at least. Then there was a bigger girl and a little boy not much older than me. And she was a fragile little thing. I lifted her down from a rock once, and she weighed almost nothing."

"But members of her own family, Evan," Bronwen insisted. "Surely not."

"I don't want to think that way, but it's funny that the same thing happens the moment they come back, isn't it? I'd like to take a look at where they're all living these days and see if there are any other missing children on the police files."

He looked up at her, noticed the makeup and earrings and silky blouse, and felt a sudden flush of guilt. "Sorry, *cariad*. You were expecting us to go out tonight, weren't you? Would you really mind if we put it off for another time? It's been quite a day, what with the skeleton and all. And you've gone to all that trouble to dress up too."

Bronwen ruffled his hair. "I suppose I'll have to get used to this if I'm going to be a policeman's wife, won't I? Are you hungry or did someone happen to shove a lamb chop into your hand while you were at the birthday party?"

"They were barbecuing lambs," Evan said, with a wistful smile. "They smelled wonderful, but no, I didn't stay to eat. I just wanted to get out of there as quickly as possible, if you want to know the truth."

"It just happens that I have lamb chops in the freezer," Bronwen said. "I can defrost them in a jiffy if you like."

Evan wrapped his arms around her, drawing her close to him so that her breasts were level with his face. "Did I ever tell you that you're a bloody miracle worker?" he asked.

She leaned down and kissed his forehead. "Being a bloody miracle worker would be teaching you to cook," she said. "I'm just a wonderful human being taking pity on a poor, undernourished public servant."

Evan snuggled his face into the silk of her blouse, conscious of the fresh, clean scent of her, with just a hint of perfume. "Of course, we could always forget about the food," he muttered.

She pushed him away, laughing. "I'll go and defrost those chops. You'll need your strength."

* * *

The last of the stragglers was finally leaving the marquee. In one corner the band was packing up instruments and amplifiers. In another old Mrs Morgan was busy stuffing leftover cheese squares into her handbag. Hugh Bosley-Thomas came up to his father and clapped him on the shoulder. "That was some party, eh, Dad? Had a good time, did you?"

"Bit noisy for my taste," the old man said. "All that modern music blasting away."

"Modern? Grandpa, that was the Beatles," Val said, laughing. "Forty years old. Positively antediluvian."

"It all sounds the same to me," Tomos said. "All thump thump thump and no decent tune to it. Not like the old days. Ivor Novello — now that was music."

"Apart from the music, did you have a good time?" Hugh asked. "You certainly have a lot of friends in the community. Look how many people turned out for you."

"Go anywhere for free food, this lot would," Tomos Thomas said. "And even further for free drink. Did you see the Misses Dawson from the rectory knocking back the wine? They always claim they're teetotallers. I suppose they'll claim this was medicinal."

"Well, I think it went splendidly." Henry joined the group. "A real compliment to your position here in the community, Grandpa." He glanced around at his sister, who was busy stripping tables and piling up primrose table centres. "Leave those, for God's sake, Suzanne. We've got people coming in the morning to pack everything up."

"But they'd just throw all these away," she said, lifting another primrose basket from a table and holding it protectively. "It seems such a shame. I was going to plant them beside the house so Grandpa could go on enjoying them."

"Sheep will make short work of those," Tomos said.

"But you don't have any sheep at the moment, apart from those few lambs," Suzanne said.

"I will soon. As soon as I've got the herd built up again, they'll be grazing down by the house and then your primroses won't last five minutes."

"Dad, I wish you'd give up this absurd idea of restocking the sheep," Hugh said. "Take it as a sign from God that your farming days are over and start enjoying life."

"Taking pottery classes and ballroom dancing lessons, you mean? Not me, boy. I'm going to die right here on my land, doing what I've done all my life. They'll find me cold and stiff one day, up on the hillside where I belong."

Nick had come to join them. "I didn't want to spoil the mood earlier, but I'm afraid I've got some unpleasant news," he said. "A policeman was here this evening — who, by the way, was none other than Evan Evans, who used to live next door. It seems they've found some — remains."

Suzanne gave a little cry and put her hand up to her mouth. The basket of primroses fell to the floor and smashed.

"They think it could be Sarah?" Hugh asked, after a long silence.

"The cop was pretty sure it was. He'll let us know when we can meet with the forensic anthropologist and work on positive identification. He mentioned dental charts and photos."

"We must call Mother right away," Suzanne said. "She'll want to be here."

"And I don't think that photos will be a problem," Henry muttered. "Mother's shrine is full of them."

"How strange that she should be found at this moment," Val said. "It's almost as if she was waiting for us all to come back."

"Bloody rubbish!" Hugh said angrily. "What nonsense you talk. Sarah is dead and gone." He pushed past them and strode away.

Tomos Thomas looked at his grandson with understanding. "Don't mind him, boy. He's been hurting too long."

"Haven't we all?" Henry said. "But I don't see what good this will do. We might have found her remains, but we won't find out who took her, will we? They couldn't do it then, and they won't do it now. It will just be opening old wounds." He glared down at Suzanne, who was now on her hands and knees attempting to salvage the primrose basket.

"For God's sake, leave that, Suzanne," he snapped. "They'll clean it up."

"But I want to plant it," she said mechanically. "Plant it in memory." She lifted the plant from the smashed pot and held it gently in front of her. "I need to keep busy, Henry, so that I don't have time to think."

CHAPTER 15

"Any news, sir?" Glynis Davies came into the incident room at eight o'clock on Sunday morning looking cool and efficient in a grey pinstripe suit. In that outfit she would have looked just right in the middle of the City of London, stockbroking or running a multinational company, Evan decided. Up here in the wilds of Wales, she'd stand out like a sore thumb. Nonetheless he gave her an appreciative look. The skirt was just short enough to show off those long legs. Glynis caught the tail end of the look, and her challenging stare let Evan know she was very well aware what he'd been thinking. "Any sightings yet?" she asked, grinning as Evan blushed.

Watkins waved a pile of paper at her. "Look at these — apparently it ran on all the evening news broadcasts, and we're inundated with bloody sightings. You and Evans are going to be spending the morning following up on these reports, deciding which ones are credible enough to warrant investigating further, and then persuading the local police to check them out for us."

"Are you sure you really need me to do that, sir?" Evan asked. "I'd sort of hoped to be there when you interview the Thomas family."

"It won't take two people to talk to them," Watkins said impatiently. "We've presumably got everything on record from the time when the child vanished. All we need are current addresses. One of the uniform boys can do that."

"But, sir — they'll leave the area, and then we'll have lost them again. Don't you think we should be checking out their backgrounds and seeing if any of their locations match with other missing children?"

"I think you're going overboard with this one, Evans," Watkins said. "I agree the discovery of your skeleton and these people showing up again is mildly interesting, but I still don't think it impacts on the crime at hand. You say they came up here for a birthday party near Llanrwst? Then what in God's name would they be doing at a caravan park on a deserted beach twenty miles away?"

"Whoever snatched Ashley must have been waiting and watching for some time," Glynis added. "He picked exactly the one moment when the mother disappeared. Either he knew the mother's habits well enough to know that she'd have to go for a cigarette, or he'd studied her enough to know that she did this from time to time."

"Good point." Watkins nodded in agreement. "Look, Evans, I know you've been right on hunches before, and I know it's an amazing coincidence that the two little girls looked alike and all that, but I have to think that's what it is — just an amazing coincidence."

"So we're not going to pursue the Thomases at all?" Evan bit back his annoyance.

"Obviously we'd like a positive identification of the skeleton from them — a DNA sample if necessary, but I've made it quite clear that we are looking for Ashley's father and we're not going off on any bloody tangent until we find him. Got it?"

"Yes sir," Evan said. He thought back longingly to the good old days when he and Watkins were mates, teaming up against the tyranny of the then DI Hughes. "So here." Watkins dropped the pile of papers on the table. "Divide these between you, see which ones look credible, and follow up on them."

"This might not take as long as you think," Glynis said kindly as they settled down at a desk together. "Listen to what this person says — 'You ought to check out the man upstairs. He looks just like your photograph and he speaks a foreign language and he's got shifty eyes. He looks just the type who'd kidnap a little girl.'" She laughed. "It's from Kent. It should be easy enough to find out if he was away long enough to drive to Wales and back."

"I wish we knew what type of car he might be driving," Evan said. "And where he'd been for the past month. That would make it so much easier to narrow these down."

"Maybe we should ask Inspector Watkins if he'd consider letting one of us go to London and take up the trail personally. Mrs Sholokhov said he had a group of Russian friends there. He must have discussed his plans with somebody."

"That doesn't mean they'd tell us, especially if they're Russians," Evan said. "They'll all gang up and want to protect their friend, won't they?"

Glynis sighed. "Oh well, I suppose we'd better get down to the task in hand or we'll be here all day."

"Right. Stuck here all day when I'm dying to find out more about those Thomases."

Glynis smiled. "You get too involved, you know. Not a good quality in a policeman."

"You're right. I am involved, but only because I don't want a murderer to slip away for a second time. If he killed little Sarah and wasn't discovered before, then he must have been pretty slick, wouldn't you say? They had search teams out everywhere that very evening. And yet he managed to get her right over the mountains and down to Llanfair — and bury her without being discovered."

"They probably didn't suspect foul play at that time," Glynis said. "He could have walked among them as one of the search team, knowing where he'd hidden her and steering them away."

Evan thumped his fist on the desk, making the pile of papers jump and teeter. "I'm going to find him, Glynis, if it's the last thing I do."

"If you don't get down to working your way through these, the DI will make sure this is the last thing you do." Glynis laughed. She had a wonderfully sexy, throaty laugh that didn't match her professional and sleek exterior.

Evan smiled as he started reading the first reports. Maybe he was being melodramatic about finding Sarah's remains. They didn't even know yet that the skeleton was Sarah. He'd look rather stupid if they found this was quite another child, buried long before his time. He picked up the phone and started dialling.

* * *

By noon they had five credible leads and had been in touch with local police in Sussex, Hampshire, Birmingham, North London, and South Wales. Of these, the one in Cardiff looked the most hopeful. A fair-haired man and child had been seen playing in a park. He was pushing her on the swings. He spoke with a foreign accent. Cardiff would be a good place to lie low and wait for a chance to slip away. There were car ferries from several points in South Wales across to Ireland and from there a flight to Europe.

"Let's leave the DI a memo about what we've done and go and get some lunch," Glynis said. "He had us in very early this morning, and I don't know about you but I'm starving."

"Me too," Evan agreed. "I wonder what delicacy the canteen ladies have thought up for us today?"

"Oh, not the canteen, please," Glynis rolled her eyes. "I'm sorry. There are many things I will do for love of my job, but eating canteen food is not one of them. And I flat out refuse to drink what they have the nerve to label coffee. There's that nice little coffee bar on the other side of the roundabout. They do a decent cappuccino and a good Greek salad."

Evan foresaw teasing if he was seen eating Greek salad for lunch, but he decided the teasing would be tempered with envy if he was seen having lunch with Glynis. “All right,” he said. “Let’s go.”

As it happened, they had a comprehensive Greek menu and Evan ordered gyros.

“Lovely,” he commented. “Lots of garlic.”

“I’m surprised at you, Evan,” Glynis commented, as he tucked in with satisfaction. “A real Welshman enjoying foreign food cooked with garlic. Won’t you be drummed out of chapel?”

“My fiancée’s been educating me,” he said. “She likes cooking exotic dishes, and I’ve developed quite a taste for them.”

“Have you now?” Her smile hovered at the very edge of flirting. “And how did she learn about foreign cooking?”

“Oh, she’s a very cultured person. She went to Cambridge, you know.”

“The university?”

“No, the bloody football club,” Evan said, half joking and half not.

Glynis blushed and had to laugh. “I’m sorry. That was very ham-fisted of me. There’s no reason at all why your fiancée shouldn’t have been to Cambridge. I was caught off guard because I was surprised that—” She broke off in embarrassment.

“That she chose to be a schoolteacher in a village school or that she chose to marry me?”

“I didn’t mean either, Evan.” She toyed awkwardly with her salad.

“It’s all right. I ask myself the same questions quite often in fact. How did someone as bright and beautiful and worldly as Bronwen wind up with an ordinary chap like me?”

“I don’t think you’re at all ordinary,” Glynis said.

“Well, compared to people like Bronwen, or like you. I mean, you’re another one I wouldn’t have expected to find in a backwater like Caernarfon.”

"I like it here," she said. "I like being a big fish in a small pond. I expect Bronwen does, too."

Evan nodded and took another bite of gyro. He was suddenly conscious that gyros were impossible to eat delicately when sitting next to a young woman. Glynis took a stab at an olive and glanced up at him. "So you're really going to get married soon?"

Evan nodded. "In August. Bronwen's school holidays."

"Ah. That's not long, is it?"

"No, not long."

She ate another mouthful in silence. "So tell me something — when we first met, did I read it wrong or did you actually fancy me?"

"Of course I fancied you," Evan said. "You're a real looker, Glynis. Any man with a pulse would fancy you. But it didn't mean I was planning to do anything about it. Just window-shopping, not intending to buy, if you get my meaning."

She laughed. "Nicely put. And if it's of any interest to you, I fancied you too." She paused, watching his reaction. "Lucky we didn't do anything about it, wasn't it? Especially now that we have to work together so closely."

"Yes, very lucky," he said. "Those sort of things can become very awkward—"

"Ah, so this is where you're hiding out!" DI Watkins exclaimed as he pushed open the coffee shop door, causing several little bells to tinkle. "So my team's turning snooty on me, are they? Cafeteria not good enough for you? Plotting behind my back — or don't tell me this is a secret assignation?"

"All of the above," Glynis said with a laugh, while Evan was still phrasing an answer.

"Well, either way, your time's up. I need you both on duty pronto. The North Wales Police doesn't pay for assignations on the firm's time." He was grinning at Evan's discomfort.

"We have actually only been here long enough for a cappuccino and a bite," he said.

"A cappuccino — you're going very upmarket suddenly, aren't you? And I don't think Bronwen will approve of the biting part either," Watkins said, as he drove them before him, like a skinny beige sheepdog.

"So has any news come in since we talked to you last?" Evan asked.

"Your Germans — criminal record in Germany. We're onto the German police about them, and I've put out the word that I want them found and brought in for questioning."

"Criminal record, eh?" Evan said, as they waited to cross at the roundabout. "They didn't look the type. Clean-cut, outdoorsy, and all that. Do we know what they were arrested for yet?"

"Civil disturbance. Probably some of these greenies or peaceniks."

"That's not exactly the same as trafficking in stolen children, is it?"

"You think those Germans could have taken Ashley?" Glynis broke into a trot to keep up with Evan as he crossed the road.

"It did cross my mind, since they were so anxious to do a bunk. I wondered whether they were being paid to take her because the father dared not show up himself."

"It's a possibility, isn't it, sir?" Glynis asked Watkins. "Anyhow, if they're driving a car with German plates and they're staying at campsites, it should be easy enough to locate them again."

"Yes, hopefully we'll have them picked up in the next day or so," Watkins said. "If the other police forces don't think we're a lot of hysterical Welshmen and sit on their rear ends, doing nothing."

"Oh, surely not," Glynis said.

"Strange though it may seem, Glynis love, the Welsh are not universally popular in the rest of Britain," Watkins said, with the hint of a smile. "I can't think why."

Evan held open the station door so that Watkins and Glynis could go through ahead of him. Watkins let Glynis go inside then stopped Evan. "Not you, Evans. Glynis, you man the shop — or do I have to say woman the shop to be PC?"

"You could try saying staff the shop," Glynis suggested.

"Right. You can reach me on my mobile if anything at all comes in. I need Evans with me."

He set off across the car park. "Where are we going, sir?" Evan asked.

"I decided that your hunches haven't been far off the mark before. I've got a free hour. We're going to talk to these Thomases."

Evan gave Watkins a quick glance and then a smile flickered across his face. "Thanks, sir."

"Nothing to thank me for," Watkins said. "It makes all the sense in the world to have you there if you've met them before. You can chat about old times and make them more relaxed." He went across to his car. "And you can drive," he said. "That way I can take five minutes' kip."

Evan took the A road out of Caernarfon, looking across the Menai Straits to the island of Anglesey with green hills and white cottages sparkling in clear light. It was one of those rare clear, glass-blue days and Evan felt a pang of regret that he never seemed to be free to take advantage of good weather anymore. How long had it been since he and Bronwen had done a day's hiking together? Life seemed to be all work and responsibility these days. His mind went back to the carefree time on his grandfather's farm when summer had seemed endless and bad weather no deterrent to a day in the outdoors. He had grown up tough and healthy and able to scramble up the hillside as nimble as any sheep. He remembered setting off after breakfast with a lump of bread and cheese and an apple wrapped in his pocket in case he got hungry and only returning from the mountains when it was getting dark.

Had anybody worried about him? he wondered now. Life had seemed so safe then. In all his long days in the hills, he had never come across anything more frightening than the occasional aggressive dog. And yet somebody had snatched Sarah from those same hills. Somebody had buried her.

* * *

He had worried that he would never see her again and had tried to recall a clear image of her during the long months of winter. Then the next summer the Jaguar had turned up again with the Thomas children. They hadn't seemed any more willing to include him in their games than the year before, even though he had hung around hopefully, watching them from the other side of the drystone wall. Sarah may have grown a little, but she hadn't changed, still looking frail and lovely. Sometimes she looked across at him and smiled before her brother and sister called her away.

It might have turned into another summer of futility except that this year the Thomases brought a puppy with them. Old Grandpa Thomas was none too pleased.

"Only dogs around here are working dogs," he said. "That thing will scare the sheep and distract my dogs from their job."

"Nonsense, Pah. It's only a tiny puppy. It can't possibly do any harm," the children's father had said. And indeed it was a sweet ball of yellow fur that might someday grow into a golden retriever. Evan had long wanted a puppy and gazed at it almost with the same longing that he felt for Sarah.

Then one day he was in his room with the window open when he heard that something was wrong. High children's voices were shouting, "Barley. Where are you, Barley? Here, boy."

He tied his sneakers hurriedly and ran outside. The Thomas children had fanned out and were walking through the sheep meadows.

"What's the matter?" he asked Nick, who was around his age and had always been the most approachable.

"We've lost our new dog," Nick said. "Only a puppy actually. Someone left the door open, and now he's gone."

"I'll help you find him," Evan said. "I know these hills really well."

"Thanks. That's awfully nice of you," Nick had said. He had the same posh English voice as the other boys, but he had a friendly smile.

Evan left them scouring the lower meadows. He scrambled up the hillside until he came to a vantage point on an outcropping of rock.

He eased himself into a position perched with the whole valley below him. Where might a puppy have gone? The road below the farm was a possibility, of course. But if the dog had come out through the back door and up the sheep track, then it would have passed this way. It was only a puppy with little legs. It couldn't have wandered too far.

As he sat there, his senses fine-tuned to the song of an invisible lark, the bleat of a distant sheep, his ears caught another sound on the breeze — the high-pitched yelp of a frightened or injured animal. He followed it across the mountainside and found the puppy at last, wedged in a deep crack in the rocks. It took time to extricate the puppy without hurting it, and by the time he clambered up, he was also scratched and bruised. But he didn't notice the hurts as he ran down the hill, the puppy in his arms, and carried it in triumph to the Thomases.

"Barley! You've found him. He's all right." They snatched the puppy, kissing it and petting it, while Evan stood awkwardly at the doorway.

Finally he controlled himself enough to say, "Well, I'll be going then."

"No, don't go. Stay and have ice cream with us." Sarah was the only one looking at him.

Then the others became aware of his presence, and one of the mothers said, "Yes, do stay and have some ice cream. We're most grateful to you. Most grateful."

Then they all turned to him and gave him the same attention they had given the puppy, patting him and telling him what a good chap he was. This was more awkward than being ignored. Evan winced with discomfort and was glad to attack the dish of ice cream. When he explained where he had found the dog, they were all impressed.

"You're allowed up in the hills by yourself?" the mother asked.

"Oh, yes. I know my way pretty well everywhere," Evan said.

"Then you can come with us next time and show us a good place to build a fort," the other big boy, not the stuck-up one, said.

And Sarah just sat opposite him, watching and smiling.

CHAPTER 16

The marquee was still standing in the Thomases' meadow, but two men were wheeling stacks of chairs out of it and into a van with the words NOSON LAWEN, EVENTS CATERING, CONWY on the side. The area beside the driveway had been churned up by tire tracks.

"Oh, we're here, are we?" Watkins asked, reviving from his doze as the tires crunched on the gravel outside the farmhouse. "Nice place. A bit of money here, I'd have thought."

"Oh, yes. They were never lacking for cash," Evan said. "Sarah's father always drove a Jag."

"But he isn't the one who owns this place, is he?" Watkins opened his door and stepped out onto the gravel.

"No, that's the grandfather, old Mr Tomos Thomas."

Watkins smiled. "Tomos Thomas. The Welsh give their kids bloody stupid names, don't they?"

"Like Evan Evans, you mean?"

"Tomos Thomas sounds even more daft somehow."

Evan grinned. "They used to call him Tomos Dau around here."

"Two times Thomas, eh?" They started for the front door. "So he's the grandfather?"

"And he had two sons, both of whom did very well for themselves, I understand, and it was their kids I played with."

"And they're all here now?"

Evan nodded. "The kids are. It was Henry and Suzanne in one family; Val and Nick are the cousins."

"And the little girl belonged to—"

"Henry and Suzanne. Their father drove the Jag. We never saw much of him. He used to be away on business all week and just showed up here on weekends."

"I hope this won't be too much of a shock for them," Watkins said. "How did they take the news last night?"

"I only spoke with Nick — he's a priest now, by the way. I thought it best not to spoil the party, but I presume he's told them all by now."

There was a brass knocker in the shape of a lion's head on the front door. Watkins gave an impressive rap, and they could hear footsteps coming down a tiled hallway.

"Yes?" The man's hair was greying at the temples, and he had deep frown lines etched into his forehead. Evan tried to work out which one of them this was but couldn't place him. He was older than any of the kids Evan had played with, but perhaps they'd had an older brother he'd never met.

Watkins produced his warrant card. "North Wales Police, sir. I'm Detective Inspector Watkins and this is Detective Constable Evans."

The man's face broke into a smile, and Evan suddenly recognized him. "It's Henry, isn't it?" he asked.

"And you're the little Evans boy. My God, you've changed."

"So have you, Henry. It has been a long time, you know."

"I do know. Twenty-five years," Henry said, and the smile faded. "Nick told us that they've found a skeleton somewhere in the mountains. I don't suppose they can tell yet . . ."

"Not definitely, sir," Watkins said. "That's where we hope you'll be able to help us out."

"Oh, of course. Won't you come in? We've all dutifully been to chapel with Grandfather, and we're just finishing up lunch." He led the way down the dark hallway into a dining room on the right. Evan only remembered the bright kitchen at the back of the house. This room was dark, with windows that faced east and brown wallpaper. The family was sitting around a large mahogany dining table, on which the remains of a roast and some serving dishes of vegetables still rested. They had evidently finished their dessert and were in the process of drinking coffee. Evan noticed there was only one woman present — easily recognizable as Suzanne. She, at least, had not changed or aged much since he'd seen her last, especially because she still wore her hair long and straight over her shoulders. She glanced up nervously as Henry showed them in.

"This is Detective Inspector Watkins," Henry said. "And this skinny little chap is young Evan from next door."

"Evan? The little boy who found the puppy?" Suzanne stared hard at him as if she somehow believed he was an imposter.

"The very same," he said. "And I recognize you all right. You haven't changed at all, Suzanne."

"So you're with the police now?"

"I am. I just moved across to the plainclothes branch."

"And you're here about Sarah?" Suzanne asked.

Evan detected a collective intake of breath.

The old man had risen to his feet. "So it's true then. They've found her at last?" In contrast to his grandson's public school tones, Tomos Thomas sounded much like Evan's own grandfather, and he was tempted to speak to him in Welsh — if DI Watkins gave him a chance to talk at all.

"We're not sure yet, sir," Watkins said, "but it's a child's skeleton of the right age. We're hoping her family has dental X rays or pictures that will help us make a positive identification."

"My mother is coming up from Surrey tomorrow," Suzanne said. "She's bringing pictures with her."

"That's good, because if we need to make a DNA match, it's maternal DNA that we use." Evan couldn't resist the chance of establishing himself as an authority here.

"They could also use Henry or me, I'm sure," Suzanne said, "since we both carry the same maternal DNA."

"Of course," Evan said quickly, "but we hope we can establish identity without DNA testing as it takes a long time and it's expensive."

"Won't we be able to tell by what she's wearing?" Val asked.

"There's nothing left, sir. Only shoes and small scraps of cloth."

A half sob escaped from Suzanne, who covered her mouth and looked away.

"And where was the body found, Inspector?" the man at the far end of the table asked. Evan focused on him for the first time. Sarah's father. He had aged well too, Evan decided, sleek and grey like his Jaguar.

"That's the strange thing, sir. It was discovered buried inside the gate of a shepherd's cottage above the village of Llanfair."

"Llanfair — but that's on the other side of the mountains, isn't it? On the Llanberis Pass?" Sarah's father asked in surprise.

Watkins nodded. "That's right."

"Then what in God's name was she doing over there?"

"That's one of the things we hope to find out, sir," Evan said. "The cottage was occupied at the time by a shepherd called Rhodri George."

"Rhodri?" Old Mr Thomas's voice was sharp. "I remember him. Cottage up above Llanfair, you say? He worked for me at one time. In fact we used to have land over on that side — right up to the top of Glyder Fach and down to the road in those days."

"So the cottage was on your land, then?" Evan asked.

"I'm not sure about the cottage any longer, but I certainly had land over there, and Rhodri worked my sheep for a while. Then I sold the land to a chap called Owens in the early eighties, and I believe Rhodri went to work for him instead."

Evan could feel his pulse had quickened. A connection at last. A piece of the puzzle maybe falling into place. "So what do you remember about Rhodri?" he asked.

Thomas shook his head. "Can't say I remember much. Didn't smell too good. One of the older generation who took a bath once a week. Had a real shrew of a wife. Knew his animals well, always had well-trained dogs — in fact, I believe one of his dogs won the county sheepdog trials once."

"But his personality, I mean," Evan insisted. "How did you get on with him? Did he have a temper?"

"What's that?" Tomos Thomas asked; then a look of amazement and horror spread across his face. "You're never suggesting that Rhodri had anything to do with — with Sarah, are you? He was as normal as you or I are."

"I just wondered if you and he ever had a falling-out? Whether he could be the kind of man who carried a grudge."

"A grudge enough to kill a little child?" Tomos was almost shouting now.

Watkins stepped in to intervene. "Easy now, Mr Thomas. We're just trying to make sense of this. There had to be some reason that the child was buried outside Rhodri's cottage, when whoever took her had the whole wilderness to bury her in. Among other things, you have to wonder how anybody could bury a child outside Rhodri's front door without his noticing."

"I think I might be able to explain that, sir," Evan said. "The water pipes to the cottage were connected around the time Sarah disappeared. The front path may have been dug up for that purpose."

"Now that could be important. Make a note to check on the timing of the water pipes installation, will you, Evans?" Watkins said.

Evan scribbled on his notepad, rather annoyed that Watkins had reduced him so clearly to subordinate.

"Old Rhodri is long gone, I suppose?" Grandfather Thomas asked. "He was older than me, I think, and I've just turned eighty."

"He was alive a couple of years ago. He sold the cottage and went to live with his daughter in Bangor," Evan said. "I'll be checking on him as soon as I can find the time."

"Find the time?" the grey-haired man demanded. "I should have thought this would become a top priority for you. God knows you boys made a balls-up of the last investigation twenty-five years ago. I'd have thought you'd have jumped at the chance to put things right."

"Oh, definitely, sir," Watkins said, "and we'll give it all the manpower we can spare, but you see we've got another case on the books at the moment — another little girl has vanished, and from what I've been told, she looks very like your daughter."

Evan noted that every single one of them reacted to this, their eyes darting around the table at their fellow diners.

"Did she live around here?" Nick, the young priest, asked.

"No, she was a visitor, staying in a caravan park on the coast."

"Oh well, that's all right then, isn't it?" the grandfather said.

What did he mean by that? Evan wondered. Was he inferring that it couldn't have been one of them?

"It's probably just coincidence that the two girls looked alike," Watkins said.

They were nodding, staring silently at their empty dessert plates, willing themselves to believe this.

"If we could just get the details on each of you while we're here," Watkins went on.

"Details — what for?" Sarah's father demanded.

"So that we can contact you again if we have any more information for you or questions we want to ask," Watkins said easily. "Are you all family members?"

"That's right," Henry said. "I'm Henry Bosley-Thomas and I think you already know Tomos Thomas, our grandfather here."

"Henry Bosley-Thomas," Watkins said. "And what relation were you to the little girl?"

"Her older brother." He stared coldly at the detective.

"And do you live in the area, sir?"

"No, I live in Surrey, just outside Guildford. Stockbroker belt." He fished in his wallet. "Here's my card."

"So you're just here for the weekend then, are you, sir?" Watkins asked.

"I was. I should have been driving back today. I've got a big case coming up in a couple of weeks and I really can't spare the time — but of course everything has to be put aside if we can finally discover what happened to Sarah."

"You're a lawyer then? Barrister?"

"No, solicitor. Mainly civil law in my practice. I had no wish to spend my life reliving what we suffered with Sarah."

"I quite understand, sir," Watkins said. "Do you have other siblings here?"

"Yes, me," Suzanne said. She pushed her long, blonde hair back from her face. "I'm Suzanne Bosley-Thomas."

"And you live?"

"Thirty-eight A Kenmore Gardens, Clapham. Not stockbroker belt. And no card."

"You're not married, madam?"

"Divorced. I have gone back to using my maiden name."

"Suzanne made an unfortunate marriage when she was very young. Naturally it didn't last," her father said.

She turned to glare at him. "Made an unfortunate marriage. I like that. And who forced me into it?"

Hugh gave her a warning frown. "Really, Suzanne, this is neither the time nor the place. You obviously haven't learned to conquer these childish outbursts. I'm sorry, Inspector. Please proceed."

Evan noticed that she flushed bright red and continued to glare at her father.

"I don't have your name and address yet, sir." Watkins addressed Hugh, who seemed unaffected by the encounter.

"Hugh Bosley-Thomas. I live in Buckinghamshire. West Wyckham — the Old Grange."

"And you are the father of these two?"

"Yes, and I was once the father of three. Sarah's father." He pressed his lips together to master himself.

"Yes. I'm sorry. It must be horrible for you having to go through this again," Watkins said.

"Better to know for sure than not to know," Grandfather Thomas said. "Let's hope it is her, so that we can get her properly buried and start mourning."

"Mourning? You don't think we've been mourning all these years?" Hugh demanded.

Evan glanced at Watkins, sensing the tension rising around the dining table.

"We'll only keep you another minute; then you can get back to your coffee," Watkins said. "But I suppose I should get details on you too, sir." He addressed the old man. "Are you Mr Bosley-Thomas too?"

"Plain old Thomas. Tomos Thomas to be exact. It was my boy here who went posh on me and started hyphenating his name."

"So the Bosley is your wife's maiden name?" Watkins turned back to Hugh.

Hugh flushed a frown of annoyance. "My mother's maiden name. I thought it only fair to honour her, too, since she came from such an old family."

"Ah." Watkins smiled as he jotted it down. He looked across the table. "That leaves these two gentlemen over here."

"We're the cousins. Our father was Uncle Hugh's younger brother," Val said. "Unfortunately, he passed away a couple of years ago."

"And your name, sir?"

"I'm Val. Short for Valentine. Bloody awful name to give a son, wouldn't you say?"

"And is it Bosley-Thomas too?"

"No, just plain Val Thomas. I'm an artist and I live in Hampstead Village. I too have a card somewhere in my jacket pocket." He fished around and produced one with bold black words on a design in red and yellow.

"And last but not least," Nick said, smiling affably, "I am Nicholas Thomas. Don't say it — the same as a character in a children's book, I know. I never lived that down at boarding school."

"Presumably you are Father Nicholas Thomas these days, unless dog collars are the latest fashion," Watkins said.

Evan shot a quick look at him. Watkins attempting to be witty? That was new, too. He remembered the prosaic sergeant and wondered if attempting witticisms was part of the training in inspector classes.

Nick laughed good-naturedly. "No, I don't go in for fashion statements. I am a Catholic priest, much to the horror of my Methodist grandfather here, no doubt. And I live in Montreal."

"And where can we reach you while you're in this country?"

"As of now at the Everest Inn, but then I'll probably be staying with my mother in Surrey. You can contact me through Val if you need me."

"Right. Thanks very much. I think that's all we need for now. Sorry to have intruded on Sunday lunch." Watkins snapped his notebook shut. "I don't know what time the forensic anthropologist will be able to meet with us tomorrow, but I'll keep you posted and try to speed this up as much as possible. Are you all staying at the Everest Inn if I need to contact you?"

"I am staying here with grandfather," Henry said. "The rest are dispersed."

"I'm at a hotel in Llandudno. The Majestic," Hugh said. "One of the few comfortable beds in this godforsaken place."

"Nick and I are at the Everest Inn, also known for its comfortable beds," Val said, giving Watkins his charming smile.

"And I am in a grotty B and B in Porthmadog," Suzanne said. "The Seaview Hotel."

"Right. That just about does it then. Thanks again, folks. Come on, Evans."

Evan had been standing unnoticed behind the inspector. The scene was painfully reminiscent of those childhood summers when he had stood by the fence, watching them, willing them to invite him to come and play. Now, all these years later, he was still the outsider and wondered why on earth Watkins had bothered to bring him along since he had hardly been allowed to say a word.

"Goodbye then," he said to the group. "Nice seeing you again."

Before he could reach the front door, he heard Suzanne's high, light voice. "Why do you think they were here?"

"The inspector told us." Hugh's lazy, upper-class drawl. "They had to get our particulars so they can contact us if needed."

Evan lingered with his hand on the front door latch.

"They could have just sent Evans if all they wanted was our names and addresses. There is more to it than that. They know something they haven't told us."

Val said, "Such as what?" at the same time as Henry said, "Don't be so bloody melodramatic, Suzanne."

"Perhaps they've found out who killed Sarah," she said.

* * *

"They were as jumpy as a bunch of grasshoppers, weren't they?" Watkins muttered, as Evan closed the door behind him.

"Definitely rattled," Evan agreed.

CHAPTER 17

They headed for the car. Watkins opened the driver's door this time and got in.

"You know them," Watkins said, "so what did you think?"

"I knew them twenty-five years ago when they were kids."

"So you didn't have any suspicions about any of them in those days."

"You mean wondering whether any of them might have killed Sarah?"

Watkins nodded.

"Never crossed my mind," Evan said. "I was a kid too, remember. When you're seven years old, you take people at face value. They were perfectly normal — Henry was always a bit pompous. When we played, he was very big on rules. Suzanne was always getting upset and saying that other people were cheating and it wasn't fair. Val often did try to cheat, and Nick was just as you saw him today, always willing to do what the others wanted."

"That's pretty much how they came across now, wasn't it? The girl is a bit highly strung, wouldn't you say?"

"But that doesn't mean that she'd be bonkers enough to kill her younger sister. And she wouldn't have had the strength to carry her over a mountain and down the other side and then bury her. Besides, none of them would have had the opportunity. If any of them had been missing for that long, they'd have been noticed."

"Then why are they so bloody jumpy?" Watkins demanded.

"It may just be that they are dreading seeing her skeleton and trying to identify her. It's like opening old wounds, isn't it?"

"Yes, I can't say I'd want to go through that, not after all these years. They've probably just about managed to put her out of their minds."

"Maybe. I bet they still dream about her," Evan said.

"You know one thing that's interesting." Watkins started the car and turned on the circle of gravel before accelerating down the driveway. "Suzanne is staying in Porthmadog."

"Yes, I did notice that," Evan said. "But then Val and Nick are at the Everest Inn. It's only a short drive down Nant Gwynant to the coast from there, isn't it?"

Watkins laughed suddenly and shook his head. "This is stupid, isn't it? There would be no reason for any of them to have driven to a caravan park on a deserted beach and just happen upon another child who looked like Sarah the moment her mother's back was turned."

"It does seem rather far-fetched when you put it like that," Evan said. "In fact, now that I've had a chance to see them again, I really can't believe any of them were involved in Sarah's death, or Ashley's disappearance."

"You're the one who made the connection in the first place. You're the one who dragged me out here."

"I know, because it seemed like too much of a connection to ignore; but now that I think about it, they all adored Sarah. She was that sort of little kid — everybody's darling."

"Everybody's darling usually means that somebody's nose is out of joint," Watkins commented dryly.

Evan's thoughts went immediately to Suzanne. He remembered her standing, hands on hips, lips pouting, shouting, "It's not fair!" "If it's okay with you, sir, I might just check on their movements since they arrived here," Evan said. "After all, they were jumpy like you said."

Watkins slapped his hand against the steering wheel. "I just wish we could find bloody Johnny Sholokhov and know whether he'd got his daughter or not. If she's safe and sound with him, then a twenty-five-year-old skeleton can wait. If she's not—" He let the rest of the sentence hang in the air.

"Maybe one of the leads will pan out," Evan said. "The ones we called sounded quite hopeful. And if he's hiding with her somewhere, he can't stay hidden forever."

"It's the waiting I hate most in this bloody game," Watkins said. "I don't mind when I feel I'm doing something, but I hate it when it's out of my hands. Knowing that I'm at the mercy of some bloody petty civil servant in London who is probably sitting on his arse picking his spots or filling in his football pools — that's what drives me up the wall."

"One of us could go to London," Evan suggested. "Maybe we'd find out more if we talked to the landlady and Sholokhov's friends, and his lawyer too, if they were in the process of getting a divorce."

"It makes you wonder why he's done a bunk now if the divorce wasn't final, doesn't it?" Watkins tapped his fingers on the steering wheel as he drove. "Why take the kid now, at this very moment? Why not wait until he's absolutely sure that he won't be awarded custody?"

"Something might have pushed him to get out of the country in a hurry," Evan suggested.

Watkins nodded. "You're right. Something not even connected with his daughter, but he can't bear to leave without her. Yes, I think you and I will try to take a little trip to the big city this week. We can leave young Glynis to hold the fort — since she's the only one who can use computers and speak to foreigners anyway." He exchanged a grin with Evan.

"And neither of us would trust ourselves on an overnight trip with her?" Evan added.

"Speak for yourself, boyo. I'm a happily married man. I gave up temptation long ago when I learned about DIY and putting up shelves."

* * *

The game was called capture the castle. The moment Evan showed them the rocks, it became their game of choice that summer. The large granite boulders littered the summit of a small peak behind the house, and the peak itself was crowned with a fissured rock that imagination easily turned into a castle. The game was a variant of hide-and-seek. One person took possession of the castle. The others had to sneak up the hillside, dodging from boulder to boulder. The first person to get to the castle without being tagged was the winner.

Evan remembered the utterly delicious thrill of lying with his face pressed to the mossy rock, hearing footsteps coming closer, holding his breath, and then letting out a sigh of relief as he wasn't spotted and sprinted triumphantly to the castle. He was good at the game and often won, so that if they played in teams, he was fought over. It was a great ego boost that they would now come to his front door to ask if he could play with them, rather than the other way around.

But he still hadn't gone on a fairy-hunting expedition with Sarah. Even though they now included him in their play, they certainly weren't going to let Sarah go off alone into the hills with him. That didn't stop Sarah from asking him questions at any opportunity she got. She would lag behind as the big boys scrambled up the hillside and call out to Evan to pull her up.

He also remembered the thrill as he took her hand.

* * *

It was five-thirty when Evan finally drove back to Llanfair. He had spent the rest of the afternoon checking out reported sightings that had come in as a result of the Sunday morning newspapers. After a couple of hours of phone calls, Evan was convinced that people had too much time on their hands on Sundays, also that too many people harboured secret prejudices against foreigners. One phone call after another found him talking to someone, and it could equally be a woman or a man, mostly older, who was reporting the man upstairs or the man across the street because he looked foreign, sounded foreign, and was therefore suspicious. As in the morning, two hours of making phone calls resulted in a handful of leads worth following. Among these was a sighting in Yorkshire, which was interesting since Ashley's mother gave her current address as Leeds. However, this was on the outskirts of Skipton, on the moors, well to the northwest of Leeds. A man resembling the picture had come into a village newsagent's to ask for directions a couple of weeks ago. The newsagent had particularly remembered the Russian accent — just like in spy films on the telly.

The fact that it was Yorkshire made this tip worth passing along to North Yorks Police, although the trail was now two weeks old. He could have come to Yorkshire to seek them out, and then found that they had gone to Wales. But surely he couldn't have lost his way to the extent that he had driven past Leeds and wound up on the moors?

Who knew how people's minds worked, Evan thought, as he drove home for the night. Perhaps Sholokhov had read *Wuthering Heights* in Russian and had taken off on a whim to see the landscape for himself? They needed to find out more about his personality, rather than blindly hunting for him.

As Evan slowed the car to a halt, he noticed a stream of people making their way up the village street. For a moment he wondered what was wrong and where they could be going. Then he saw his former landlady, Mrs Williams, in her Sunday hat, and realized that they were heading for evening chapel. He had completely forgotten that it was Sunday and was stricken with that pang of conscience that remains with those raised in strict, religious households throughout their lifetimes.

Mrs Williams spotted the car and was standing, waiting for him, arms folded, as he opened the door.

“Don’t tell me they’ve made you work again on the Sabbath, is it?” she said, shaking her head. “What sort of heathen institution are they running, I’d like to know?”

“Crimes don’t take weekends off, Mrs W.” He smiled at her.

“Well, I hope you’ve got time to change and make it to chapel tonight,” she said accusingly. “You missed a beautiful sermon this morning — lovely just, it was. The reverend was in fine form. About the camel going through the eye of the needle and it being so hard to get into heaven that almost nobody’s going to make it — except for us, of course. Those people who go to chapel regular on Sundays, I mean.” She gave him a reassuring smile. “And the music was very uplifting, I must say.” She paused and examined him critically. “You’re looking peaky these days. I hope you’re eating proper. You need to hurry up with that wedding so that Miss Price can look after you. Toad in the hole in the pub — whatever next?”

And she went on her way up the street, leaving Evan staring after her. The Llanfair bush telegraph was so impressive that she had even heard about the toad in the hole! The smile faded as a thought struck him. Even though it was twenty-five years ago now, was it possible that someone in Llanfair knew something about the skeleton buried outside Rhodri’s cottage?

Evan sighed and went indoors to get changed for chapel. There was only one way into the Red Dragon pub on Sunday nights, and that was to follow Harry-the-Pub in through the back door after chapel was over. Although almost the whole of Wales now officially allowed pubs to stay open on Sundays, Harry had bowed to pressure from the two ministers and their wives and at least kept the front door firmly closed. It was almost six by the time Evan had changed into a clean shirt and trousers. He hurried up the street to make it into Capel Bethel before the big double doors were shut, thus making it impossible to sneak in late without being heard. As he approached the two chapels, he heard an imperious voice calling him.

"Constable Evans!"

He didn't need to look around to know that the voice belonged to Mrs Powell-Jones, wife of the Reverend Powell-Jones, minister of Capel Beulah across the street — the one he didn't attend.

"A word with you before you disappear into — that place," she said, her voice loud and clear enough for all those now entering Capel Bethel to hear. She made the words "that place" sound like a strip club or the anteroom of hell.

Evan dutifully crossed the street. "Can I help you with something, Mrs Powell-Jones?"

"You most certainly can, young man. I know you are no longer officially in charge of the welfare of this village, but you are still a policeman and you do still live among us. Now that we have nobody watching over us and those wretched squad cars never turn up when summoned, I have nobody else to go to."

"Is something wrong?" he asked, and wished instantly that he hadn't.

"Of course something is wrong. Tell me, am I not right in thinking there is an ordinance on the books against excessive noise on Sundays?"

"If it's causing a nuisance."

"It is causing an extreme nuisance," she said. "Electric guitars. One of those dreadful pop groups."

"There's a pop group in the village? I didn't know that."

"Oh, yes. Dreadful loud heathen music desecrating the Sabbath, making it impossible for good Christians to worship. I tried calling your so-called police hotline, and they refused to do anything about it."

"I'm sorry. I'll speak to them about it. Do you happen to know where the music was coming from?"

She pointed dramatically. "From that place."

"From the chapel?"

She sighed. "Well, what can you expect? That Parry Davies man has to lure in people somehow, knowing that he doesn't possess my husband's ability to preach. So what have they got now but electric music — amplified music blasting out so that we couldn't hear ourselves pray."

"Dear me," Evan said. "Well, I'm just about to go in there, so I'll have a word, shall I?"

Mrs Powell-Jones managed a smile. "I would be most grateful."

Evan was intrigued as he joined the last of the worshippers to beat Charlie Hopkins closing the doors. He couldn't imagine where Rev Parry Davies had dug up a rock group to play in chapel. The question was answered almost immediately. Mr Parry Davies came out of the vestry, wearing his black gown, and faced the congregation.

"For those of you who were here this morning, you'll know we've had a slight mishap," he said. "Mice have eaten through the organ bellows, and we can't get any sound out of it. So until we can afford to have it fixed, Betsy Edwards has kindly volunteered her young man to accompany our singing. And we are most grateful to him for stepping into the breach like this."

Barry-the-Bucket, still looking remarkably clean and well scrubbed, but also remarkably embarrassed, stepped out beside the altar, an electric guitar in his hands, and started strumming the chords to "Cwm Rhondda."

CHAPTER 18

As soon as the service was over, the congregation filed out — the women out of the front door and home down the street to prepare dinner, the men out of the side door and along the footpath to the Red Dragon. Evan was about to follow when he thought of Bronwen. She'd had a weekend all alone — she certainly wouldn't take kindly to his heading straight for the pub.

He ran out past the last of the women and sprinted up the street to the schoolhouse.

"Evan, what is it?" Bronwen sounded anxious as she saw him standing there, breathing heavily after his run.

"Do you fancy a drink?"

She laughed. "You ran all the way here to ask me that?"

"Well, you see, I want to go to the Dragon to ask some questions and then I thought we could go out for dinner somewhere, but you know how you have to be let in with the crowd on Sundays or you don't get in at all."

Bronwen laughed. "Oh, I see. I'm not exactly dressed for going out tonight."

She was wearing jeans and a big navy sweater.

"You look just fine to me."

"You always say that," Bronwen said, "but I wouldn't feel comfortable going to a restaurant looking as if I'd just been hiking."

"We can always come back for you to change after we've been to the Dragon. No rush."

"All right then. Come on." She took his hand. "Before they lock us out."

* * *

The bar at the Red Dragon was subdued, as befitted a Sunday evening — a low murmur of conversation being considered suitable and not even Frank Sinatra on the jukebox. Bronwen followed Evan to the bar, even though most women still took their drinks through to the lounge. It was considered fast and loose to hang around with the men.

"What'll you have?" he asked. "And please don't say Perrier."

She laughed. "All right. Ginger beer shandy then."

"Ginger beer shandy and a pint of Guinness, please, Betsy *fach*," Evan said, making sure not to call her *cariad*, with Bronwen and Barry both listening.

Betsy looked up to see who the shandy was for. "Oh, hello, Miss Price. Fancy seeing you here. I noticed Evan in chapel, coming in at the last minute, but I didn't see you with him."

"No, I wasn't with him."

"You weren't raised chapel, were you?"

"I wasn't raised much of anything, but I was taken to chapel when I stayed with my *nain*."

Evan watched them and noted, with relief, that the tension had gone from their interactions these days. Since Barry-the-Bucket had come on the scene and Evan had become engaged to Bronwen, Betsy was no longer seen as a potential threat.

He took his drink and moved toward the men. While he was still considering when and how he should tackle the subject of the skeleton, they beat him to it.

"So what's this about finding a skeleton at Rhodri's old place then?" Evans-the-Meat asked him. "They say some woman from the university came to take a look at it. And Charlie says that if it's old enough, they'll want to dig up the whole place and you'll not be allowed to finish your building, is it?"

Another point scored for the Llanfair bush telegraph, Evan thought. It was only surprising that they hadn't found out who the skeleton was.

"It's a child's skeleton," he said. "And not so old. Less than forty years, the anthropologist says."

"Anthro— what?" Barry asked.

"Forensic anthropologist," Evan said. "She's an expert at identifying old bones."

"Yes, you know, like you see on the telly when they can take a bit of rock or an old skull and tell you that it's ten million years old." Charlie Hopkins came to join them, pint in hand. "Wonderful what they can do now with science, isn't it?"

Evans-the-Meat sniffed. "I always think they're making it up, personally," he said. "I mean, who's going to tell them they're wrong? It's the same when they tell me some star is a billion light-years away. I mean, nobody's got a tape measure that long, have they?"

Evan noticed Bronwen listening and about to tell the butcher how light-years are measured. Not wanting to get off topic, he forestalled her.

"So about this skeleton, then," he said. "Who do you think it could be?"

"A child, you say?" Owens-the-Sheep asked. "How old?"

"About four, five, they think."

The men looked at each other and shrugged. "I never heard of a child going missing from around here."

"There was that little girl outside Bethesda." Evan managed to keep his voice even and casual. "Remember, about twenty years ago?"

"Oh, yes," Charlie Hopkins said. "I do remember now. Summer visitor, wasn't it? But that was a good way from here. And she was never found?"

Evan shook his head. "Never found."

"I can't see why she'd end up here, though, can you? Rhodri's cottage?"

"Rhodri was living in it then?" Evan asked.

"I'm sure he was," Charlie said. "Twenty years ago?"

"More like twenty-five," Evan said.

"That would make it — seventy-eight? Seventy-nine?"

"And you said something about water pipes being put in around that time, Charlie?" Evan suggested.

"You're right. Around that time. I remember Rhodri getting angry because they had to dig up all his plants to put that pipe in. Not that he had much of what you'd call a garden anyway, but he liked it."

"So those bushes by the gate would have been planted after the pipes went in, or did they leave those?"

"I think he had to plant everything new when the men had gone. I know he was hopping mad about the mess they left. Bloody great mounds of mud and dirt everywhere, he said."

"And who put in these pipes?" Evan asked. "Was it a local contractor?"

Charlie shrugged. "I can't remember anymore. Wasn't it the water board? But I couldn't say who they used. They did your farm at the same time, didn't they, Bill?" He turned to Mr Owens.

"That's right. They connected all the hill farms at the same time. Seventy-eight, it was, because that was the year our Sioned was born. The wife was expecting any day, and she was worried that they'd dig up the track and we wouldn't be able to drive down the hill to the hospital. But they were through and out very quickly."

"And I understand that you didn't own all this land in those days." Evan turned to the farmer.

"No, I only owned about half what I have now. I bought the rest from some bloke over in the next valley. Not long afterward that would have been. He asked a really fair price so we took out a second mortgage and snapped it up."

"So Rhodri wasn't working for you until you bought the extra land?"

"He didn't work for me for some time after that. I couldn't afford to employ an extra shepherd in those days. We were very hard up, what with getting the farm going, building up the breeding stock, and then producing young ones of our own. Rhodri only came to work for me in the late eighties, after he had a falling-out with the farmer he worked for. Thomas, his name was, on the other side of the Glyders."

"Was Rhodri the sort who had fallings-out?" Evan asked the general company. "I hardly knew him. He was a very old man by the time I moved here, and then he went to live with his daughter. But you said he was hopping mad, so I wondered if he had a bad temper."

"Oh, a terrible temper," Charlie said. "Especially when he'd had a couple. He liked his whisky chasers, you know. I recall him having many a set-to with the barman in those days. That was before Harry's time. It was Dai Roberts then — and he'd refuse to serve Rhodri when he'd had too much. Oh, and Rhodri would get that riled. 'As long as I'm paying, your job's to keep pouring,' he'd say. Didn't he, Sam?" He turned to Betsy's father, Sam Edwards, sitting in his usual seat, nursing his pint.

"Terrible, just." Sam said. "And when he got home, it was worse. You could hear him and the wife going at it right down here in the valley. It's a wonder they didn't kill each other, the way they shouted. Of course, her temper was worse than his even, and that's saying something. My, but she was a dreadful old woman."

"But she was dead by then, wasn't she?" Evan asked.

"By when?"

"When they put the water pipes in."

"Oh, yes. She went long before that." Sam looked up and laughed. "You're not saying that it's her lying in that grave outside the front door? Well, I wouldn't have put it past him, but she died of cancer when their daughter was still a little child."

"Best thing that could have happened for that kid," Charlie said. "Rhodri sent her to live with her auntie in Bangor. Not only did she get a decent upbringing in a God-fearing home, but she inherited the house and that's where she's still living. And he lives with her now, of course."

"He's still alive then?"

"Oh, yes. I saw him only a few weeks ago. Miserable as ever, of course. Complains about everything, but still hale and hearty and gets around."

"I'll be going to visit him this week," Evan said. "Let's hope his temper has calmed down a little with age."

"Just don't let him think you're accusing him," Charlie suggested.

"I'm not accusing him of anything," Evan said. "But if someone buried a child outside his front door, you'd have thought that he might have seen something or his dog might have smelled something."

The men nodded. "Yes, you would have thought so, wouldn't you? Of course, he was off roving the hills from light until dark. Anyone could have sneaked up while he was gone, especially if it was lambing season."

* * *

"So did you get anything out of that?" Bronwen slipped her arm through Evan's as they stepped out into the chill wind.

"Not really, only that Rhodri had a terrible temper and he's still alive."

"But men with terrible tempers don't go around killing strange children, do they? They get into fights and kill their mates."

"There's one more thing I hadn't considered," Evan said. "There would have been a team of labourers up here digging the trench for those pipes. The local council will have a record of who they are, I expect. It will be worth checking to see if any of them have any kind of history of subsequent child abuse."

"I'm sure they must have checked them at the time, surely," Bronwen said, snuggling closer to Evan as they caught the full force of the wind rushing down the pass. "A team of strange men working on the mountain would have been prime suspects."

"I'm not so sure," Evan said. "From what I remember about those days, foul play wasn't even suspected, not even hinted at. Of course the police may have been investigating on the quiet, but we all thought she'd had a nasty accident and fallen into a disused mine or a pothole."

Bronwen nodded. "The world was a different place in those days, wasn't it? People let their children roam free without worrying about them."

"I can't say they ever let Sarah roam free," Evan said. He paused outside the wall of the school playground. "You run in and put on something stunning and sexy, and I'll go and warm up the car. Then we'll forget about my work and go and paint the town."

Bronwen laughed. "Paint the town at eight o'clock on a Sunday night? We'll be lucky if we find anything open!"

* * *

"Are there any pools around here?" Sarah asked him, as they followed the older children up the hillside.

"Swimming pools? There's one in Bangor."

She laughed. She had a delightful, musical laugh. "Not swimming pools, silly. I meant magic pools, where the Tylwyth Teg would live."

Evan considered. "There's plenty of lakes and ponds up in the mountains. My grandfather would know."

"Yes, but we can't ask him, can we? I want you to take me."

Evan was torn between wanting to please her and knowing that he'd never be asked to play with them again if he led her off without permission.

"We'd get into trouble," he said. "Your family wouldn't let you go off alone with me. Your brother never lets you out of his sight."

She wrinkled her little nose. "I know," she said. "Let's slip away when they're playing their stupid castle game. Henry doesn't worry about me so much when he wants to win. They'd just think we were hiding." Her face lit up with anticipation, and she laughed again. "That would be such fun, wouldn't it?"

CHAPTER 19

The woman who stepped off the train at Bangor station was thin to the point of looking haggard. She wore a smart navy suit and remarkably high heels. Her grey hair was swept back into a severe chignon, accentuating the thin face and high cheekbones. She stood, holding a weekend case, looking around with annoyance, then set out for the exit, the tap of her high heels echoing across the now-deserted platform.

"Ah, there you are." Her voice betrayed her annoyance. "I thought nobody had come to meet me."

Henry Bosley-Thomas stepped forward to take her bag. "Sorry, Mother, but they won't let anyone onto the platform these days. Security, you know."

"Bloody terrorists," Mrs Bosley-Thomas said. "We shouldn't give in to them. If we change our lifestyles and let them know we're afraid, then they've won, haven't they? Where are the others?"

"We're going to meet at a hotel in Bangor at noon," Henry said. "We thought you'd probably not want to go to the farm."

"No," she said. "I most certainly wouldn't want to go to the farm. Your father's here, I take it?"

"We're all here."

"He hasn't brought HER with him, has he?"

"No. He's alone. I'm alone. We're all alone. No spouses or hangers-on. Just family. You'll be fine, Mother."

"I hope so," she said. "I really didn't know what to think when Suzanne called to tell me the news. Not whether to be glad or sorry, I mean."

"Surely it's a relief to have found her. Not knowing was so hard."

"I'm not sure." She eased herself into the car as Henry held the door open for her, then sat, staring straight ahead until he got in beside her. "Of course I always hoped we'd find her and know what happened to her, but finding her like this — until now I had always convinced myself that she'd had a horrible accident, but now knowing that somebody buried her" — she put her handkerchief up to her mouth — "one can't help wondering what he did to her before he buried her."

"Don't think about it, Mother. It's too awful for words," Henry said. "But they've got a forensic anthropologist working on it at the moment. Maybe at last they'll find out who took her, and he'll finally pay for what he's put us through."

She nodded, but didn't speak. Then she collected herself and put the handkerchief away. "Of course, we don't even know that it's Sarah yet, do we? We can't go jumping to conclusions. I hope this hotel has food. I had a most ghastly breakfast on the train. I'm sure they precooked the eggs and then warmed them in a microwave. I was absolutely horrified the way the standard of rail travel has gone down since privatization. You'd have thought private companies would know how to make a better job of it than British Rail, wouldn't you?"

She was not going to speak of it again, Henry saw. She had allowed herself one brief outburst and was ashamed of it, and now it was not going to be mentioned. It would be as it had been throughout the rest of their childhood. Sarah's room was kept as it had been, but outside of it Sarah had never existed.

* * *

Evan arrived at the tall, redbrick-and-glass building that was North Wales Police headquarters early on Monday morning and asked for the Records Department. He was surprised how slim the file was on Sarah Bosley-Thomas. Apart from a full-scale search on the mountain, precious little seemed to have been done. If they had considered abduction a possibility, then it hadn't made its way into the records. Evan scanned down the pages of the report and noticed a name he recognized. PC Meredith had been on the search team.

He ran out of the building and jumped into his car. PC Meredith was now Superintendent Meredith, his former boss. Luckily the super was of the old school who believed in hard work, punctuality, and keeping noses to the grindstone. He was already in his office when Evan arrived there at eight-thirty, his uniform jacket hanging over the back of his chair, his tie off, and his shirt sleeves rolled up.

"Ah, Evans, what can I do for you?" he asked genially. "You haven't come begging for me to take you back, have you?" He laughed loudly at his own joke.

Evan smiled. "I wanted to ask you a couple of questions about a search you conducted when you were a PC," he said. "I saw your name on the list. A missing child, twenty-five years ago. She was staying at a farm above Bethesda. Her name was Sarah Bosley-Thomas. Do you remember it?"

The smile faded from the superintendent's large, flabby face, immediately causing his jowls to return to their customary droop. "Oh, I remember it very well," he said. "I'd only just joined the force, and I was very cut up about it. They showed us the little girl's photo. Pretty little thing, she was. So what's your interest in it now?"

"A skeleton has been uncovered, about the right age. The family is going to meet with the forensic anthropologist today and hopefully provide positive ID."

"Well, that's good to know, isn't it? So they've finally found her. Where was this skeleton?"

"Above Llanfair."

"Llanfair? Good God. That's a long way from where she vanished. How on earth did she get there?"

"We don't know. Maybe somebody carried her. She was buried in a grave."

"Good God. So it was foul play after all. I remember suggesting that might be the case, and my superiors pooh-poohed the idea. They did check the area for known child molesters and the news was relayed to other forces, but the general opinion was that she had met with an accident up in the mountains and that maybe foxes or wild dogs or birds of prey had made short work of what was left of her."

Evan swallowed hard. "You were part of the search team. You found nothing? No trace of her?"

Meredith shook his head. "It was late afternoon before she was reported missing. We had men out on the mountain right away. We combed the immediate area. It wasn't thought that she could have wandered too far because she was only a small child. And it was most definitely assumed that she'd just lost her way. Dogs were brought in. One of them seemed to pick up a scent for a while, going up, not down, but then darkness fell."

"The search went on all night," Evan said. "I remember because I went along with my father. Everyone had torches."

"Yes, it went on all night, but remember, it rained heavily before morning. That pretty much obliterated any scent the dogs might have picked up."

Evan hesitated before asking, "Tell me, sir. Was the family ever suspected? There is no mention of it in the records."

"The child's family? Suspected of doing her in? Good God, man, they were in shock. In terrible grief. It never crossed my mind. Of course, I was only a PC and I'd no idea what the plainclothes blokes were thinking, but I certainly didn't get an inkling that their thoughts were moving in that direction." His eyes narrowed. "Why — have you new evidence that implicates one of them?"

"No sir, but I can't help wondering."

Superintendent Meredith looked up sharply. "You're thinking about the child that's just been reported missing, aren't you? Putting two and two together?"

"I can't help it, sir. Especially since the entire Thomas family is back in this part of the world for the first time in twenty-five years and they're as jumpy as kittens."

"I'd understood that our missing child's father is thought to have snatched her and taken her back to Russia. Are we now discounting that theory, because if so, nobody has informed me."

"No sir. The child's father is still our number one suspect, but the two little girls look so similar that I felt we had to look into this angle."

"Your boss is thinking along these lines too? Or is this another of your lone maverick actions? Because if it is, Evans, let me give you a word of warning. You're still on probation in the detective branch, and superiors do not always like probationary constables stepping on their toes."

Evan had to grin. "No sir. I quite understand, but my boss had me accompany him yesterday to interview the Thomases. He's keeping an open mind, I'm sure."

"I'm glad to hear it. So the Russian chap hasn't been found yet?"

"I haven't checked in today yet. There were several more reported sightings yesterday. We've got people working on them for us."

"Ten to one he's taken the kid back to Russia, and the Thomases appearing from out of the blue is just a remarkable coincidence. Having been on the force for twenty-six years now, I can tell you that my work has been punctuated with plenty of coincidences." He flexed his hands together, cracking his knuckles in a way that set Evan's teeth on edge. "So don't get carried away, will you, Evans? Eliminate one suspect before you go dancing all over the place looking for others — right?"

"Thank you, sir. I'd best be getting to work then," Evan said. "I appreciate your help."

* * *

Glynis Davies was already working her way through a stack of papers in the incident room as Evan came in. Today she was wearing a dark green turtleneck that accentuated her sleek auburn hair. She gave Evan one of her dazzling smiles.

"We're both in before the boss today — we must be keen," she said. "But it doesn't look as if we're getting anywhere." She waved a pile of papers at him. "None of our sightings has panned out so far. We've got a few more come in overnight, and we'll have to check those, of course."

Evan nodded. "I hope we're not wasting too much time looking in the wrong direction."

"You really don't think it was the father, do you?" Glynis looked up from her papers.

Evan shrugged. "He does seem the most likely suspect because of the way it happened, because the window of opportunity was so small. If the mother's telling the truth, that is."

"What do you mean? Why should she be lying?"

"Guilt? She only meant to go to the van, grab a cigarette, and come straight back, but she wasn't supposed to smoke anywhere near her daughter, remember. What if she stayed up there and had quite a few puffs before returning to the beach? Smoked the whole cigarette, maybe?"

"So she was away long enough for someone to have spotted a lone child, grabbed her, and made off with her?"

"Exactly."

Glynis flicked through the papers then let them drop to the desk. "I wish the bloody Russian government would get moving and let us know if Sholokhov has been traced there. It really shouldn't be too hard to ask questions of his family and friends and find out if he's returned home."

"If he really did take the child, he could be anywhere, I suppose." Evan pulled out a chair and sat at the table opposite her. "He might be waiting it out somewhere in Europe until the fuss dies down."

"But he had no money, Evan."

"He must be somewhere. Even if he's being hidden by friends at the moment, he'll have to go out sometime, won't he? The little girl will need her prescriptions renewed."

"I take it we haven't heard back from any chemists yet then?"

"Not yet, but it's been the weekend, hasn't it? They'll have been closed."

"Oh, right."

"Maybe that will be our lucky break eventually. If he has got her, he'll have to refill that prescription sooner or later, won't he?" Glynis looked up at him.

"And if he hasn't — if she's been kidnapped by someone who doesn't know about her heart condition, then she could be in a bad way very quickly."

Glynis nodded. "You're right. We should send out a general alert to hospital emergency rooms, in case someone brings her in."

"This is presupposing that whoever took her has kept her alive," Evan said.

Glynis shuddered. "Don't. It's too horrible to think about, isn't it? I criticized you for getting personally involved the other day, but it's hard not to when it's a child's life at stake." Her eyes met Evan's.

"Seeing that little skeleton made it more real to me — knowing that Ashley might wind up like that and that I might have the power to stop it, if I'm not too late. That's what gets to me — wasting all this time."

"Who's wasting time? Surely none of my team." DI Watkins came into the room and dropped his briefcase down on the table.

"We're just feeling frustrated that we don't seem to be getting anywhere with Sholokhov, sir," Glynis said.

"Yes, I agree, it is dragging on, isn't it?" Watkins said. "It's a bugger. I don't think we'll sit here holding our breath to hear back from Interpol or NCIS or whoever they are. I'll get Evans to drive me to London tomorrow, and we'll see if we can sniff out where Johnny boy might have gone."

"You and Evans, sir?" Glynis looked disappointed.

Watkins grinned. "Constable Davies, I know you're the senior constable, but my wife would never understand if I went on a jaunt to London with someone who looked like you. Besides, you're the only one who—"

"I know, who can operate the computer."

"I was going to say hold the fort. Indispensable."

"Oh, right," she said, giving him a sideways smile. "If you lay it on thick enough, I'll begin to believe it myself."

Watkins pulled out a chair and sat at the head of the table. "So I take it there's no news come in overnight?"

"A few more sightings, sir," Glynis said. "I'll start working on those right away, if you like."

"And I stopped off on my way here to check the records on the Bosley-Thomas case," Evan said. "It doesn't seem they did very much, apart from search for her. They were sure she'd wandered off and met with an accident. They haven't even kept a list of people they interviewed, so we've no way of telling if there were any known child molesters in the area at that time."

"I don't remember authorizing a records check," Watkins said, looking up sharply at Evan.

"No sir, but I just thought it might be helpful to be one jump ahead, rather than sitting here waiting for the phone to ring."

"Evans, if I want you to be one jump ahead, I'll tell you."

Evan felt his face becoming uncomfortably hot. "Sorry, sir. I didn't think you'd mind."

"I do mind. I'm running the show around here, and I decide what line of investigation we're taking, not you. I've already made it clear that we eliminate Sholokhov before we look for other suspects. We're going to London tomorrow, and hopefully we'll come back wiser than we left."

"So you're not going to follow up on the Thomases before they leave the area?"

"We saw the Thomases yesterday. I'm not convinced that there's anything to follow up. We have the numbers to contact them, if we need to."

"But, sir, isn't there an element of time involved here?" The words came out before Evan had time to consider whether pursuing this was wise. "I mean, in the remote possibility that one of them had taken Ashley?"

"I don't mean to be blunt, Evans, but if one of them had taken Ashley, then she's already dead and buried. Now let's get down to today's schedule. Davies, you're following up on those latest sightings. Evans" — he paused and glanced up — "someone needs to be there for the meeting with the forensic anthropologist. I can do without you for a couple of hours, I suppose."

Evan tried not to smile. "Thank you, sir," he said.

CHAPTER 20

Evan was not too familiar with the University of Wales at Bangor. He always felt uneasy in university situations, having not attended one himself. Those young people who surged out of buildings in great, noisy groups always seemed so confident and at ease, as if this sort of life was their due and right. He never passed among them without a pang of resentment that he hadn't sampled those years of freedom and exploration and gained the sort of knowledge that Bronwen tossed out so effortlessly. Nietzsche? Bach? Freud? No problem. All stored somewhere in the brain.

He had to ask twice before he found the modern square block, well away from the ornate Victorian buildings he had always thought of as the university. He was directed up a flight of concrete stairs, then thought he might have made a mistake and entered a cold storage room. The room was even cooler than the brisk wind outside.

"Hi, there." Dr Jan Telesky was standing at the far end in a white lab coat in the process of arranging a row of glass dishes. "Come on in," she said. "I'm glad it's you."

It took Evan a moment to realize that the skeleton lay between them on a stainless steel gurney. He started visibly. Now that it was out of its grave, cleaned and rearranged with every bone in place, he was amazed how very small it was, how very delicate the bones were.

"Are the Thomases here yet?" he asked, wrenching his eyes from the table.

"No, they won't be here for another half hour or so." There was something in her gaze that was challenging. "Do you want a cup of coffee? I've got some brewing in my office — real American coffee, not the weak stuff they serve here."

"All right. Thanks." Anything to get out of this room and away from that table.

"This way then." She led him through a back door to a bright, neat office. Sun shone in through large windows with a view of the Menai Straits between houses. "Sit down. Make yourself at home."

She smiled at him and he sank onto the stainless steel and plastic chair beside her desk.

"I was hoping they'd send you," she said, pouring coffee into two handmade pottery mugs. "I asked them to."

"Yes, you were right. One of us should definitely be present when they identify the remains," he said.

"Not one of you. You. I asked for you."

"Because I'd known her. I might remember something important."

"No, because I wanted an excuse to meet you again." She noted his look of confusion and laughed. "I'm obviously being too forward, but I'm American. We're taught to be pushy broads."

She put the mug in front of him. "I suppose, being British, you'll want cream and sugar?"

"If it's all right."

"No problem." She produced a canister of sugar and one of non-dairy creamer from a cupboard and put them beside him with a plastic spoon. "Help yourself."

Evan took one look at the non-dairy creamer and tried to conceal the shudder. "Thanks. Cheers."

"Explain that to me," she said. "Don't you say 'cheers' when you're drinking? But surely not when you're drinking coffee?"

Evan laughed. "It's come to mean about the same as thanks these days. 'Thanks' or 'cheers'. Same thing really."

"Ah. It's quite a challenge." She pulled up a stool beside him and sat, crossing her long legs so that one toe almost brushed his trousers. "Not only do I have to master the British form of English, but half the people here speak goddamned Welsh. I suppose you do, don't you?"

"Yes, it's my first language actually. I grew up speaking it."

"I'll never learn it. I tried a couple of classes, but my tongue won't go around those sounds. Too much like spitting to me." She laughed and Evan smiled too, but his brain was trying to interpret the messages she was sending him. Was she making a play for him, or was this the American version of being friendly? He didn't have to ponder the question for long before she said, "I noticed you weren't wearing a ring. Does that mean you're not married?"

"Most men don't wear rings over here," Evan said, "but no, I'm not."

"That's good to know." Her face lit up in a smile before he could finish his sentence.

"I'm engaged, actually," he said. "We're getting married in August."

"No problem," she said again, smiling at his discomfort. "I'm sure she'd understand if you took pity on a lonely American girl. I'm just starved for young male company, really. I've been here two months and most of my colleagues are older than the hills and boring as hell, and I'm not allowed per contract to date students, so here I am stuck in the middle, dying of boredom."

"I'd be happy to show you around someday when I'm not working," Evan said cautiously.

"Great! What you guys call a pub crawl Saturday night?"

"I was thinking more of a hike up one of the mountains."

"A hike? Jesus, you are all so fit and outdoorsy here. I usually go in more for indoor sports."

"Indoor sports?"

"I guess I hadn't considered that a sabbatical year might also mean a sex-free year," she said, making Evan choke on his coffee. So he hadn't been misreading the signals.

"Do you have a boyfriend at home?" he asked.

"Yeah, but that's three thousand miles away. I'm here now and he understands that."

"I could introduce you to some of our unmarried policemen if you'd like."

"God, aren't most policemen thicker than planks?"

"I'm a pretty average policeman."

"But you're a detective, so you must be one of the smart ones."

"Please, Dr Telesky—"

"It's Jan."

"Look, Jan. I'm here on official business, and I think we'd better keep it that way, if you don't mind. If the Thomases are coming in half an hour, maybe you should be briefing me on what you've discovered so far."

"Okay, if you insist." She gave a dramatic sigh and pushed a strand of long hair back from her face. "I've managed to locate a botanist who was able to interpret the plant rings on the root that went through her foot. We're right on the time frame — between twenty and thirty years. He could be more accurate if he has to."

"Anything more?"

"It was either a little girl or a boy with exceptionally long hair. We recovered a couple of strands of long, blonde hair."

Evan swallowed. "Yes, she had long, blonde hair."

"And we've got a couple of fibre scraps and the shoes in good enough condition to be identified. I'm hoping the mother will be bringing dental records; otherwise we'd have to go ahead with the DNA sample to make sure."

"But you can't say — how she died?"

"Not through any kind of violent trauma, that's for sure. No broken bones or cracked skull. But of course there are plenty of ways to kill a kid that don't break bones."

Again he was startled by the easy way she said it.

He drained his coffee cup. "Right, then. Thanks for the coffee. It hit the spot."

"Hit the spot. I just love your quaint expressions. What spot is that exactly?" Her eyes teased him with double meaning, making him get to his feet and put on a business-like expression. "Will they phone through to you when the Thomases arrive or should we go to the lab to wait for them?"

"I'm making you nervous, am I?"

"To be frank with you, a little."

"Don't worry. I'm not about to seduce you."

"I'm not about to be seduced — and I'm not worried."

She looked at Evan and laughed. "You should see your face. It's as if you were in a room with a tiger. I'm looking for company, Evan, nothing more."

The sound of voices echoed up the stairwell. "Oh, it sounds like the Thomases have arrived," Evan said with relief in his voice, and opened the door to greet them.

"Oh, there you are, Evans," Hugh Thomas called up the stairs to him. "Good. We are in the right place then." He noticed Jan Telesky standing beside Evan. "And would you be an angel and please tell your professor that we've arrived and maybe find a cup of tea for Mrs Thomas? This is all very upsetting for her."

Evan glanced at Jan's face with anticipation.

She was wearing a frozen smile. "I am Dr Telesky, visiting professor of forensic anthropology. And you are?"

Evan had to admit that Hugh handled it perfectly. "Good heavens! Are you really? I must apologize, but you look so young I thought you had to be a student. I'm Hugh Bosley-Thomas, the child's father."

"Apology accepted, Mr Bosley-Thomas. This way please." She pushed open the lab door and held it as they filed in, one by one. "Are you all family members?" she asked.

"All of us," Henry said, as he passed her. "I'm Sarah's brother, Henry. My mother and father and my sister, Suzanne. These gentlemen are cousins, Val and Nick Thomas. My grandfather chose not to come today. He apologizes but he says his eyesight is poor and he'd have been no use anyway."

Evan recognized Sarah's mother and was horrified at how old and drawn she looked, her face almost like a living skull itself. She was holding onto Henry's arm as she went through into the room, and Evan heard the half-stifled cry as she saw the skeleton.

"Oh, no. My Sarah!" she exclaimed.

"We don't even know that it's her yet, Mother," Henry said.

"It is her. I know it," Mrs Thomas said. "Look at the way her front teeth stick out. Remember how we always told her she'd have buck teeth if she kept on sucking her thumb, and Daddy used to paint that bitter-tasting stuff on her thumb before she went to bed?"

"Did you bring any dental records, Mrs Bosley-Thomas?" Jan Telesky asked.

"She didn't have any. She still had her baby teeth. She'd never even seen a dentist."

"Had she lost any of her baby teeth?"

"No, but one of the lower teeth was wobbly. She was very excited that it was going to fall out soon."

Dr Telesky went over to the skeleton, put on a latex glove, and touched the teeth. One of them moved as she manipulated it. She looked up at Sarah's mother and nodded.

"And you brought photos like I asked you?"

Mrs Bosley-Thomas fumbled with a portfolio. "They're in here," she said. "I brought a whole lot of them, just in case."

Dr Telesky took the pile of photos and spread them out on a counter. There was complete silence in the room as she examined them. Evan tried to look over her shoulder and was shocked at the stab of pain he felt as he saw Sarah smiling back at him with that wicked, impish smile.

"And we have retrieved some scraps of clothing," Jan Telesky said, moving to the row of glass dishes along the counter. "Do you happen to remember what she was wearing the day she disappeared?"

"Of course I do." Mrs Bosley-Thomas's voice was high and tight. "She was wearing a white short-sleeved T-shirt and a flowery red skirt, white tennis shoes and socks. And she had her hair tied back in red ribbons. She said it got in her face, and she couldn't play the game when it was blowing around." She put her hand to her mouth again and turned away from the group.

"The T-shirt would have been cotton, and cotton just doesn't hold up long term," Dr Telesky said, "but was the skirt a man-made fibre?"

"Yes, it was. Sarah liked soft wispy fabrics."

"We've recovered a couple of samples large enough to see traces of a pattern. Of course it's more dirty brown than red these days, but would you take a look?"

Henry led his mother over to the glass dishes. She stared for a moment. "It's hard to tell, isn't it?" she said. "I know it was a flowery pattern, but I can't really see enough of it."

"And the shoes? Were they man-made, too?"

Mrs Bosley-Thomas frowned in concentration. "I can picture them," she said. "Little white trainers with flower shapes cut out of the toe. She loved those shoes." And for a moment she smiled.

"Then would you look in here?"

Mrs Bosley-Thomas stared at the dish. "I'm afraid it's hard to tell again. I suppose these were white once. And that does look like the kind of sole they had. I don't see the little flower shape . . ."

"That could be a flower petal there," Henry pointed out.

"Yes, maybe." Mrs Bosley-Thomas nodded. "Oh, dear. This is even harder than I thought," she said. "I thought we'd know. The loose tooth and the clothing seem to be right, but we still don't *know*, not one hundred percent. And I'll never rest until we do know. Isn't there some test they can do these days?"

"There is DNA testing, but it takes time and it's expensive."

"Expense is of no consequence," Hugh said briskly. "If you need us to pay for the DNA testing, then we'll pay. My — Sarah's mother is right. We do need to know one hundred percent."

"Then let me arrange to have samples taken from Mrs Bosley-Thomas and her children. We always use the maternal DNA to make the match. If the rest of you would like to wait in my office?"

Evan held the door open as Hugh pushed Val and Nick through before him then commandeered the one good chair in the office. Val remained in the hallway, staring down the stairs. Evan went to stand beside him.

"I don't suppose I'm allowed to smoke in a lab building, am I?" Val asked.

"I don't suppose you are," Evan said.

"Damn. I need a cigarette."

"This has been getting to you then?"

"Well, of course it has; what do you think?" Val snapped. "I had managed to put it out of my mind. I hadn't thought about it for years and now we have to go through it all again. Bloody kid. Just the annoying kind of thing she would have done."

"Got herself killed, on purpose?"

Val gave a half laugh. "No, I didn't really mean that, but she was good at getting her own way, wasn't she? And she was quite good at paying people back."

Evan looked up, startled. "What do you mean?"

"She was annoyed when Henry wouldn't take her home. I've always thought she got herself lost deliberately so that Henry got into trouble."

Evan continued to stare. "What exactly happened that day? I've never really known."

"You weren't with us? No, of course you weren't. We were playing capture the castle as usual. Sarah announced that she was hot and tired and wanted to go home. We were all having a good time, and we weren't ready to leave. Henry told her to go down to the big oak tree and wait for us in the shade. We'd left a bottle of water there. When we finished the game and came down to the tree, there was no sign of her. We naturally assumed she had gone home without us. Henry was angry, but I think it was because he was sure he'd get in trouble. We ran all the way down to the house, but she wasn't there."

"So you were all playing capture the castle together, and Sarah went down to the oak tree by herself? Nobody took her?"

"No. Nobody wanted to stop playing because Henry and Nick and I had each won twice. It was going to be winner takes all."

"And who was king?"

"Nick."

"So Nick was up in the castle." Evan processed this thought. That meant that Val and Suzanne and Henry were spread out, hiding on the slopes. Any one of them could have slipped away for a few moments and not be noticed. He shuddered at the absurdity of what he was thinking, and Val picked up on it instantly.

"You don't think it was one of us, do you?"

"No, of course not," Evan said. "None of you would have had the opportunity, or the strength, to take her over the mountain all the way to Llanfair."

"Henry was pretty strong," Val said, still staring down the stairwell, "and he often went up into the hills with Grandfather to help with the sheep."

"Well, that wasn't too bad." Suzanne emerged from the lab. "They only took a saliva sample. I thought they were going to have to take blood."

She smiled at Evan and came to stand beside him on the landing. "Do you think they'll ever find out what happened to her?"

"I hope so," Evan said.

"That American woman says there's no way to know how she died — just that somebody laid her out nicely. It's horrible not knowing, isn't it? I've had nightmares about it all these years — Sarah's face coming back to haunt me again and again."

"Did she tell you anything in your dreams?" Val looked up with interest.

Suzanne shrugged. "Nothing that ever made sense. I remember she said she couldn't play capture the castle with us anymore because the castle was upside down — garbled nonsense like that."

"Do you want to sit down?" Evan asked. "There are chairs in Dr Telesky's office."

"Is my father in there?"

Evan nodded.

"Then I'll stand, thanks."

"You two don't get along very well, I take it?"

"Don't get along is an understatement," Suzanne said. "He hates my guts."

"Why?"

"It's obvious, isn't it?" she said bitterly. "He thinks I'm to blame."

The lab door opened and Mrs Thomas came out, still leaning on her son for support. "Well, that's over. Not too terrible, was it, Suzie? Now let's go and get something to eat, shall we? I need to be fortified."

"I think Grandfather was expecting us back at the house for a late lunch," Henry said. "Are you sure you won't come and say hello?"

"Not if your father's going to be there."

"Mother — it all happened years ago. Isn't this a good time to get over the past and start moving on?"

"Do you think I can ever forgive him for what he did?" she asked. "He wrecked our lives. All our lives."

"Why don't you at least stay the night, Aunt Margaret?" Val asked. "Nick and I haven't seen you for years, and Nick goes back to Canada in a few days. We'll treat you to dinner at the Everest Inn. The food's damned good."

"The Everest Inn?" She looked inquiringly at Evan.

"It's a new five-star hotel on the Llanberis Pass," Evan said.

"And you can drive down with me tomorrow, Mummy — that will save you from taking the train," Suzanne said.

"In your old boneshaker? Do you think it will make it all the way down the M6?"

"It made it up here," Suzanne said. "It's quite a good little car, actually."

"If you don't want Suzanne to drive you, I've got my Beemer," Val said. "She'll do a hundred and ten when nobody's watching. Get you back to London in a couple of hours."

Mrs Bosley-Thomas looked from Val to Suzanne. "Thank you, Val dear, but I think I'll risk the boneshaker. It will give Suzanne and I a chance to talk. We see each other so seldom these days."

"Only because you won't come to Clapham, and it's hard for me to get away."

"Of course I won't come to Clapham. I don't know what possessed you to move to such a racially mixed area. I feared for my life the moment I left the tube station."

"I have to live where I can afford the rent, Mother."

"I'm surprised old whatshisname hasn't set you up with a nice flat by Regent's Park," Henry said.

Suzanne shot him a look of pure venom. "My private life has nothing to do with you. And be careful, or I'll swing the conversation around to the lovely Camilla."

"Children, please — and with your sister lying on that table, too." Mrs Bosley-Thomas stepped between them.

Evan stood unnoticed, studying them. If ever there was a dysfunctional family, then this was it. Hate and blame were flying in all directions. And then there was Val, leaning lazily on the landing rail — Val who was an artist who drove a BMW and stayed at the Everest Inn.

Evan managed to make a graceful retreat from the lab at the same time as the Thomases, rather than risk finding himself alone again with Dr Telesky.

Nick Thomas fell into step beside him. "The little girl that's missing — any luck yet?"

"Not so far. We're going to London to try and find out more about the father tomorrow."

"Another child is missing?" Mrs Bosley-Thomas turned around, almost stumbling down the stairs.

"Yes, and they say she looked like Sarah," Nick told her.

"Oh, my God. You don't think" — she looked appealingly at Evan — "you don't think there's any connection, do you? But that's absurd. How can there be? Twenty-five years ago? It can't be the same person. It absolutely can't."

She reached out blindly to grab Henry's arm and let him lead her like a blind woman across the car park and into his car. Evan wondered if he'd persuade her to go to the farm with them after all. And by tomorrow most of them would be gone. He felt frustration boiling up inside him at his limitations as a detective. A good detective would know how to have questioned them subtly, to have observed their body language, and thus to have deduced if any of them was guilty.

He ran through them in his mind as he got into his own car. Henry, who had been Sarah's main protector; Val, who managed to live very well and looked at life through cynic's eyes; affable, easy-going Nick; and sharp-tongued, highly strung Suzanne. Did any of them really believe that one of the others was responsible? If not, then why did those sideways glances dart between them? Why were they so much on edge?

CHAPTER 21

Glynis Davies was sitting at the computer as Evan came into the Caernarfon police station.

"Any news?" he asked.

She shook her head. "I've been following up on the last sightings and so far nothing. Oh, we've located the Germans, by the way, but it seems they're in the clear. Nothing but clothes and camping equipment in their car. And their brush with the law was during an anti-immigrant rally."

"Neo-Nazis?"

"Could be, but they were only arrested for blocking a public street, not for violence or antiracial attacks."

"Then why did they make such a hurried escape when they heard about the missing child?"

Glynis shrugged. "They weren't asked that. But we'll keep tabs on them until they leave the country."

"So we're still getting nowhere." Evan pulled out a chair and sat beside her.

"So it would seem."

Evan glanced around before he said, "Look, Glynis, would you do me a favour? Could you run a background check on the Thomases? I don't really see how one of them can be involved, but they are really nervous and I just get the feeling that they are keeping things from me."

"Shouldn't you clear this with the DI first?" Glynis smiled.

"You know what he'll say — that we don't do anything until we've located Sholokhov. But the Thomases leave the area tomorrow, and I'd just like to be one jump ahead."

"One jump ahead got you in trouble this morning."

Evan grinned. "I know. Am I imagining things or is DI Watkins going through a personality change and transforming into another Hughes?"

"He's under a lot of strain, Evan. Don't forget, he's got a daughter of his own. He's personalizing this whole thing more than we suspect."

Evan nodded. "Right. Yes, I suppose he would. I didn't think of that."

"So what came out of the autopsy? Did they identify her?"

"Not positively, but they're doing a DNA match, and everything pointed to its being Sarah — clothing scraps, shoes, blonde hairs."

"Poor little kid. Poor family. How horrible for them. No wonder they're jumpy. It's making them go through the whole thing again, isn't it?"

"I'd just like to be sure it's nothing more than that," Evan said. "I couldn't tell whether they were dropping hints when they spoke to me. It was almost as if they suspected each other."

Glynis looked up with a sigh. "All right. Tell you what. Give me their names and addresses, and I'll see what turns up when the DI's not around."

Exactly on cue the door opened and DI Watkins came in. "What are you conspirators muttering about now?" he asked, looking at their guilty faces.

"Nothing, sir. Just talking," Glynis said quickly. "I've gone through the last of the sightings and turned up nothing so far. The one in Cardiff that looked hopeful — they've located him. A Norwegian man and his daughter. They live nearby."

"Blast." Watkins slapped his fist into his palm. "Let's hope we find out something useful finally when we go down to London tomorrow. What about you, Evans? How did the anthropologist go?"

"They weren't able to make an absolute identification. No dental records, you see. They've taken DNA samples from the mother and siblings, but it seems pretty certain that it is her — plenty of clues."

"Did you pick up any clues of your own?" Watkins asked.

"I'm not sure, sir. A couple of times it seemed as if someone was dropping me a hint and there was some accusing going on, but that might just have been because it was stressful for them."

"So do you think we should still keep them in mind and do any additional follow-up on them?"

"It might be worth running a background check on them, just in case." Evan looked away so that he didn't meet Glynis's eyes. "Just to see if anything strange comes up."

"By all means. What have we got to lose at this stage?" Watkins said.

"And I'd also like to talk to the old shepherd who used to own the cottage when Sarah was buried there. He may be quite gaga by now, but I think we should at least speak to him."

"He's still alive, is he?"

"He was quite recently. Lives with his daughter in Bangor."

"Then we should definitely talk to him right away. It better be you because I'm sure he's Welsh speaking, and you know my Welsh isn't too wonderful. Oh, and Evans, I think you might have another word with Mrs Sholokhov before we go tomorrow. Find out all you can about where they lived, who they knew, where the husband hung out — anything to put us on the right track."

"Right-o, sir. I'll start right away, if you don't need me here."

"Bloody useless here, aren't you?" Watkins said with a grin.

* * *

He decided to get Mrs Sholokhov over first so that he could devote enough time to interviewing Rhodri. He also put a call in to HQ to see if Rhodri had any kind of police record. Then he took the A487 cutting across the fields and farmland of the lower Llŷn Peninsula to the seaside town of Criccieth, past the ruins of the old castle and on down the coast toward the caravan park. A shower had just passed through, leaving behind a dazzlingly bright afternoon. The sky seemed to be a dome of blue glass over mountains so clear that Evan felt he could pick out every tree and rock on them. One lone cloud clung to the summit of Cader Idris to the south, sitting on top like a jaunty white beret. A stiff wind blew from the sea, making holidaymakers along the esplanade at Criccieth walk with anorak hoods up and backs to the wind. Just the sort of day he liked to spend outdoors.

The caravan park still had a deserted air about it. Evan suspected that all the publicity about the missing child wouldn't have done much for future bookings either. He parked outside and went in through a gap in the hedge. When he reached the small caravan, he was surprised to find nobody there. He peeked in through the window. The interior was completely neat and clean as if it was unoccupied. It seemed as if Shirley Sholokhov had also vanished. He was alarmed at this train of thought and broke into a run as he crossed the meadow, almost bumping into the large, muscular form of Richard Gwynne, who was coming toward him carrying a box full of rusty auto parts.

"Watch out!" he yelled, as Evan swerved to avoid him. "Where's the fire?"

"Oh, hello," Evan said. "I've just been to Mrs Sholokhov's caravan, and she's gone. Any idea what happened to her?"

"Don't ask me. I mind my own business, mate. Ask the old bat at the office. She likes to know everything about everybody."

"Right. Thanks."

Evan was about to move on when Gwynne called after him, "So they didn't find the little girl yet?"

"No, not yet. We're still looking."

"I don't expect they'll find her. They never know where to look, do they?"

"We think she's with her father. We'll locate him soon."

"Good luck." Gwynne nodded and stomped on his way.

Evan stared after him for a moment, then went to Mrs Paul's bungalow. In response to the bell, she came to the office window, a startling apparition in a voluminous purple muumuu that contrasted violently with her orange hair.

"Hello, love," she said, her face breaking into a smile as she recognized Evan. "Is there any news yet?"

Evan shook his head. "I'm afraid not. We're going to London tomorrow to see if we can find out any more about the child's father."

"You won't find him there, love." Mrs Paul gave him a pitying smile. "He's gone back to Russia, sure as eggs are eggs and bacon's bacon."

"We've had an alert out at all the ports of exit, and there's been no sign of him."

Again the pitying smile. "He won't have used his own name, love, Shirley said. You can buy passports, two a penny, if you know where to look. He knew all the fiddles, Shirley said. He and his foreign mates. Crooked as bent pins they were."

"And where is Shirley?" Evan asked.

The woman's face clouded. "She's gone, love. Gone home."

"When was this?"

"This morning. You just missed her."

"She went home without telling the police?"

"Oh no, she said she was going to stop in at the police station on her way past. She said it was giving her the willies staying there alone in that little van, and I don't blame her. Hardly room to breathe in there, so I invited her to stay in my spare room, but I could understand that she'd rather be at home, in familiar surroundings, at a time like this."

"You mean back to Leeds? Is that her home?"

"I'm not sure that she actually comes from there."

"Does she have relatives living nearby, do you know?"

"She has an auntie somewhere in Yorkshire, and she shares her place with a good friend, she said."

"Ah." Evan digested these facts. "You don't think anything happened to make her decide to leave suddenly, do you?"

"Just depression, I expect, love. She couldn't take all the waiting and not knowing — and it's not the same when you're in strange surroundings, is it? You need your own things around you at times like this. I remember how comforting it was to come home to my own armchair after I'd been to visit my husband at the hospital. How about a nice cup of tea? I was just going to put the kettle on."

"No thanks, this time," Evan said. "I've got a lot to do today."

His mind was racing as he left the bungalow and squeezed through the gap in the hedge to his car. What had made Shirley Sholokhov up and leave without telling anyone? If it had been his child, he wouldn't have wanted to leave the place where she vanished, not until he knew one hundred percent that she wasn't there. The word "Russian" played over in his mind. Sholokhov had fled to England because he had upset the Russian Mafia. Evan had heard enough about the Russian Mafia to know that they made the Cosa Nostra look like pussycats. Had they somehow caught up with Sholokhov and taken his daughter in punishment or as a hostage to make sure he came back to Russia? Were they somehow threatening Shirley Sholokhov so that she feared to tell the truth?

He picked up his mobile and dialled Inspector Watkins.

"I thought you'd want to know, sir. Mrs Sholokhov has hopped it — gone home to Leeds, so the caravan park owner says."

"Bloody hell. Did she say why?"

"Got fed up with being stuck in a little caravan, so the woman says."

"So she ups and goes without telling us?"

"That's what I thought. I'm just wondering if there's more to it than that."

"Like what?"

"I'm wondering whether Shirley Sholokhov knows more than she's willing to tell us. Her husband fled from Russia to get away from the Mafia, supposedly. Is it possible they've caught up with him, and they're using his daughter as bait?"

"Possible, I suppose. Well, that does put a new angle on things, doesn't it? I suppose we ought to pay our Shirley a visit at home in Leeds after we've checked out her husband's haunts in London. Have you talked to your shepherd yet?"

"I'm on my way there right now."

He pushed the end call button and found himself entering the outskirts of Porthmadog. As he passed the police station on the high street, he decided to stop, just in case Mrs Sholokhov had told the officers there that she was going home and nobody had bothered to report this fact to the plainclothes branch.

His nemesis, Constable Roberts, was sitting at the duty desk. "Hello, Evans. Been caught raiding any more dustbins lately?" he asked, with a broad grin on his face.

"No, the other officers seem to be able to tell a copper from a crook." He had longed to say something like this to Roberts for ages. Now he realized that he was a detective constable and Roberts wasn't. He didn't have to take any more rubbish from him.

Roberts laughed at the reply, then quickly became serious again. "No news on the little girl yet, I take it?"

"No good news. She's been sighted all over the country, of course, but none of the sightings has panned out so far. The only surprise is that her mother has upped and left without telling us. I just wondered whether she told anybody here."

"She did stop in a couple of days ago as a matter of fact."

"To say she was leaving?"

"To ask us if we thought she should stick around. She said she couldn't stand being in that caravan any longer. We said that we could contact her just as easily from her home."

"And you didn't think of mentioning it to DI Watkins?" Evan's voice rose.

Roberts looked surprised. "Of course we assumed she'd tell you blokes. Listen, mate. She asked our opinion and we gave it. Nothing more."

"Right. Sorry. It was just a shock to find that she'd gone. Makes you wonder if there's more to it that she hasn't told us."

"That's what you blokes are paid to find out," Roberts said. "Tell you what. I'll give you a buzz if she comes back."

The message was only one step away from insolence, but Evan ignored it. No sense in widening the lack of communication between the branches or fuelling Roberts's jealousy.

"Keep in touch," Evan said with a smile. "Drop us a postcard if she comes back."

CHAPTER 22

Evan got back in his car and was about to drive to interview Rhodri the shepherd in Bangor when he realized he was in Porthmadog, where Suzanne Bosley-Thomas was staying at a bed-and-breakfast. He swung the car off the high street and down to the waterfront, which was lined with a row of small, unprepossessing hotels, most of them dismal in the extreme. He realized it was unlikely that she'd be there, alone, in the late afternoon, but it was worth a shot. To his surprise the landlady at the grandly named Seaview Hotel nodded up the flight of narrow stairs.

"Yes, she's up there. Got in a few minutes ago. Who wants her?"

"Police," Evan said.

"I never did like the look of her. Shifty eyes," the landlady said. "What has she done?"

"Nothing, except identify the body of her sister, who disappeared years ago," Evan replied, watching with satisfaction the embarrassment spread over her face.

"Oh dear. I'm sorry. How dreadful for her, poor thing." She nodded up the stairs again. "She's in room twelve. Third floor."

Evan went up two flights and tapped on the door. It opened an inch or two.

"Yes?" Suzanne asked.

"It's Constable Evans, Suzanne. Do you have a moment?"

"Just a second. I was in the middle of changing. Val's treating us to dinner at his hotel tonight, so I thought I'd better look respectable."

He waited, studying the pattern of grapes and garlands on the wallpaper until the door opened again. "Sorry about that. Come on in. Excuse the mess. There's no room to put anything."

The room was scarcely bigger than Shirley Sholokhov's caravan had been and every surface was piled with clothes, makeup, toiletries. Suzanne moved her discarded garments from the bed and cleared a space for him to sit on the coverlet. "Sorry, but they don't provide a chair. Not exactly the Ritz, is it?"

"What about you?" he asked. "Where are you going to sit?'

"It's all right. I can perch on the window ledge."

"No, don't do that. Let's go out for a coffee."

"I haven't got long," she said. "I'm supposed to be picking up Mummy soon, but I'd love a coffee actually. Fortification before I have to face the family again."

"Is it that much of a strain for you?"

"What do you think?" she asked. "Do you think I like being 'poor Suzie' all the time?"

"Do they mean financially? In which case why aren't they helping you? They all seem very comfortably off."

"Oh, they are. Very comfortable, except for Mummy, who manages to keep up appearances on the pittance Daddy gives her."

"But surely your father is rich, isn't he? I remember the Jaguar he used to drive."

"Still drives," she said. "And yes, he's loaded. He's also very sharp and he hired the better lawyer. Mummy was too upset at his walking out like that and agreed to pretty much everything as long as she could keep the house. So there was no provision for a cost-of-living increase in the maintenance payments."

"That's tough."

Suzanne picked up her handbag, and Evan held the door open for her. They walked down the stairs and through the front hall in silence. The landlady poked her head out as they passed.

"It's all right, Mrs Mathias, he's not arresting me. He's a childhood friend," Suzanne said, as she pushed open the glass front door and stepped out into the wind. "Nosy old cow," she muttered, as the door swung shut behind them. "I had to say that because she'll obviously find out that you're a policeman."

"It's all right. I told her why I was visiting you. Now she's sorry for you—" He looked at her and grinned. "Sorry, that probably isn't what you wanted to hear, is it?"

"I'm used to it by now."

"So tell me," Evan said. He opened his car door for Suzanne to get in. "Why are they all sorry for you? Money isn't everything in this life."

He climbed in beside her and slammed shut the door. Suzanne sat staring down at her handbag. "They're sorry for me because I screwed my life up, because I've never managed to make a go of anything." Evan waited for her to go on. "I had a baby when I was sixteen, you know. They persuaded me to marry the father, to prevent any more scandal, of course. Well, 'persuaded' is an understatement. They pretty much forced me to marry the father — either you accept our offer and we'll give you some money to set up a home or you're out on your own, kiddo." She laughed bitterly. "Of course it didn't work. I didn't really have strong feelings for my husband in the first place. He was interested in me enough to take me to bed, and that was all I wanted — someone who was willing to pay me attention. But of course, he wasn't the greatest husband material. He felt trapped, as I did. He drank, became abusive, and it lasted all of two years before he split and found someone prettier and unencumbered."

Evan found a parking space and squeezed into it.

"I can't guarantee the quality of the coffee," he said, as he steered her toward the Copper Kettle Tearoom, "but they do good Welsh cakes, which you have to have if you're in the area."

"Welsh cakes? Those little round scones? Oh yes, I haven't had them since we were here as children." She looked almost like a child herself as her face lit up.

They decided on tea rather than the pale grey liquid that passed for coffee, and Evan poured it as they waited for the Welsh cakes. "Tell me," he said, "why does your father blame you for what happened to Sarah? Does he really imagine you had anything to do with her death?"

She looked startled. "No, of course not. You don't think — that one of us—?"

"No. I just meant that you and Henry were older, and perhaps he thought you could have looked after her better."

"Yes, I should have looked after her better," she said. "But that's not why he blames me."

"Then why?"

She looked at him directly this time. "Because she died and I lived," she said. "He adored her. Everyone adored her — well, who wouldn't? She was sweet and lovely and she was everybody's favourite, especially my father's. After Sarah died, I used to catch him looking at me, and it was so clear what he was thinking — Why are you here, when she's dead? He couldn't stand to be in the same room as me. I couldn't do anything to please him, no matter how hard I tried. When he walked out on us, I was sure it was all my fault."

There was a catch in her voice and she turned away.

"You know now that wasn't true," Evan said. "When people have been hurt, they have to blame somebody. Your parents obviously blamed each other. That's why they couldn't live together any longer."

"Maybe, but I was the last straw — having me alive, knowing how much better Sarah would have done everything. Henry was fine because he was a high achiever, and he went to boarding school. I stayed home with Mother after Daddy left us. He had to take me at weekends, but it was clear he didn't want me around. Then, of course, getting pregnant only confirmed what he'd been saying all along — that I was no good."

The Welsh cakes arrived, warm and dipped in powdered sugar. Evan offered her the plate. She took a bite, then finished it before she went on. "Strangely enough, having the baby was the one thing I've done right so far. Charlie is a great kid. He's turned out okay. Apart from him, my life has been pretty much of a mess. A steady downhill slope, winding up with this job as Sir Toby Handwell's assistant. You've heard about that, presumably. I'm sure the others will have told you."

Evan shook his head. "They've told me nothing, and it's none of my business."

"Another reason to pity me, you see. More than assistant, of course, and he's never going to divorce his wife, but he's kind and he's funny and I like the attention he gives me. I know he's so much older than me . . ."

"The father figure you never had?" Evan suggested.

She nodded. "Probably. Mmm. These are delicious, aren't they?"

Evan watched her as she ate a second Welsh cake. She looked much younger than her thirty-something years and now he saw why. The long, blonde hair, the fresh-scrubbed look, the jeans and T-shirt — she had spent her life trying to re-create Sarah. He felt a wave of pity for her but tried not to show it.

"This must be really hard for you," he said. "Hard for the whole family, but especially you."

"Yup." She sighed. "But if they can find out how she died and who killed her, at least we can put her to rest."

"We'll do our best, I promise you," Evan said.

Suzanne drank her tea in silence; then she looked up. "It's funny about what you just said — remember how Henry and Val liked to win?"

"At capture the castle. Oh yes, they liked to win all right."

"They didn't win that day," Suzanne said, toying with the powdered sugar on her plate. "I did. I was surprised when I got to the top and found I was the first one. I beat Henry and Val by quite a lot actually. I was really pleased with myself. I couldn't wait to get down and tell Mummy, but then Sarah was missing and I never got the chance to tell anyone."

She continued drawing lines in the powdered sugar with the tip of her fingernail.

Then she pushed her cup away and stood up. "I really should be getting back if I'm to make myself presentable before I pick up Mummy."

* * *

Evan dropped Suzanne back at her B and B then drove to Bangor, up and over the mountains by way of the Nant Gwynant Pass, and then down the Nant Ffrancon, past the Thomases' farm. As he passed the farmhouse, he slowed and pulled off the road to stare up at the mountains. He couldn't see the exact rocky outcropping where they had played capture the castle from here, but he could still picture it clearly in his mind. Had Suzanne really been dropping a hint that she suspected Henry or Val? He remembered how fiercely competitive Henry especially had been. And he had been tied for first place at that moment that day. How could he possibly have let Suzanne, of all people, win?

But Henry had been Sarah's main protector and bodyguard. He had watched over her every minute, until that one afternoon when he had sent her down to wait at the tree because the game was too important to quit. And then he hadn't won. Evan wondered if he'd have a chance to talk to Henry again, and if he did, what questions he could ask him.

CHAPTER 23

The woman who opened the door of the plain, terraced house in a back street of the city of Bangor had that archetypal Welshwoman's face from which caricatures of witches are usually drawn: long and thin with pointed chin, high forehead, and long nose. The fact that she was looking at Evan as if he was something the cat had dropped on her doorstep made her look even more objectionable.

"I'm not buying anything," she said in Welsh.

"That's good because I'm not selling anything," Evan replied. "I'm a detective with the North Wales Police." He was pleased at the look of alarm this provoked.

"Has something happened in the neighbourhood? I knew there would be trouble when that Pakistani family moved in down the block. Foreigners everywhere nowadays, aren't they? You're not even safe walking in Bangor after dark."

When she paused for breath, Evan said quietly, "Are you the daughter of Rhodri Morgan, who used to live above the village of Llanfair?"

"I am. What of it?"

"I understand that your father was living with you until recently."

"Still is. Sitting in front of the telly in the sitting room at this very moment."

"I wonder if I might have a word with him, Mrs—"

"Jones," she said. "Look, it's nothing upsetting, is it? He's getting rather frail, I'm afraid, and I don't want him upset."

"No, nothing upsetting," Evan said. "I just need to ask him some questions about the cottage he used to live in."

"That place — not fit for a dog, that hovel," Mrs Jones said, almost spitting out the words. "Luckiest day in my life when my mother died and my auntie took me to live with her in this house."

The daughter seemed to have inherited her mother's temperament. Evan didn't envy Rhodri.

"Come on in, then," she said. "Wipe your feet."

Evan followed her down a dark, narrow hallway into a living room at the back of the house. French windows opened onto a small square of garden, bordered by high fences. On the telly channel S Pedwar C was blasting out the early news in Welsh. An old man sat on a straight-backed chair, bending forward to catch the words. His daughter strode right past him and turned off the set.

"What did you want to go and do that for?" Rhodri shouted.

"Visitor!" she yelled back. "You've got a visitor."

"If it's that woman from the National Health again, I'm not having my toenails clipped."

"It's a policeman."

Rhodri swivelled in his seat and his gaze fastened on Evan. Evan was surprised to note that the eyes in that grizzled old face were remarkably clear and bright. He stared at Evan and, just as the latter was about to speak, said, "I know you. You're the young lad in Llanfair."

Evan smiled. "Good memory you've got, Mr Morgan."

Rhodri nodded. "Not much I forget, is there, Eiryl?"

"No, there's not much wrong with your memory, I'll say that for you."

"Excellent," Evan said, pulling up another chair beside him, "because I want to ask you some questions about your cottage long ago."

"It burned down, so they say," Rhodri said. "I sold it to some English people and it got burned down — serves them right. Never did like them much, coming in here and talking me to be as if I was a simpleton. But I made them pay a good price. So who's the simpleton now, eh? I've got the money stored away in the bank, and all they've got is a few burned bricks." And he cackled with laughter.

"The time I'm talking about is many years ago," Evan said, "About twenty-five years ago now. The council came to lay on the mains water. Do you remember that?"

Rhodri nodded. "I remember. It was about time, too. We'd been asking for it for years."

"I suppose they must have had to dig a trench up to your house?"

"A trench? I'll say they did — they left a horrible bloody mess — great piles of dirt all over the place, all my plants ruined. I called the council to complain, but nothing ever came of it."

"So was it a team of men who put in the pipes? How many would you say?"

"I've no idea. I wasn't there, was I?"

"What do you mean, you weren't there?"

"That was the year I fell and broke my leg. It was very nasty because I didn't get help right away and then gangrene set in. They thought I might lose my foot for a time. I was in hospital for over a month, and then I stayed down here with Eiryl, recuperating."

"And a right pain in the neck you were, too," Eiryl said, making Evan aware for the first time that she had been hovering in the doorway listening to them. "Pacing around the house like a trapped tiger, saying you couldn't wait to get back to your cottage and your sheep."

"Well, when you're used to the outdoors and to walking miles every day, it drives you crazy being cooped up indoors.

My old dog felt it too, didn't she? She'd spend the day running between the back door and the front, whining."

"You're lucky I put up with the pair of you. Many daughters wouldn't have," Eiryl said graciously.

"So you were away when the pipes were put in?" Evan asked.

"I just told you, didn't I? They'd been in for a month when I came back. That's why I was so annoyed to find those great heaps of earth and my plants all dug up."

"And the trench was all filled in by this time?"

"Oh yes. They'd done a good job with that. All nicely tamped down."

"So who were you working for at that time, Rhodri?" Evan asked.

The old man frowned. "Let me see. That was before I went to work for Bill Owens, wasn't it? Yes, that's right. Mr Thomas sold him the land the very next year, so I went to work for him instead. But at that time, I'd have been working for Mr Thomas of Maes Gwyn. He owned land right up from Nant Ffrancon, over the Glyders and down to Llanfair at that time."

"So why did he decide to sell? Was it getting to be too much for him?"

"Too much? He was in his prime in those days, like I was," Rhodri said.

"So much in your prime that you had to fall and break your leg," his daughter commented from the doorway.

"So what made him sell?" Evan persisted.

"Bill Owens was keen to get more land. I expect he made him a good offer. And Mr Thomas sort of lost heart after the family tragedy."

"Family tragedy?" Evan asked.

"Mr Thomas had lost a granddaughter the year before. She went up into the hills and was never seen again. Terribly cut up about it, he was."

"Yes, I heard about that."

"He sold me my cottage at the same time," Rhodri said. "Before then I'd just been renting it from him, but he offered me a really low price and good terms. It seemed stupid to refuse." He looked up at Evan. "So what's happening to it now? Burned to the ground, so I heard? Are they just going to let it lie there and go to ruin?"

"Not at all," Evan said. "As a matter of fact I bought it. I'm just waiting for the planning permission before I put a new roof on it. The walls are still sound."

"Well, I never. Good luck to you then, young man. May you be as happy there as I was." He took Evan's hand and shook it. Given the rumours of terrible fights and the sour-faced daughter, Evan wasn't sure if this counted as a blessing or not.

"So you got on well with old Mr Thomas, did you?" Evan asked.

"What's all this about?" Eiryl Jones interrupted from the doorway. "Don't tell me the old man has died and left him money?"

"Sorry to disappoint you, but he's just celebrated his eightieth birthday and he's still hale and hearty."

"That old bugger will live forever," Rhodri muttered, "and why shouldn't he? He's still got his farm, his freedom, hills to go walking in. Not like me, trapped down here with these four walls."

"I like that! After all I've done for you, all you do is complain," his daughter said. "You should consider yourself lucky. It's a lot better than the old people's home, and you get three square meals a day. You can always go there if you want."

"I didn't mean that, did I? It's just that after a life outdoors, it's hard to take bricks and concrete." He looked at Evan, appealing with him to understand. Evan did.

"I can't say I'd want to live in a city myself," he said, "but at least you can see the mountains when you go out." He looked around the room. "You don't have your dog anymore?"

"No, she's not with us anymore," the old man said. There was something in his voice that made Evan suspect that maybe she had died before her time. He got to his feet.

"Well, thanks for your help, Mr Morgan."

The old man's handshake was still firm. "Thank you for coming, young man. I'm not sure what I'm supposed to have helped with."

"Oh, didn't I tell you?" Evan said. "They found a child's skeleton buried under your front path."

There was a gasp from Rhodri's daughter.

"A skeleton, you say? From long ago, like?" Rhodri asked.

"We think it was from the time those water pipes were put in. It could be Mr Thomas's missing granddaughter."

"Then I'd ask those blokes who left all that mess in my front garden," Rhodri said. "I'd ask them a few questions."

Eiryl Jones escorted Evan back to the front door. "Lucky he was with me all summer, wasn't it?" she said, with a smirk on her face that somehow made her look even more unpleasant. "Otherwise you'd have him handcuffed and locked up by now, wouldn't you?"

* * *

As Evan pulled out from the curb, his mobile phone rang.

"Evans, where the devil are you?" Watkins's voice echoed through the car on the speakerphone.

"Just on my way in now, sir. I've been with Rhodri Morgan."

"And?"

"He was away from his cottage all that summer. He broke his leg and was in the hospital, then with his daughter."

"Well that's one theory shot to pieces then. We've been more successful here. We've just found out that Ashley's prescription was filled a couple of weeks ago in North Yorkshire — same area where we had the reported sighting of the child's father."

CHAPTER 24

It was eight-thirty when Evan opened his front door. He felt as if the day had gone on forever and tried to remember if he had stopped for a meal. He didn't think so, apart from the Welsh cakes with Suzanne Bosley-Thomas. His stomach was certainly growling for food, and he wondered whether he could barge in on Bronwen at this hour. On school nights she was usually up to her eyes in marking and preparing for the next day. The other option was the pub. Betsy's microwaved toad in the hole was better than nothing and certainly better than what he had in the fridge.

He pushed open his front door, then froze as he heard a noise coming from his kitchen. The door was closed and he always left it open. He moved forward cautiously then flung open the door.

"Evan — you scared the daylights out of me. You nearly made me drop this. What on earth was the James Bond imitation in aid of?" Bronwen demanded. She was standing at his stove, wearing an apron and holding a casserole in a gloved hand.

"I didn't expect to come home and find anyone in my house," Evan said. "So naturally I thought . . ."

"That the Mafia had invaded?" Bronwen was laughing now.

"Well, I am a policeman."

"And you did give me a key." Bronwen put the casserole on a mat on the table. "Is this liable to be a nightly occurrence when I'm married to you? Because I need to know whether I should be taking martial arts lessons now, just in case."

Evan came over to her and enveloped her in his arms. "I'm sorry, *cariad*. It's been a long day. I'm bushed and my brain is obviously not functioning."

"I know you've been working very long hours. That's why I decided to come over with the lamb *cawl*. Sit down. It's all ready."

"Bron, you're a miracle worker." He kissed her forehead then pulled out a stool.

"Tough day, was it?" She ladled out a generous helping of lamb pieces and vegetables, swimming in a rich brown gravy.

"Frustrating. We're not getting anywhere."

"So they didn't manage to identify the remains as being the little girl you knew?"

"Not conclusively, but I'd say it's pretty definite."

"Well, that's one piece of progress, isn't it?"

"About the only one. Oh, and we may be getting somewhere with the missing child's father at last. A man matching his description was seen in a remote area of North Yorkshire a couple of weeks ago. Now we find that the child's prescription was filled in that same area."

"So are you going up there?"

"I wanted to, but Inspector Watkins still wants to check out the father's haunts in London first. We've got the North Yorks Police conducting a search for us up there and showing the photos around. If we get any confirmation of a more recent sighting, we'll head in that direction."

Bronwen frowned as she helped herself to the hotpot. "But wait a minute — two weeks ago is no good to you, is it? The child was safely with her mother until last Friday."

"Unless the father was establishing a hideout in Yorkshire, planning for when he had a chance to kidnap her. He probably assumed they were still in Leeds and it would only be a short drive to North Yorks. He would have wanted to make sure he had enough of her prescription drugs on hand."

"Did the chemist recognize him?"

"No, unfortunately the chemist couldn't remember who picked it up. The signature is illegible. It may have been his young assistant who was behind the counter that day. The North Yorks Police will be showing him the photos we've sent them."

"What about the address? Don't you have to fill in the address on a prescription?"

"It was the child's own home address."

"And the child and her mother were already here at the caravan two weeks ago?"

"Yes, they were." Evan paused to eat a couple of forkfuls, then chewed hard to finish a mouthful. "You know what else is interesting? The mother has left without telling us. Apparently she told the local police station, but she never contacted the DI."

"Do they know where she's gone?"

"Home, she said. We're checking that out, of course."

"I can understand that," Bronwen said. "If you're sick with worry, you wouldn't want to be stuck in a caravan all alone, would you? You'd want the support of loved ones."

"If she has any loved ones," Evan said. "I got the impression she didn't live near any family members. But I suppose you're right. If you're really worried, you don't think logically, do you?"

"So what happened when the family came to identify the child's skeleton today?" Bronwen asked. "I imagine that must have been awfully hard for them."

"It was."

"Did anything come out of it?"

"Like what?"

"You suspected it might be one of them, didn't you? You didn't get any sense that one of them was guilty?"

Evan ate slowly before saying, "I really don't know what to think, Bron. It just seemed so much of a coincidence that a second child disappeared when they all came back to the area for the first time. But now that I've met them again, I find it so hard to believe that one of them could have killed Sarah. We were all little kids."

"You should know better than anyone that kids do terrible things sometimes."

Evan nodded. "Yes, but it's just hard to equate any of those children I knew with a clever killer."

"What do they think?" she asked. "None of them have had suspicions?"

Evan paused. "Now that you mention it, a couple of them did drop hints. At least I think they were trying to drop hints." He ran through the conversations in his mind. Suzanne had surely hinted her suspicions about Val and Henry — more definitely about Henry and how it was strange that he hadn't won the game of capture the castle. And hadn't Val mentioned how strong Henry was and how he was the only one allowed out alone? Had they really been hinting that they suspected him, or was it just their desperate need to have this case solved at last?

"I presume they've all gone home now so you've lost your chance to interview them," Bronwen said.

"No, actually they're having a family dinner up at the Everest Inn," Evan said.

"In that case, if you wanted to follow up on those hints, then it would seem like now or never, wouldn't it?"

Evan looked up, a cube of lamb skewered on his fork. "You think I should go up there tonight?"

"It might be your only chance."

"But what could I say? I've no authority to pursue this matter. I'd get in terrible trouble if they complained about me."

"I don't recall that ever hindering you in the past." Bronwen met his eyes with a smile. "In fact, I'd go as far as to say that you deliberately went against your superior officers on certain occasions."

"That was different. I was going against that pompous twit Inspector Hughes."

"Inspector Watkins knows you well enough, Evan. If you start doing some investigating on your own, he'll understand."

"I'm not so sure. The old Watkins would have, but he's into his 'I'm the boss around here' mode at the moment. Very touchy, in fact."

"Then make it look as if you bumped into the family by accident," Bronwen said. "Come on. Finish your dinner and then you can take me for a drink at the Everest Inn."

"At those prices," Evan said with a chuckle, "you'll be getting lemonade."

* * *

The foyer at the Everest Inn was deserted when Evan and Bronwen came through the etched-glass doors. A big fire burned in the fireplace. Soft music was playing.

"I hope they haven't finished dinner and gone," Evan said.

"If it's their last night together, they won't want to leave in a hurry, will they?" Bronwen slipped her arm through his. "Come on, let's go to the bar and order drinks; then we can have them at that table by the fire."

They settled on Irish coffees.

"This is really nice," Bronwen said, looking around her with satisfaction. "We should do this more often."

"Then you'd better find yourself a high-paying job, my love, because my policeman's pay isn't going to stretch to this more often."

Bronwen smiled and sipped her drink. Evan studied her. She had grown up in this sort of life. Irish coffees at five pounds a head were probably nothing in her mind, even though she was only earning a schoolteacher's salary at the moment. Would there come a time when she was dissatisfied with living humbly? Would she suddenly find that she wanted her old life back again?

As if she sensed what he was thinking, she looked up and smiled. "Come to think of it, there's nothing here that we can't have at home. We'll get the chimney working at the cottage and we'll have armchairs in front of a roaring fire and we can make Irish coffees every night and look out at a better view than this. I wish those stupid planning people would get on with it. I can't wait."

Evan looked up at the sound of voices and saw Mrs Bosley-Thomas come into the foyer on her son's arm. Suzanne hovered behind them. She was clearly ill at ease, her eyes darting around nervously as they crossed the foyer and exited through the front door. Evan rose to his feet, not sure whether to follow them. Bronwen was signalling him to go after them. However, he was only halfway across the floor when the door opened again and Henry came back in. He seemed preoccupied and didn't notice Evan until he almost bumped into him.

"Oh, hello," he said. "What are you doing here? Not looking for us again, I hope."

"Not at all," Evan said. "I live in the village. I bring my fiancée up here from time to time for a quiet drink." He saw Bronwen smirk.

Henry nodded. "It's not bad by Welsh standards, is it?"

"So your sister and mother have left, have they?" Evan asked.

"That's right. Suzanne's going to drive Mummy home tomorrow. It's been a bit of an ordeal for her, I'm afraid."

"Your mother or Suzanne, did you mean?"

"Mummy, of course. Everything's an ordeal for Suzanne. She always has been a bag of nerves, poor thing. You remember her as a child, don't you? Always having outbursts and completely overreacting. Always with a grievance about something too."

He looked Evan directly in the eye for a second.

"I've never mentioned this before," he said, "but that day, when Sarah — when Sarah went missing, we were playing that silly game. I spotted Suzanne. She was going down, not up to the castle."

"She says she won," Evan said.

Henry shook his head with a pitying smile. "Oh, I don't think so. Truthfully, I can't remember anymore who won, but I don't think it was Suzanne."

"Are you suggesting that your sister may have had something to do with Sarah's disappearance?"

"Oh, Good Lord, no. Not at all. Nothing like that. I mean, that's totally absurd. How could you ever suggest such a thing?" Henry laughed. He slapped Evan on the shoulder. "Good seeing you again, even if it was in such distressing circumstances. Must join the others in the bar, or they'll wonder where I've got to."

He strode across the floor, his leather soles making brisk tapping noises. Evan went back to join Bronwen.

"Well?" she asked.

"What a family," Evan said. "It appears that the brother and the sister suspect each other."

"And which one do you suspect?"

"I have no idea. I don't think I can be the kind of detective I thought I was, Bron. I just have no idea."

CHAPTER 25

"I didn't like London the first time I came here," DI Watkins said, as they inched forward through a traffic jam, "and I like it even less each time I come back."

Evan, who had done all the driving, was concentrating too hard on avoiding other vehicles to talk. It had been a long, stressful drive through a rainstorm that had stalled traffic on the M4. He winced as a double-decker bus drew up beside him, seemingly only inches away. He noticed the sign to Shepherd's Bush on the left and wondered how he'd ever get across to it. He had been feeling keyed up and uncomfortable since before they started that morning. Knowing that the Thomases were going their separate ways worried him. He had tried telling DI Watkins that they shouldn't let the Thomases go but had been overruled.

"It's not as if they're going to flee the country, is it?" he had laughed. "Look, Evan, you said yourself that you can't really believe one of them was involved. I agree with that. They were little kids and you said it yourself — they were distraught about losing her."

All the way down in the car, Evan had chided himself for not acting. He should have acquired photographs of the Thomases and shown these around the caravan park. He should have taken their car numbers. He realized he could get these if he needed them, but he sensed that the window of opportunity had closed. Now they had gone home, and he'd probably never find out who had buried Sarah at his front gate.

He closed his eyes and slid in between a taxi and a van. The van honked at him.

"There, that was easy, wasn't it?" Watkins said, as they pulled up outside a row of faceless, three-story Victorian houses. "Piece of cake, I'd say."

Evan, who was sweating, glanced at him, opened his mouth, then changed his mind. "When you've got a driver who knows his north from his south," he said.

"I don't deny I've got a rotten sense of direction," Watkins said. "Right. Number thirty-one. That must be the one with the letter box hanging off." He opened the car door and got out. Evan followed him. The neighbourhood was definitely what could be described as racially mixed. There was an Indian grocery on the corner. The small row of shops opposite contained a video rental shop with signs advertising films in a language that could have been Arabic, a Chinese takeaway, and a curry-and-chips place. Three little West Indian boys were riding skateboards along the pavement. But the woman who opened the door had the hard, big-boned face of a Londoner.

"Mrs Strutt?" Watkins said.

"What do you want?"

"We're from the North Wales Police. We'd like to talk to you about your former tenants, Mr and Mrs Sholokhov."

"The police have already been round here asking questions." She stood, tree trunk arms folded over broad chest, defying them to get past her into the house. "I told 'em 'e don't live here no more. And didn't leave no forwarding address neither."

"We know that the local police have spoken to you, but we have a few more questions we need to ask, if you don't mind," Watkins said. "There may be some things that they overlooked because it wasn't their case and they didn't realize what was important. Can we come in for a moment?"

She tried to stare them down. "I'm due at bingo in half an hour."

"Then we'll try to keep it brief," Watkins said.

"Mrs Strutt, it's about the little girl who used to live here," Evan said. "Little Ashley. Did you hear that she's missing? Her mother thinks that her father might have kidnapped her. You'd want us to find her before he took her back to Russia with him, wouldn't you?"

The hard face softened a little. "Nice little thing she was. Sweet as anything. All right. Come on in then, but I'm not missing the start of bingo."

She led them into an old-fashioned front room that looked as if it was never used. There were antimacassars on the three-piece suite, and the fireplace looked as if it had never had a fire in it. She sat on the sofa, leaving Watkins and Evan to take the uncomfortable, straight-backed armchairs.

"I told the other bloke everything what I know," she said. "They lived upstairs for three years. They come here when little Ashley was one year old. I think they'd had a hard time finding a flat what would take kids."

"And what sort of tenants were they?"

"Oh, not too bad, considering," she said. "They had their fights, but what couple don't? And he was a bit on the highly strung side like most foreigners, you know."

"Did he work at all while he was here?"

"Odd jobs from time to time, but no steady work. His English wasn't too good. But she worked, of course. They paid their rent regular enough, and he got money from the social services. If you really want to know, it made my blood boil. I said to Mrs Finch next door — we've sweated and slaved all our lives and they hand out the public assistance to these bloody foreigners, pardon my French."

"What sort of job did she have?" Evan asked.

"Hairdresser. She did quite well at it, I believe. The little kid was always nicely dressed."

"What kind of parents were they?"

"Well, I can't say you could fault them as parents, either of them. They both adored that child. You never heard either of them raise their voices to her, no matter how much they fought with each other. They were both dead worried when she had the operation. Didn't leave her bedside the whole time, but she pulled through nicely and now she's just like any other normal kiddy, running around and singing and playing."

"When Mr Sholokhov left here, did he talk about going home to Russia?" Watkins asked.

"We never talked much. I had a hard time understanding him on account of his poor English, if you really want to know. I think he just lost heart after she left him. And he was probably having a hard time coming up with the rent money. He just come to me one day and said the place was too big for him and he was moving out at the end of the week. Then he packed up his stuff and left."

"Did he have much furniture to move?" Watkins asked.

"She took most of it with her. There was only odds and ends what she left — a table, a bed, that kind of thing, and they went into a friend's van."

"Tell us about his friends," Evan said, leaning toward her. "Did they have friends come to visit here often?"

"What do you think I am, a bleeding spy?" she demanded. "What they did was their own business. But I did notice the occasional person going up and down the stairs. She had some women friends and sometimes one of them Russians would come round for him and they'd come down the stairs together, jabbering away."

"Would you happen to know the name of any of his friends?"

"The police already asked me that and I told them I'd no idea. I've got three tenants in the building and what they do is up to them so long as they don't make noise and they keep the place clean."

She glanced at her watch and Evan sensed that they'd better move quickly before she escaped. "So the father looked after Ashley during the day, while his wife worked as a hairdresser, did he?" he asked.

"He was supposed to. Sometimes I babysat her, rather than have her taken down to that club with all the smoke. She wasn't supposed to be near smoke, you know, on account of her weak heart, but both her parents smoked."

Evan shifted on his seat. "What club was this, Mrs Strutt?"

"Some place where all the Ruskies get together and talk about how to fiddle the British government. He used to go down there all the time. She didn't like him going, but he still went."

"Is it around here?"

"It must be. I can't say I've gone looking for it myself, but I know she went to find him once when she came home from work and he wasn't here. Was she angry! You should have heard the language. 'He's taken my daughter down that effing place again,' she said. She stormed out and they were all back here within ten minutes."

"Thank you, Mrs Strutt. That's most helpful," Watkins said. "Anything else you can tell us that might be of help locating him? Anything at all, no matter how small?"

She screwed up her face in concentration, then shook her head. "I'm blowed I can think of anything, but I hope you find him with the little girl. I wouldn't want her taken to Russia — nasty cold horrible place."

"Well, that's something to go on," Watkins said, as they came out into another rain shower. "Good of you to pick up on the club business. Let's pop into the local police. They'll know what's on their turf."

"Why didn't they mention the club to us if they knew about it?" Evan asked.

"They might have asked there and not come up with anything," Watkins said. "Come on, then. Let's see if you can find the police station."

* * *

Instead of the sleazy nightclub Evan had pictured, the club turned out to be a Russian tearoom with a Greek restaurant on one side of it and a laundrette on the other. A large woman in a sari was negotiating a pramful of laundry across the pavement while two little children clung to her skirts. Evan held open the door for the inspector. At first glance the tearoom was empty, but voices were coming from a room at the back.

As they closed the door, a bell rang and an elderly man appeared. "Good afternoon, gentlemen. A table for two?"

"We're police officers," Watkins said, and a look of alarm shot across the elderly face. "We're trying to find out the whereabouts of Ivan Sholokhov. We understand he used to come here."

"Yes, but no more. He hasn't been here for one month maybe." He spoke with a strong accent, but his English was fluent.

"I understand this is a place where Russian immigrants meet. Would it be possible to speak with some of them? It's very important that we track down Mr Sholokhov."

The man hesitated then shrugged expressively. "You can ask these men, but they don't know where he is." He shuffled ahead of them down past rows of white-clothed tables and through a bead curtain. Several men were sitting in the gloomy area beyond and, as Mrs Strutt had predicted, the air was full of cigarette smoke. And some kind of foreign tobacco too — sweet and herby. Faces looked up at them and one man had half risen to his feet.

Watkins raised his hand in a calming gesture. "Sit down, fellows. No cause for alarm. We just want to ask you a few questions about your mate Ivan."

"Ivan has gone," a large man with round cheeks and piggy eyes said.

"We know that. We need to trace him. We think he took his daughter with him."

"And why should he not take his daughter?" a younger, bonier man demanded in clipped, heavily accented English.

He was wearing red braces to hold up his trousers. "A man can travel with his child if he wishes."

"Not if he wasn't the parent with custody."

Evan saw the word didn't mean anything to them. "The court said the mother must have the child with her, and the father could only come to visit."

"Which court is this?" the young man demanded.

"The divorce court?" Watkins said. "You mean they're not officially divorced yet?"

"Of course not." The young man shook his head fiercely. "Johnny and his wife met once with the woman from social service to decide what is best for the child. Then the wife takes the child and goes pffft. Just like that."

Watkins pulled out a chair and sat beside the young man. "Are you sure of this? They hadn't awarded custody to the mother? They hadn't told the mother that Ashley could stay with her?"

"I tell you, it has not yet come to any court. Johnny wants to cause no fuss for his child. He says we must talk with the child welfare lady, and she will help us decide how things will be. But his wife no — she does not want this. She does not want Johnny to see his child no more. So she takes her away."

A sallow, hollow-eyed man leaned across the table. "Johnny is heartbroken. He has to search for his child. He has no money, no car. What can he do?"

"So what did he do?" Watkins asked patiently.

"He find that his wife now lives far away in the north, in another city. He goes to see her. Then he comes home and we tell him, Johnny — you must see lawyer or this woman will make sure you never be with child again."

"So he went to a lawyer?"

"We give him money. We take him to immigration lawyer — he is a good man; he will help us. He says he will find us the right kind of lawyer to help Johnny get back his child. He says don't worry. We go to court and we show them you are good father, and the judge will say that child must be with you."

"When did this happen?" Watkins asked.

"One month ago Johnny meets with the lawyer. They make date to go to court. Then one day Johnny does not come here anymore." He spread his hands in a gesture of futility. "We don't know where he has gone."

The one with the braces put his hand on his friend's shoulder. "I have Johnny's things at my home. We wait for him to call us, but there is no phone call."

"Is it possible that he went back to Russia?" Watkins asked.

"To Russia? Pah!" The man almost spat. "Why should he go back to Russia? No good there. Not good life. Johnny likes England. He says England is good place to raise my daughter."

"Then he must have taken his daughter and gone into hiding with her," Watkins said. "Look, I'm going to give you my telephone number. If he contacts you, will you please have him telephone us? If there has been no custody hearing — if the judge hasn't decided — then he's not going to get into trouble. It's just that everybody needs to know that the little girl is okay."

"Johnny would do nothing to harm his child," the fat man said defiantly. "This child was the light of his life."

Evan had been standing behind the group in the murk. Now he moved forward. "Perhaps he was afraid the judge wouldn't let him have his daughter when they went to court."

"Pah!" The man almost spat again. "The judge will see who is the good parent and who is the bad. Johnny does everything he can to make things good for daughter. He finds a job where he can work at night, and the daughter can sleep with my two girls. He finds a good place to live."

"But maybe the judge would favour the English parent?" Watkins suggested.

"This woman? She can be called good parent? Huh! What about men?"

"Men?"

"She is not content to stay home and be a good wife, good mother. No, not she. She likes a good time. She wants to go dancing, and she thinks it's okay to flirt with other men. Johnny says no. He forbids her to act this way. That is why they fight."

* * *

"It may just be that we've been looking at this the wrong way round." Evan stood outside the tearoom, breathing deeply to rid his lungs of the smoke. "We've always assumed that Mrs Sholokhov was the one in the right. But now we know she lied to us about the custody, don't we?"

Watkins nodded. "Maybe not flat out lied, but she led us to think that she'd been awarded custody."

"So what if she was scared that he'd get full custody, and she's the one who took the child to a remote beach?" Evan asked. "It's understandable if he wanted his daughter back and came looking for her, isn't it?"

"That doesn't give him the right to take the child without the other parent's permission," Watkins said. "Two wrongs don't make a right."

"Well, from what those men said, it certainly doesn't sound as if he's gone back to Russia. I wonder why his wife was so convinced that he had?"

Evan opened the car door for the inspector. Watkins looked up at him as he climbed in. "I'm beginning to think that Mrs S may have been leading us up the garden path, Evans."

"So what do we do now?" Evan started the engine and pulled out into the traffic.

"First of all we have to verify what those Russians told us. They're obviously on his side. Let's hear what the mediator at the child protective services really has to say before we go jumping to conclusions. But then I think we have to pay Mrs Sholokhov a visit in Leeds."

CHAPTER 26

The caseworker at the child protective services remembered Ashley and her parents very well. "They both seemed to want what was best for her," she said, "which always makes it easier. Then the mother decided to move back to Yorkshire, where she came from. Naturally we were going to make sure that this didn't prevent the other parent from his share of the custody. We tried to persuade her to remain in London until custody was decided, but she just upped and went."

"She seems to make a habit of that," Watkins muttered. "So at this moment they were supposed to be sharing her?"

"They were supposed to be working out how they could both have a relationship with the child that imposed the least stress and disturbance on her. Mr Sholokhov was trying to be accommodating, I must say. He even volunteered to move up to Leeds so that Ashley wouldn't have to travel when she went to her mother. Then we lost contact with both of them."

"So have we, seemingly," Watkins said.

The woman looked up from the file in front of her. "Please do let us know when you relocate them. I don't like people taking the law into their own hands, especially not where a child is concerned."

"That's about it, then," Watkins said, as the interview concluded. "Not much more we can do down here, so we won't have to spend the night, thank God."

Evan looked around him uneasily. "Of course, it is possible that Sholokhov's Russian friends are the ones hiding him. He could be upstairs at that very tearoom right now."

Watkins nodded agreement. "Always possible. I'll have another word with the DI at the local police station and have his men keep their ears to the ground. Maybe we should post a reward — that brings people out of the woodwork, doesn't it?"

"Not a bad idea," Evan agreed, "if the DCI is going to find you any money in the budget for a reward."

"Probably not, mean bastard. I may just go over his head and ask the chief constable myself. Let me call the Met then and you can check in with Glynis, just to make sure she's not sitting there doing her nails while we're away."

"That is definitely a sexist remark," Evan said with a grin. "You'll get yourself in trouble one day."

"Nonsense. Men do their nails too, don't they?" Watkins smiled back.

Evan got into the car to shut out the street noise before dialling Glynis Davies. He brought her up to date on their interviews.

"So he is really the good guy?" she asked.

"Maybe he's not the villain."

"So are we still going to pursue him? He hasn't committed an offence at this point if he hasn't tried to leave the country with her. We know Ashley's being taken care of. It's up to her parents and the social services to sort things out."

"All assuming that Johnny S is the one who has taken his daughter. Did you have any chance to do a background check on the Thomas family?"

"I couldn't come up with anything on Henry Bosley-Thomas, except for his passing his law exams and his membership at a golf club. There are hundreds of references to Val Thomas. He's quite famous, so it seems. He's even got pictures hanging in the Tate Gallery. The *Observer* called him one of the brightest young stars of the art world."

"Did they? Good for Val. What about Suzanne and Nick?"

"I haven't had a chance to get around to them yet, but I will. It's been quite busy in here, what with one thing and another."

"One thing and another?"

"DCI Hughes attempting to take over the whole thing and make me redo everything we've done so far."

"DCI Hughes? What's he poking his nose in for?"

"You tell me. Maybe because the case is getting media attention, and you know how he loves the limelight. Anyway, he showed up and grilled me about everything we had done."

Evan chuckled. "Tough luck."

"You're going to pay for this when you get back," she said. "I'll expect no weekends and assignments that end at five o'clock for the next month."

"I'll pass on the message to the DI."

"See you tomorrow then," Glynis said. "Oh, and Evan, drive safely, won't you?"

* * *

"If your friends at the rugby club knew that you'd asked to visit an art gallery," DI Watkins muttered.

"It's research," Evan said. "I thought we should at least see one of Val Thomas's pictures while we were in London."

"And I thought I'd be home in time for the nine o'clock news. What a load of old rubbish this is," he added. "They call it art?"

Evan had to agree. In this exhibit of current British artists at the new Tate, there were few pictures that were actual representations of anything he could recognize. There was one painting of a black square on a white background, which Evan thought even he could have done just as well. There was even a pile of bricks in the middle of the floor with a label beside it saying, "Destruction of civilization." Art seemed to be an easy profession these days.

Then at last they saw the plate on the wall beside a large painting. "Valentine Thomas. *Lost Bird*. 1997."

Evan stared at it for a long while, then the picture next to it, also by Val. These were no facile squares or piles of bricks, but dark, brooding, frightening scenes reminding Evan of his own nightmares. He saw the fear and the suffering, and he began to understand. Sarah's death had affected Val as deeply as any of them, but he had only allowed his anguish to spill out onto his paintings.

"Not my cup of tea," Watkins commented. "Wouldn't fancy that on the living room wall, would you?"

* * *

They had just passed Droitwich on the M6 when the phone rang.

"Inspector Watkins, it's DC Davies here."

"You're working late, Glynis," Watkins said. "Have you got some news for us?'

"I think I might have. Listen, sir, Evan asked me to check into the backgrounds of the Thomas family. I've been in touch with the Royal Canadian Mounted Police. It seems that Nick Thomas stood trial for child molestation two years ago. He was acquitted, but I thought you'd want to know."

"Bloody 'ell, Evans. You were right all along," Watkins exclaimed, as Glynis hung up.

Evan shook his head. "Nick? I can't believe Nick had anything to do with any of this. He couldn't have had anything to do with Sarah — for one thing he was only a little boy at the time, and for another, he was king in the game they were playing. He was guarding the top of the hill. He couldn't have come down without being seen."

"But what about Ashley's disappearance? What if you were right, and it wasn't her father after all? Sometimes an upsetting event like that in early childhood can unhinge a person. You know that as well as I do."

"But he's a priest. He always seemed like a nice bloke."

"You know damned well that even serial killers come across as nice blokes. Do we know where to find him? He hasn't left the country, has he?"

"As far as I know, he's still at the Everest Inn. He and his brother were going to stay a couple of extra days."

"Everest Inn, is it? Quite an easy drive down to the caravan park from there. Well, put your foot down, boyo. We're going to call on Father Thomas tonight, before he vanishes on us like everyone else."

Rain peppered the windscreen and flew off the wipers as Evan drove as fast as he dared. Giant lorries hauling one, two, or even three trailers threw up curtains of spray, making passing them a breath-holding experience, but Evan was driven by the same sense of urgency as the inspector. Nick Thomas — the quiet one whom everyone liked. Was it possible that he had anything to do with Ashley's disappearance. If so, would they get him to confess? He didn't want to believe it, and it still didn't explain what had happened to Sarah. Did Nick know something about her disappearance that he'd kept to himself? Had he witnessed something from his hilltop vantage point that day?

The miles seemed to pass frustratingly slowly as they were swallowed into darkness. They turned off at Chester, then had to endure another eternity on the A55, almost deserted at this time of night and made unreal by pockets of mist that floated in the valleys. Then finally the twinkling lights of the outskirts of Caernarfon. The mist grew thicker as they passed Llanberis and climbed the pass. Llanfair loomed like a ghost town, then the monstrous shape of the Everest Inn, its lights only dimly visible across the car park. They hurried toward the front door, raincoat collars turned up against the bitter chill.

"Like the middle of bloody winter again," Watkins complained.

The Thomas brothers were sitting together in the bar. They looked up as the two policemen approached them.

"Any news yet, Inspector?" Val asked.

"I wonder if we could have a word, sir," Watkins asked.

"By all means. Grab a pew," Val said. "Can we get you gentlemen a drink?"

"No, thanks all the same, sir," Watkins said. Evan's gaze met Nick's, and Nick gave him a big smile of recognition. "It's actually Father Thomas we'd like to talk to — in private, if you don't mind."

Val shot his brother a questioning glance.

Nick rose to his feet. "Of course. Maybe we should go up to my room. See you later then, Val."

They followed Nick up the staircase. The room on the first floor was spacious with windows opening onto a balcony.

"Take a seat." Nick indicated leather armchairs beside the desk. He waited until they were seated before he said, "You've found out, haven't you?"

"We've been in touch with the Canadian police, yes."

Nick sighed. "I was trying to keep it from my family. It was bound to come out in the end, I suppose, and obviously you'd pick up on it. The charges were dropped, you know."

"Yes sir, we know. Would you like to tell us about it?"

"It's still too horrible to think about," Nick said. "You probably can't imagine what it's like to stand in the dock and see people staring at you with loathing — people you trusted and liked."

"We know none of the details of the case, sir. You were accused of molesting a child?"

Nick looked down at his hands, toying with the signet ring on his little finger. "It was all part of the epidemic of priest bashing. Half the Catholics in the world were suddenly accusing their priests of molesting them. The motives weren't always the purest, I have to tell you. There was a bob or two to be made when the church was still paying people to keep quiet."

"We're only interested in your particular case, sir."

"I'm coming to it," Nick said. "It's not easy to talk about. I've always been a friendly sort of guy. I love children. So when I talk to a child, it's natural for me to put an arm around them, to take little kids on my knee — that sort of thing. Well, a do-gooding woman in my parish saw me with my arm around a little girl. She had been crying because she'd lost the doll she'd brought to school with her. I told her I'd help her find it." He looked up at them. "This woman interviewed the child after I left her. She twisted the child's words — that I'd tried to lure her into my study with the promise that we'd find her a doll there, that the child had felt uncomfortable with my arm around her, that I'd made her cry, that it wasn't the first child I'd touched. Next thing I knew I was relieved of my parish duties and I was up in court. I can't begin to tell you — it was like a horrible nightmare. You try to wake up and you can't. Fortunately the charges didn't hold up in court. There were plenty of witnesses to speak up on my behalf. I was acquitted, but the damage was done. Everywhere I go now I can hear the whispers, 'He was the one who molested that little girl.'"

He looked away and sighed. "I've been reassigned to the cathedral, where I'm safely shielded from contact with real people. I'll probably never be a parish priest again. They made me a handsome cash payment for my suffering, but what good does that do? All the reasons I wanted to become a priest — they're all denied to me now." He got up and went to look out of the window. "You know what it was like? It was like going through Sarah all over again."

CHAPTER 27

Evan was relieved to see lights on in the schoolhouse, even though it was after eleven. The long drive through the rain and then this last emotional session with Nick Thomas had left him feeling drained. He crossed the playground, tapped on the front door, found it unlocked, and let himself in. Bronwen, already in her silky blue robe and slipper socks, appeared from the bedroom.

"Hello, Bron, sorry to come round so late, but I need a hug," he said.

"From whom?" she asked, staying where she was at the bedroom door.

"From you, of course."

"Oh, I wasn't sure if you wanted one from another of your girlfriends," she said. Her tone was half joking, half not.

"What are you talking about?" Evan was tired, confused, and irritable.

"I've had an interesting evening, Evan," Bronwen said, coming out now and crossing to the fireplace, in which embers still glowed. "Knowing that you had a long drive today, I decided to be the dutiful fiancée and make you a lovely dinner for when you came home. So there I was, working in your kitchen, when there's a tap on the front door. In comes Betsy, wearing a dress that was so short and revealing that it left nothing to the imagination. She looked startled to see me, muttered that she'd just come over to show Evan something, and left."

"Betsy? Does this mean she's broken up with Barry?"

Bronwen shrugged. "She was certainly armed for battle. But that wasn't all. I'd just put the casserole in the oven when there was another knock at the door. A strange woman was standing there, and she said she was taking you up on your invitation to show her around the place, starting with the Red Dragon."

"A strange woman?" Evan's brain refused to cooperate. "Did she tell you her name?"

"She sounded American, if that's any help."

"Oh, *cachwr*," Evan swore under his breath. "It must have been that lady anthropologist again."

"Lady anthropologist. I don't think you mentioned her."

"The one who dug out the skeleton."

Bronwen had fixed him in a cold stare. "You said the anthropologist from the university. I don't think you used the word 'she'."

"Look, Bron, I didn't tell you because it wasn't important, but she came on to me the other day. I told her I was getting married and I wasn't interested. I guess she just doesn't take no for an answer."

"Popular chap, aren't you?" Bronwen said.

"I can't help it if I'm irresistible," Evan said. "I swear I do nothing to encourage them."

Bronwen finally laughed. "No, I'm sure you don't. And I'm acting like a jealous shrew for no reason. Sorry." She went over to him and wrapped her arms around his neck. "I was thrown by Betsy in the slinky dress, and then I was quite startled to hear that you'd promised to take some strange woman to the pub."

"I actually offered to take her hiking with us," Evan said. "She's very persistent."

"American women are supposed to be aggressive, aren't they? Sometimes I wish I could be more assertive myself. Then I'd put my foot down and forbid you to talk to anything in skirts that doesn't play bagpipes."

"Glynis Davies usually wears trousers," Evan said, his eyes teasing her as he pulled her close to him. "Now give me that hug."

Bronwen rested her head on his shoulder, and he stood there, letting peace flow through him.

"You must be starving or did you stop for dinner on the way?"

"We grabbed sausage rolls at the motorway place. Bloody disgusting they were."

"So you must have left London very late."

"We had another errand to run when we got back." And he told her about Nick Thomas.

"But he was falsely accused, Evan," she said, when he had finished talking. "Poor man. I feel sorry for him. I bet there's a lot of that kind of thing going on."

"I feel sorry for him too, but we're still going to have to check him out. We've only had his side of the story, after all. Watkins is going to have his picture shown around at the caravan park and throughout the area."

"If I'd kidnapped a little girl and done God knows what to her, I wouldn't stick around in the area any longer than I had to," Bronwen said. "Now the others have gone home, and he's lounging in the bar with his brother."

"I agree with you, but we have to cover our rear ends," Evan said. "Personally I can't believe anything bad of Nick Thomas, but I'm beginning to see how easy it is to twist the truth," and he told her about Ivan Sholokhov. "So I'm off to Yorkshire in the morning to trace the elusive Mrs S," he said. "Watkins doesn't want me involved with the Nick Thomas stuff. He thinks I may be biased, and he's right. Besides, I can't wait to confront Shirley Sholokhov. This is the first real thing he's let me do alone, Bron."

"Just so long as he doesn't change his mind and send Glynis Davies off to the wilds of Yorkshire with you," Bronwen teased. "I'd offer you food, but your supper is sitting in your own oven."

"Thanks," Evan said, still holding her firmly around the waist, "but I think I'm too tired to feel hungry. You didn't leave the gas on, did you?'

"Of course not. I had no idea when you'd be back, and you do have a microwave."

"In that case," Evan said, nuzzling at her long, soft hair, "I'm in no hurry to go home, am I?"

* * *

It was under a grey and leaden sky with the promise of more rain that Evan started for Yorkshire the next day. He left at first light, wanting to beat the traffic that always clogged the junctions around Manchester. It was one industrial city after another all the way to Leeds, old wool and cotton towns like Huddersfield and Bradford. These days there was no pall of smog hanging over them since strict pollution standards had been introduced. Most of the old industries had died anyway, and gangs of unemployed youths, lounging outside pubs, were a feature on many street corners as he drove into Leeds. Leeds, of course, was bigger and more prosperous than those towns that had relied on only one dead industry. He drove through areas that looked positively yuppie, with fancy foreign cars parked outside reinvented town houses and new flats. The address he had for Shirley Sholokhov was not like that.

It was in a development of former council houses, now mostly privately owned, but with little attempt at improvement. They were similar to those he had visited in Swansea — eight front doors to a building, pebble dash exterior, lacking any kind of ornamentation to make them attractive or unique. What had been small front gardens once had been paved over to make room for off-street parking, except for the house at the end, which still sported a small square of lawn with a birdbath in the middle.

The door at number thirty-eight opened abruptly in response to Evan's knock, and he was startled to see a large, unshaven man wearing only an undershirt and jeans.

"Yeah? What do you want?" the man demanded.

"I'm looking for Shirley Sholokhov," Evan began.

"She's out," the man cut off the last of his sentence. He went to close the door.

"But she does live here?" Evan's foot prevented the door from closing.

"Yeah."

"And you are?" Evan asked.

"None of your bloody business, mate."

Evan reached into a pocket and produced a warrant card. "Police. It is my business. Now give me your name."

"Joe Bingham. What's all this about?"

"What do you think? Mrs Sholokhov's missing daughter. Now, are you going to let me come in or leave me standing on the doorstep where all the neighbours can see us?"

Bingham opened the door wider. "Okay. Come in then." He led Evan to a spartan front room with mismatched furniture and full ashtrays. A television in the corner was going full blast.

"Go on then." Bingham eyed him insolently as Evan took an orange vinyl chair at the table.

"Are you a relative?" Evan asked.

"No."

"But you live here?"

"What are you — the bleeding morality police?"

Evan ignored the remark. "Mrs Sholokhov reported her daughter missing in North Wales."

"That where you're from? I thought you had a funny accent."

"She reported her daughter missing in North Wales. We've had the entire police force out looking for her. We've put out nation-wide bulletins and now, in the middle of all this, we find that Mrs Sholokhov has upped and left without telling us."

Bingham shifted uncomfortably under Evan's stare. "Yeah, well, she got cheesed off there by herself. She wanted to be home with me."

"Have you been living together long?"

"Nah. I moved in about a month ago. She got scared when her old man paid her a visit, so I told her I'd keep an eye on her. Too bad I couldn't go to the caravan with her — I'd have knocked his block off if he'd tried to take Ashley, bloody foreign git."

"So why didn't she tell the police she was leaving the area?"

Bingham shrugged. "Search me, mate. I don't know what goes on inside her head, do I? I can tell you one thing — she's very upset. She probably don't know what she's doing. She's upset with you blokes, that you haven't found her daughter yet. Not too good, is it — the whole bloody police force after that Russian git and nobody can find him?"

"So where is she now?"

"I can't tell you, mate. Out somewhere. Shopping maybe. I got up and she wasn't here. That's all I know."

"So you don't know when she'll be back?"

"No idea."

"She hasn't gone back to work, has she?"

"Too upset to work. Says she can't settle to anything until Ashley's brought home. She loves that kid, you know."

"Why did she go to the caravan in Wales?" Evan asked.

"Why? Because he found out where she'd moved to, didn't he? He came hanging around. Made her nervous."

"So she left your protection and fled to a lonely coast where she knew nobody? That doesn't seem too smart to me."

Bingham took a step toward him. The intent to be threatening was obvious. "Listen, mate, she thought he'd never find her there."

“So she went into hiding because she didn’t have full custody of Ashley, and she was scared the courts would make her hand over the child to her father?”

“Something like that. She’s terrified of that man. She said he came across as quiet and well behaved, but if he lost his temper, he’d just explode. Knocked her around a bit, you know. If he’s gone back to Russia, then I say good riddance. We don’t need his sort here.”

“But not if he’s taken Ashley with him.”

“Oh, right.” He corrected himself. “It would break her heart if she lost that kid. The kid is her whole life.”

“We’re doing everything we can, I assure you, Mr Bingham. We’ve got the national crime people, the Foreign Office, Interpol all working on it. We’ve followed up on God knows how many leads. If he’s still in the country, he can’t stay hidden forever. Someone will come forward.”

“And when they do, he’s going to be sorry.”

Evan got out his notebook. “So you really don’t know when she’ll be back? And she doesn’t have a mobile phone with her?”

“What do you think we are, bleedin’ millionaires?”

“All right then. I’ll give you my mobile number, and you are to call me as soon as she comes home. I’m not leaving until I’ve spoken to her. There are still some things we need to clear up — she may be in violation of the law just as much as he is, running off with the child without his permission.”

“His permission? She don’t need no sodding permission, mate. They’re separated.”

“Still legally married and sharing joint custody until the hearing.”

The big man shrugged again. “I wouldn’t know. I just met her, as a matter of fact. At a club.”

Evan got up and handed him a slip of paper. “Here’s the number she’s to call. Make sure she does, or we could haul her in for questioning.” He was pleased to see that he was slightly the taller of the two when he matched Bingham, eye to eye.

He started toward the door, then turned back. "You're not worried about the fact that she's not here when you wake up, then? You're not worried that her husband has come back for her if he's got such a violent temper?"

He noticed a spasm of alarm cross the man's face; then he shook his head. "He wouldn't do that."

"And if, by any chance, the child wasn't taken by her father?"

"Someone else, you mean?"

"Nobody near the caravan park ever saw who it was. It could have been anybody — it could have been the Russian Mafia caught up with them."

"Go on. Russian Mafia?" A smirk crossed the big man's face.

"Sholokhov did leave Russia because he had a run-in with the Mafia, you know. They may have a score to settle with him. You haven't noticed anyone hanging about outside the house at all?"

Bingham shook his head. "Can't say I have. Why don't you ask the old biddy next door. She spends her life watching through the curtains, minding other people's business."

"Thanks," Evan said. "I'll do that. And I'll be back as soon as Shirley comes home."

He got as far as the door.

"You don't think anything really might have happened to Shirley, do you?" Bingham asked.

"No idea," Evan said and left.

CHAPTER 28

The next-door house was the only one on the block with some attempt at a front garden, although it was little more than a few sorry tulips now dying around the birdbath. Before Evan could reach the front door, it opened and an old woman in carpet slippers and overall stood there.

"You're with the police," she said, a satisfied smile on her face.

"How did you know?"

"Stands to reason, doesn't it. The police have been round several times recently, about the little girl, I suppose. But she's been away. He's been there alone. A nasty bit of goods he is, if you ask me — and she's no better than she should be — dumping the child on me when she wanted to go out and then not coming home until morning. Have you come about him?"

"What do you think he might have done?"

"You're the policeman not me."

Evan produced his notebook. He had discovered that this somehow made an interview official, rather like the warning "everything you say may be used in evidence". "I'm Detective Constable Evans, of the North Wales Police, madam, and what is your name?"

"Mrs Hardcastle," she said. "Gloria Hardcastle."

"Right, Mrs Hardcastle. If I could ask you a couple of questions?"

"You'd better come in," she said. "I wouldn't want the neighbours thinking I'd done anything that required a visit from the police."

She led him into the front room, overdecorated with knick-knacks, lots of photos, and potted plants. She pointed to the photos. "My grandchildren in Australia," she said proudly.

"Very nice." Evan smiled, and the smile was returned.

"Now, Mrs Hardcastle — do I understand that you don't get out much?"

"I can't, on account of my arthritis," she said.

"You say you looked after the little girl next door sometimes?"

"Just a couple of times, when the mother couldn't find anyone to babysit at the last minute. Nice little thing. I didn't mind at all, really. It was a bit of company for me, and she was no trouble."

"So, Mrs Sholokhov had no relatives in the area she could ask?"

"Not that I know of. In fact I remember that she said her parents were both dead and she only had the one auntie left in the world. Sad, isn't it? Still, that's how it goes. I've got five grandchildren, but I've never even seen them."

"I expect you've heard that the little girl has been kidnapped," Evan said.

"I saw it on the telly," she said. "You could have knocked me down with a feather when I saw her picture."

"We think her father has taken her," Evan said. "I just wondered if you'd happened to notice any strange men hanging around here in the last few weeks — the father is a tall, blond bloke — foreign looking."

She shook her head. "I can't say I saw anyone like that. In fact the only man I've ever noticed watching the house is that old geezer with his dog."

"Old geezer with a dog?" Evan looked up.

"Yes, he used to come here a lot. I haven't seen him lately, but for a while he'd walk that dog up and down, up and down in front of the houses, and he'd always slow down when he passed next door."

"Can you describe him?"

"Well, he was a pleasant-enough looking man. About my age. Stout. White hair."

"And the dog. Was that white, too?"

"Why, yes it was. Clever of you to guess that. Nice little dog. Well behaved. And the man had nice manners, too. I was putting the milk bottles out once, and he raised his hat and said good morning. You don't get that type of thing much anymore, do you? Most young people are being raised with no manners at all. They push past you to get on the bus. Shocking, isn't it?"

Evan nodded with sympathy, but his brain was racing. "He didn't ask you anything about the family next door?"

"No. He didn't say anything apart from good morning."

"And you say you haven't seen him recently?"

She shook her head. "Not for a couple of weeks, anyway."

Evan held out his hand. "Thank you, Mrs Hardcastle. You've been most helpful."

"Have I?" She looked pleased.

Evan hurried back to his car, drove around the corner, away from prying eyes, and then dialled on his mobile. He was informed that Inspector Watkins was out but that Constable Davies was available. Almost immediately Glynis's high, clear voice came on the line.

"Listen, Glynis. I think we're onto something," Evan almost yelled into the phone. "There was an old man who used to walk his dog on the beach at the caravan park. Distinguished-looking old bloke, rather old-fashioned in his dress — you know, tweed hat, that kind of thing, and he had a little white dog. He asked about Ashley. He said he was staying at one of the bungalows on that road. I want you to find out about him right away. I think he could be the same one who has been spying on Ashley here in Leeds."

"Wow — that's a turn up for the books, isn't it? I'll get Inspector Watkins on the phone immediately. He's down at the caravan park right now. I'll call you back as soon as I've got something."

Evan drove to the nearest café and ordered a cup of coffee, trying to concentrate on reading the paper while waiting for the phone to ring. He finished his coffee, finished his paper, and cruised past Shirley's house a few times. Still the phone didn't ring. He wondered whether he should talk to Joe Bingham again and try to get a list of Shirley's friends out of him. He rather felt it would be like pulling teeth. He brought the car to a halt beside a park and sat watching the children in the playground. *The old man with a white dog could be pure coincidence*, he thought, as he watched several old men walking several white dogs around the park. But on the other hand, he knew that it wasn't unusual for a kidnapper or child molester to appear concerned and even to volunteer to help with the search.

The sun came out, warm on his face in the car, and he closed his eyes. He was just nodding off when the phone rang, and his heart gave a great lurch.

"Evans here," he barked into it.

"Listen, Evan, you're right. You may be onto something," Glynis said. "The old man moved out of the bungalow this weekend and went home, saying the weather was too cold for him. I've got the name and address he gave the landlady. He comes from Colchester in Essex. Now listen to this — you know we talked about putting together a list of unsolved child abductions and murders. Well, I've just been looking at it. Eighteen months ago a little girl was murdered in Colchester. They haven't found the perpetrator, and she looks a lot like Ashley."

"Bloody hell! This could be it, Glyn."

"Inspector Watkins is calling the Colchester Police right now. I'll keep you posted."

"So what does he want me to do — come straight back or wait around for Shirley Sholokhov?"

"You haven't seen her yet?"

"No, she's out — according to her live-in boyfriend."

"You'd better stick around until she comes back," Glynis said. "There's not much any of us can do here until the Essex police get back to us. Don't worry, I'll keep you posted."

"Right." Evan hung up, feeling excited and frustrated at the same time. It was annoying to be stuck so far away when things were happening, waiting for Shirley Sholokhov to reappear in her own sweet time. He came to the decision that he had waited long enough and drove back to the house. Joe Bingham looked as if he had probably gone straight back to bed after Evan left. His stubble was more noticeable, his hair uncombed, and the unwashed smell drove Evan to take a step back, even at the doorway.

"Oh, it's you again. She ain't home yet."

"And you're not worried about the fact that she's been gone for several hours."

Joe shrugged. "I'm not her jailer, you know. She comes and goes as she pleases. That was one of the things that drove her up the wall about her old man — he wanted to keep her in a cage, always tell him where she was going. She couldn't stand it. So I keep my mouth shut and don't ask questions."

The thought flashed across Evan's mind that what Shirley Sholokhov was doing might not be legal, but he dismissed it. "Look, I need to talk to her today. We might have found the man who took her child."

"Really?" He was definitely interested now, Evan could tell. "Where did you find him — in Wales?"

"I can't tell you any details at the moment, but I'm sure she'll want to know and we'll need her to identify him. So if you can give me any suggestion of where she might be — names of close friends, places she likes to hang out."

Joe shrugged again. "Look, I wish I could help you, but I can't. I know she's got some girlfriends and she likes to natter with them, but I don't know their addresses, honest to God."

"Then the name of the hair salon where she works?"

"I can tell you that all right. It's Flair for Hair, and it's in the big new shopping centre. You'll pass it on the right as you drive into the city centre. Can't miss it."

"Thanks," Evan said. "I'm going there right now, but I'll be back. If she comes home, you tell her she's not to go out again until I've spoken to her. Got it?"

"I never got your name, mate," Joe said, and Evan realized that he had only flashed a warrant card at him.

"It's Evans," he said. "Detective Constable Evans."

A look of scorn crossed the man's face. "You mean I've been wasting all this time speaking to a bleeding constable?"

"If you're not careful, I'll bring you in for questioning next time, and you can wait in a cell until I'm good and ready to talk to you."

"Go on! Pull the other one. You can't do nothing unless your boss tells you to. Constables are ten a penny."

"We'll see when I come back," Evan said. He hoped it looked as if he was sauntering back to his car, but his pulse was racing. He wondered just what he'd do if he tried to bring someone in and they refused. Call for backup, obviously, but the only backup he could count on was a hundred miles away.

He drove to the shopping centre, located the hair salon, but got nothing out of the girls who worked there. Shirley had taken time off work because her kid was poorly and she hadn't said when she'd be back. They hadn't even heard about the kidnapping. Both the girls seemed so clueless that Evan couldn't believe they were lying.

He walked through the shopping centre, past the heavy beat blaring from music stores, past the bright lights and the prams and gaggles of teenage girls. Smells of frying onions and cinnamon enticed him from the food court, reminding him that he hadn't had lunch yet, so he stopped to grab a slice of pizza. He was halfway through it, with a full mouth, when his phone rang again.

"Evans," he mumbled.

"Evan, it's Glynis. No news yet on our Mr Johnson in Colchester, but something else has come up. I'm not sure if it's even relevant now, but we got a call from some hikers in Yorkshire who have just seen a little girl who looks like Ashley. And since you're our man on the spot, so to speak, the DI thought you should follow up on this."

Evan wrote down the mobile phone number. As soon as she hung up, he dialled it.

"Look, this may be a false alarm," the man who answered him said with an embarrassed laugh. He had a smooth, well-bred voice and Evan was unable to trace a regional accent. "But my wife was very insistent that we call you, so—"

"I appreciate your calling, sir," Evan said. "It's always better to be safe than sorry, isn't it? Too many opportunities are lost because the public doesn't want to get involved. If I could have your name, please?"

"Francis," the man said. Evan was about to ask for his last name when he continued, "Rodney Francis. My wife and I are currently hiking the Pennine Way."

"Oh, that's great. I'm a hiker myself," Evan said. "So, Mr Francis, you say you saw a child who could be Ashley Sholokhov?"

"My wife did. We stayed the night in a village called Newby on the A65," the man said, "and then we hiked up and over Ingleborough. I don't know if you are familiar with the area, but that's one of what they call the Three Peaks. It's a big, flat slab of rock — very bleak and wild. We stopped for lunch high up on a shelf of limestone, and my wife was looking through the binoculars — she's very keen on birding, you know. She spotted this child, playing outside a cottage down in the valley — she was a little thing with long, blonde hair. Then a woman came out, grabbed her arm, and dragged her back inside, as if she was doing something wrong. My wife thought this was strange, and then she remembered the picture we'd seen on the news of the girl who was kidnapped. So she thought we ought to report this as soon as possible."

"Thank you. We'll certainly go and take a look straightaway," Evan said.

"It may be nothing." The man said. "The child may well have just been misbehaving and outside when she should have been doing chores, but my wife says the woman looked around nervously as she dragged the child back inside, as if she was afraid they'd been seen. And my wife is not the kind of woman given to dramatic fancies."

Evan thought that somebody who hiked the Pennine Way probably wouldn't be.

"Right." He took a deep breath. "If you could give me the location of this cottage."

"The problem is that we only saw it from above. I can tell you the route we took. The trail started in a village called Clapham, just off the A road. It was signposted to the Ingleborough Cave, past the Gaping Gill, then up and over the mountain. I'm pretty sure we were looking due west from the limestone outcropping down at this cottage. It was quite remote, not near any village and not even on the road, I think. I'm sorry I can't be more helpful, but we have to press on to our next destination by nightfall, or we'll fall behind our schedule."

"That's all right, sir. We'll take it from here. Thanks again for your help."

"I hope it turns out to be your kidnapped child," the man said. "We've got two daughters at boarding school. My God, if anything happened to one of them . . ."

"I hope so too, sir."

The moment the phone call ended, Evan found the nearest WHSmith stationery store and bought a map of Yorkshire. His knowledge of English geography was somewhat hazy, and he was amazed to locate Ingleborough so far west that it was only a few miles from the West Coast. He had always thought of Yorkshire as a strictly eastern county. Now he was impressed by its size, and by the distance from Leeds to Ingleborough. At least it was on an A road, even if that road did climb up and over the crest of the Pennines. He traced the route with his finger. As he did so, names leaped off the page at him, first one and then another — names that had not made sense before because he wasn't looking at a map. Skipton — that was where the chemist had reported that Ashley's prescription had been filled; then a little farther along, just off the A road, was Settle, where there had been a report of someone who sounded foreign and looked like Ivan Sholokhov a couple of weeks ago. Both of them on the A65 leading to Ingleborough. It couldn't possibly be coincidence.

CHAPTER 29

It took a frustrating hour driving through one-way systems and clogged traffic before Evan located the A65 and was finally clear of the city. At any moment he expected the phone to ring with instructions that he was to return home and that the matter was being handled by someone with more seniority and experience. Suburban sprawl went on and on. One housing estate after another, one factory after another, and still he hadn't even reached Skipton. Then at last houses gave way to moors. The A65 wound up hill and down dale, through patches of woodland and past signs to such tantalizing places as Ilkley, famed of song, where you were supposed to catch your death of cold by going out *bar tat*.

Skipton came at last, and the road skirted around it. It looked like a fair-sized town, and Evan wondered whether he should stop to check in with the local police or at least with his own DI. He knew that protocol demanded that he report to local police when he came onto their turf, and he'd certainly have to do so if he needed to obtain a search warrant. But he kept on going, telling himself that there was time for that kind of thing later. He was consumed by a great sense of urgency. Although his rational self knew that the child had only been spotted through field glasses, he couldn't help fearing that the spotters had themselves been observed and plans were being made to move her elsewhere.

After Skipton the country became truly wild. Bleak hills rose on either side as the road followed a valley steadily upward toward the spine of the Pennines. There were no more villages, just the odd, remote house built in solid grey stone to survive the worst of the weather. The few trees he passed were bent by the force of the wind, and even in May they were only just coming into leaf. A patch of daffodils in front of a cottage lent the one splash of colour in a grey-green landscape. As in Wales, there were few sheep to be seen in the fields. Foot-and-mouth disease had passed this way too.

The sun was sinking on the western horizon so that he caught it full in the face, almost blinding him at times. How long could this bloody road go on? He must have been driving at least two hours and still he had seen no signs to either Newby or Clapham or Ingleborough. Momentary panic set in that he had passed them and would wind up on the Lancashire Coast any second. Then he spotted the sign to Ingleborough Cave almost too late and had to jam on the brakes. The village of Clapham was off on a small road to the right, a pretty cluster of stone houses, sheltered by trees and with enough tearooms and souvenir shops to show that the caves attracted some tourism. Evan parked the car, crossed the rushing mountain stream by way of a footbridge, and followed the signs to the footpath. An old man sitting on a bench outside a row of cottages shook his head as Evan walked by.

"If tha's hoping to visit t'cave, tha's too late." He looked pleased at delivering this bad news. Evan was tempted to sound him out about a possible cottage that might now contain a visiting child, but decided not to. He couldn't risk putting one foot wrong from now on. But he did say, "Is there a police station in the village?"

"Not no more. Used to be when I were a lad. Closest copper is in Ingleton now."

"How far's that?"

"About five mile." He made this sound like it was close to the end of the earth.

"Thanks," Evan said, and went to continue on his way.

"I suppose tha's wanting to ask t'police about t'tragedy then? I expect it'll be on t'evening news," the old man said.

"Tragedy?"

"Some poor bugger fell down one of t'potholes. Another of they hikers. They only found him today. He'd been there awhile, they say. They're always doing it, you know — trying to climb down and then falling."

"Was he badly injured?"

"No. Dead as a doornail, poor bugger. Been there for weeks. That's the second this year." He gave a macabre grin, revealing a mouth of missing teeth. "Tha wants to be careful if tha goes up there. Observe the warnings, young man."

"I'll be careful then," Evan said, and again went to pass on his way.

"I told thee that t'cave's closed, didn't I?" the old man called after him.

"Thanks, but I'm not going to the cave, just for a hike. And I'll be careful of potholes."

"You do that, young man." The words echoed after him as he passed between two of the stone houses and found a smooth, well-used path stretching out ahead of him. To begin with it wound through pleasant woodland. He had to pass through a gate with a notice announcing he was entering Ingleborough Hall Estate and a fee would be collected. But there was nobody to take his money, so he kept on going through more woodland, with a small ornamental lake to his left. He came to the entrance to the cave, which was, as the old man had predicted, well and truly closed, with an iron grille across the gate.

After the cave the smooth path became a rocky track beside a noisy, dancing beck. He continued on upward, feeling the fresh breeze in his face and the fresh smell of upland air and pines. He came to a small limestone gorge with cliffs rising on either side of the path and fir trees clinging precariously. Then out of the gorge and the first sense of high moor — no more trees, just rocky fields and drystone walls. To the north he caught his first view of the peak that had been described to him — Ingleborough, one of the big three and recognizable by its flat top, as if a giant hand had sawn it off. He began to realize his own folly in taking this on alone and without preparation. He hadn't stopped to consider how far it might be and how much real hiking would be involved. Now he realized that he might not reach the viewpoint from which the child had been spotted and get down again by nightfall. Not a comforting thought as he had just passed a notice board warning DANGER. POTHOLES AHEAD. PROCEED WITH CAUTION. DO NOT CROSS ANY BARBED WIRE FENCES.

The moment he had taken in the notice, he was conscious that the gurgle of the stream had turned to a roar and he found himself standing beside a wire fence, looking down in awe as the stream plunged suddenly into a black, gaping hole in the ground. The sign at a locked gate identified it as GAPING GILL and mentioned that the winch operated only on weekends. As one who suffered from claustrophobia, Evan could hardly imagine anything worse than being winched down into that blackness. He remembered the hiker who had plunged to his death and had only been found after several weeks. Had that been here or were there other, even more terrifying holes opening up into the earth nearby? He glanced nervously toward the west and saw the sun turning into a red ball as it moved closer to the horizon. Another hour or two of daylight, that was all.

After the Gaping Gill, the trail began its stiff ascent of Ingleborough Peak. Evan slithered on smooth rock and wished for his sturdy hiking boots. He was conscious of rings of wire fencing around what must be smaller potholes and couldn't help wondering if others were unfenced. His eyes scanned the horizon ahead, trying to pick out the limestone outcropping where the couple had spotted the cottage. Why hadn't he thought to ask them how many miles it had been from Clapham? He realized to his annoyance that he'd left their phone number in the car. He doubted that he'd pick up a signal up here anyway.

Then the path curved around the side of the mountain, and he found himself staring into the sunset with a rocky outcropping immediately ahead of him. Cautiously, remembering he was wearing work shoes that lacked good tread, he climbed out onto it and lowered himself to the still-warm rock. The view that spread out below him was spectacular — hills and valleys, clumps of trees with hamlets nestled in them, and in the far west maybe the glint of the Irish Sea. The whole scene was bathed in slanting evening sunlight, making the limestone glow almost pink. But the sense of urgency was still pumping adrenaline. He wrenched his eyes from the view and peered down the slope, looking for the cottage the hikers had seen. Again he didn't know how powerful their binoculars had been and cursed himself for not asking more questions.

Then he saw it, half-hidden by some trees, directly below him. There was no sign of a road or other houses nearby. Not in a village then. He tried to pick out landmarks that would help him to identify it from below. Probably northwest from Clapham, with the summit of Ingleborough due east behind it. And three trees. And a stone wall coming down in a direct line from the mountain. Would that be enough? He decided not to take the chance of losing it again. The slope below him was steep, but not impassable. Someone had managed to build and maintain a wall down it. All he had to do was follow that wall, and he'd get a look at the cottage for himself. If the worst happened and he was seen, he'd be a hiker who had lost his way. Ivan Sholokhov had no idea what he looked like and probably wouldn't even recognize a Welsh accent. He was quite safe.

He lowered himself down the outcrop and began the descent. It was hard going, slithering over patches of limestone in places, making sure he didn't turn his ankles on rocks hidden in the grass. Down and down until the bright sunlight on the peaks was replaced by shadow. The wind that had blown fresh in his face had now become icy cold, and he realized again what a stupid chance he had taken, going into the high country so ill prepared. Every year he had had to rescue tourists who had been stranded on Mount Snowdon when the weather turned ugly, and he had not been able to believe their stupidity at starting out in sandals and shorts. Now he had been equally guilty and just lucky that the weather hadn't turned on him yet.

A light came on, farther down in the valley, identifying possibly where the road ran. Still no lights shone out from the cottage. He came closer, hoping that they hadn't a watchdog. Then he froze as he heard something — through an open window a child was singing. The sound sent his spirits soaring. If it was indeed Ashley, then she was still alive and well and happy enough to sing.

He moved more slowly now, circling away from the drystone wall to give the cottage a wide berth. He passed the cottage and on the other side of it, he picked up a rutted track that led down to the nearest road. At least cars could get to it. That was good to know. Now all he had to do was make his way down to the road, call the local police, and wait for them. Before he went down to the road, however, he decided he should at least see if the cottage had a name, which would make it easier to find. He found a battered front gate, standing open, and saw that his hunch had been right. There was a board tacked onto the gatepost identifying it as FERNDALE COTTAGE.

At that moment his mobile phone rang. His tension level was so high that his heart gave a huge lurch at the sound, and he almost dropped the phone as he fumbled to get it out of his pocket before it rang again.

"Evans, where the hell are you?" DI Watkins's voice demanded. The crackling indicated that the connection was tenuous.

"In Yorkshire, sir, following up on the reported sighting of the child, like you told me." Evan struggled to make his voice sound calm.

"Have you got in touch with the local police yet?"

"No sir, I tried to do that when I got here, but they've closed the police station."

"They can't have closed every police station in the whole bloody area," Watkins said. "Make sure you contact them at once. You don't tread on someone's turf without permission — you know that full well."

"Yessir, I know. I was just about to call them. I just thought I should check out the cottage for myself first."

"For yourself? I'm not having any of my team playing lone ranger, Evans. You go in with backup or not at all. If we've really located Ashley, we're not going to risk a screwup because you're too bloody pig-headed to hand over to the local boys."

"Don't worry, sir. I wasn't planning to go in alone. I'll call them right away."

"And you stay put until they get there, Evans. That's an order."

"Right, sir." He had to smile at this last order. If Watkins really knew where he was.

"And Evans? Don't do anything daft, you hear me?"

"I won't, sir."

He hung up and dialled 999, only to be told that there was no one at the Ingleton station at the moment because the policeman on duty had escorted the hiker's body to the morgue in Skipton. Evan tried to give details to a patient, but slow-moving, girl on the switchboard and impressed upon her that she should send someone as soon as possible. At some point during the conversation, the penny dropped. "The little girl whose picture was on the telly, you mean?" she blurted out. "You've found her?"

"I hope so. I think she's being held at this Ferndale Cottage, so we need to be careful. I'll give you my mobile number so that your blokes can contact me. Tell them I'm watching the place now."

"Ooh, how exciting," she said, most unprofessionally. "Right. I'll get them onto it straightaway."

Feeling more confident now, Evan pocketed his phone and was about to head for the road when he heard a sound behind him. Instinctively he turned toward it. A door had opened and somebody had come out. She was standing on the doorstep, looking directly at him. It took him a second or two to recognize her in the gathering twilight. It was Shirley Sholokhov.

CHAPTER 30

Before he could hide in the bushes that flanked the path, she spotted him and the look of surprise on her face matched his own.

"Bloody hell," she muttered. "What are you doing here?"

"I was about to ask you the same thing," Evan said, coming steadily up the path toward her. "But I think I know the answer to that one. I've been on a wild-goose chase looking for you in Leeds, where your boyfriend assured me you'd be back any moment."

"This is my auntie's house," she said. "I decided to stay with her for a few days. I felt trapped in Leeds. I needed to be with family at a time like this. Is there anything wrong with that?"

"Nothing at all. I think family members should stick together. I just don't go along with lies and deceit."

She had her hands on her hips. "I don't know what you're talking about."

"I think you do." He was eye to eye with her now. "It's funny, but I felt that something was wrong all the time. There never was a kidnapping, was there? You brought Ashley here, out of the way, and then pretended that your husband had kidnapped her." He shook his head. "I could never really believe that a child had been playing on that beach. No child goes to a beach without digging in the sand. It's part of their nature."

She was still looking at him defiantly. "All right. What if I did? I only wanted to make sure we were free of him forever. He had some high-powered lawyer paid for by his Russian friends — they were trying to make out I was a bad mother, and they were going to give him custody of Ashley. I couldn't give her up — I just couldn't." She stared at him for a moment. "So how did you find us?"

"We've been running a hotline. Some hikers spotted a little blonde girl playing outside the cottage this morning and called us. I just happened to be trying to visit you in Leeds. If you'd come to us and told us you were going home, I'd never have come looking for you."

"Bloody stupid of me, wasn't it? But I just didn't want you blokes questioning me again. I did tell your local Mr Plod."

"Who conveniently forgot to mention it to us," Evan said. "But you left some other clues too. You had her prescription filled in Skipton — that's the nearest big town, isn't it? And that was also something that never made sense to me. If my child had had a major operation like Ashley, I'd have been frantic about her medications. You never even mentioned it to us the first time."

"Shit," she muttered. "So what will happen now? It's not a crime, hiding my own child, is it?"

"Falsely reporting a crime and mobilizing all those policemen is not going to be taken too kindly. It could also go against you when you have your custody hearing."

"Have you found Johnny yet?" she asked.

"No. He may have gone into hiding when he heard we were looking for him. He may have feared being deported."

"That's rubbish. I bet he's gone home to Russia like I told you. He did nothing but talk about it and how much he missed it."

"Not according to his friends," Evan said. "They say he wanted to stay in England. Look, are you going to invite me in? I'd like to meet Ashley for myself, since we've all been so worried about her."

"All right. I suppose so," she said grudgingly and passed through the door ahead of him. Evan followed her into a low-ceilinged, dark kitchen. The lights had not yet been turned on, and the house was in strange, flickering shadow. Evan saw the reason for this, as he looked through the doorway to a living room beyond. A television set was showing cartoons and in front of it a blonde-haired girl was sitting. At that moment a stout, older woman came through into the kitchen and gasped when she saw Evan.

"Who's he?" she demanded.

"North Wales Police. He's found us. The game's up. Still it was worth a try, wasn't it?"

The little girl spun around too at the sound of voices. She jumped to her feet and rushed to her mother. "Have they come to take me away?" she wailed.

"Hush. No, love. You're quite safe." Her mother stroked her hair as the child clung to her leg.

Now that Evan had a chance to look at her, he saw that she didn't bear that strong a resemblance to Sarah, apart from the hair. She had a rounder, flatter, more Eastern European face, like her father.

"Don't worry, Ashley," Evan said, smiling down at her. "Nothing bad's going to happen to you, I promise." Even as he said it, he wondered if this was a lie. Shirley would almost certainly be charged with parental abduction and custody could well be handed to the father, as soon as they located him. Which of them would be better for her? he wondered. It was hard to tell.

"I suppose you'd like a cup of tea?" the old woman asked in a broad Yorkshire accent. She pronounced it coopatee.

"Thanks. I would. I've been up a mountain and down looking for this place." Evan sat at the bench at the kitchen table, glad that the whole thing was going to be civilized. DI Watkins would have no complaints about the way he'd handled it until the local police got there. A cup was put in front of him. He hadn't even taken his first sip when he heard the sound of an engine straining as it climbed the track toward the cottage. So the local police had got here quickly after all. Shirley pulled back the curtain, then ran to open the front door.

"It's all right, Mrs Sholokhov, don't be alarmed," Evan started to say, then heard Shirley shouting, "What the hell are you doing here?"

"I came to warn you," the voice shouted back. "There's some damned copper nosing around the house today. He said he wasn't leaving until he'd seen you. I think we may have a problem if you don't—"

Evan came to stand beside her at the door. "If she doesn't what, Mr Bingham?" he asked.

Joe Bingham reacted quickly. "Shit. How did he get here?"

"You and your big mouth, I expect, Joe."

"I swear I didn't tell him nothing, Shirley." He came up to them, not taking his eyes for a second off Evan. "Still, no matter. He's all on his own, is he? I didn't pass a car as I came up here. They send out one lousy constable on foot? That was rather stupid, wasn't it? We'll just get rid of him like we did the other one."

And with a mighty shove, he pushed Evan back into the house. Evan was unprepared for it and fell against the kitchen table, knocking over crockery and making the little girl cry out in alarm.

"Get her out of here," Joe Bingham instructed to the aunt.

Evan had regained his balance. "Don't be so bloody stupid," he said, fighting to keep his voice calm and reasonable. "You're in minor trouble at the moment. You touch a police officer and you'll be away for life."

"He's right, Joe," Shirley began, but Bingham cut her off.

"Who's to ever know, eh? We dump him down a pothole, and they'll never find him. I'll get his car and drive it back to Wales and leave it somewhere. They'll never know he's been here."

"Sorry to disappoint you, Joe," Evan said, still amazed that he could sound so relaxed when his heart was racing a mile a minute, "but I called in my location just a few minutes ago. We've got squad cars on their way right now." A thought suddenly struck him, with such remarkable clarity that it was almost like having a vision. "And you're wrong about something else, too. They found a body in a pothole today. I'd like to bet it turns out to be Johnny Sholokhov."

He was satisfied to see the look of alarm that passed between them.

"It wasn't me. I didn't want to do it," Shirley said quickly. "It was his idea."

"Shut your mouth, woman. Of course you wanted to do it. You begged me to get rid of him. Come on. Let's take our chances again. We get rid of this bloke, and we can be out of here before the rest of them turn up."

"You won't find me so easy to get rid of," Evan said.

"Won't find you easy?" Joe Bingham laughed, opened a kitchen drawer, and produced a long carving knife. "I'll slice you to ribbons, mate."

"And how will you clean up the blood before the police arrive? You're cooked, Bingham. Your fingerprints are all over the room — yours and Shirley's and Ashley's, too. The smartest thing you can do now is come quietly." As he spoke, he was backing, inch by inch, toward the front door. To his great relief he heard the sound of an approaching car engine. "Looks like my backup just arrived," he said. "Now why don't you put down the knife before someone gets hurt."

Joe Bingham glanced at the door, then reached out and made a grab for Ashley, who was cowering in the doorway between the kitchen and living room.

"We've got the kid," he said, holding her in front of him with one big arm while the other hand still wielded the knife. "They won't dare touch us. We can get away."

"Are you out of your mind?" Shirley Sholokhov screamed. "Take your hands off my child. You're hurting her."

Instead, Bingham eased his way around the table, with Ashley still in front of him and the knife still ready. "I'm not staying here to be caught. And I'm not going to jail, neither. You made me do it."

"Let go of her, you bastard!" Shirley shrieked. She rushed at him. The moment his eyes turned away from Evan, Evan made a grab for the hand with the knife and brought it smashing down on the table with all his force. Bingham yelled out in pain. The knife clattered to the floor as the North Yorks Police burst into the room.

* * *

"So the local police were able to pick up Ashley and her mother with no trouble, then?" Detective Inspector Watkins asked Evan at their eight o'clock briefing the next morning. He had returned home well after midnight and had been so wound up that he had not been able to sleep. He had had a couple of close calls before in his life, but he suspected that this was the closest. If the local boys hadn't shown up in time, would Joe Bingham have risked the blood in the room? Would he have been able to fight his way out? And what if Joe had had a gun instead of a knife? Evan would be lying now down some deep pothole, maybe not properly dead, but dying in darkness.

It seemed from the autopsy that Johnny Sholokhov had not been dead when he was dropped down an unnamed pothole above the cottage. He had slowly bled to death and died of thirst in the next couple of days. The thought brought Evan out in a cold sweat, and he realized he was suffering from delayed shock. Now he was feeling hollow eyed and frazzled.

"Shirley's boyfriend was a bit of a nuisance, but otherwise no problem," Evan said.

"Well done, boyo," DI Watkins said. "Of course, it was lucky that Shirley Sholokhov was stupid enough to come out and let you see her."

Evan was glad that he hadn't phrased that the other way around. If Joe Bingham had got there first. If they'd spotted him before he saw them — then he could well have been taken off guard and now be lying, like poor Johnny Sholokhov, at the bottom of some pothole.

"You look terrible," Watkins said. "Are you coming down with something?"

"I didn't get any sleep. It took a while to write reports and identify the body in the morgue as Sholokhov. By the time I got home, it was almost time to wake up again."

Watkins got up. "Come on, then. Let's go down to the cafeteria and get something in your stomach." He marched Evan down the hall and soon he was sitting with a plate of egg and chips and a cup of tea in front of him.

"So now the poor kid's wound up with neither parent," Watkins said, stirring his own cup of tea as Evan tucked into the egg and chips. "She'll be placed in custody, I suppose."

"They may let her live with the great aunt who was looking after her in the cottage," Evan said. "She seemed a nice enough old girl. Offered me a cup of tea."

Watkins laughed. "She was probably planning to poison you."

Evan didn't laugh and wondered if that had been true. "I wish I'd followed my hunch all along," he said. "I kept feeling that something was wrong when we were on that beach. No sand toys, no sign that a child had been playing there at all. And what mother wouldn't be frantic if her child had had major surgery and might not get her proper medicine?"

Watkins nodded. "No wonder we thought she was a cool customer. Well, she was, wasn't she? Calmly lying, deceiving half of Britain — and dumping her old man down a pothole. Well, I'm glad we know the outcome. I always hate it in those cases when we never know. Especially when kids are involved."

"Speaking of that," Evan said, suddenly coming wide-awake, "did you hear anything from Essex — about the old man and the white dog, and the unsolved child murder down there?"

Watkins looked smug. "You'll never guess," he said. "Turns out he was the child's grandfather — the little girl who was killed in Colchester, I mean. That unsolved murder on the books. It was her heart they used for Ashley. He's been following Ashley around ever since, as though watching her alive somehow makes sense of losing his own grandchild."

"Poor old man," Evan said. "No wonder he seemed so concerned for her. It would have been a double blow if Ashley had been killed, too."

"So that's pretty much that, isn't it?" Watkins said. "And I'm delighted to say that you were wrong, for once. All those suspicions about the Thomas family. The two cases were obviously totally unrelated."

Evan nodded. "Yes, I'm afraid you're right," he said. "And we may never know who killed Sarah Bosley-Thomas. It just seemed like too much of a coincidence, digging up those bones at the same time as the whole Thomas family was here. It was almost as if she was asking to be found — and they were jittery, you said it yourself."

"But you don't think now that any of them was responsible, do you?" Watkins asked.

"If they were, we'll never prove it," Evan said. "We'll never know."

"I've been thinking of one possible explanation," Watkins said, putting down his teacup and looking up at Evan. "What if Sarah met with a horrible accident — she fell off some rocks and was killed, say? Henry was sure he'd get into trouble because he should have been watching her, so he swore the others to silence. They buried her quietly and said nothing."

"Sounds daft to me," Evan said, "but then children don't always make the best decisions. It may have seemed like the best solution at the time, and then they were stuck with it. Possible, I suppose."

"So how are we going to get the truth out of them?" Watkins asked.

"They've all gone home, haven't they? I'd say Father Nick was the best bet. Priests are supposed to be honest. We could catch up with him before he leaves the country."

"He's staying at a hotel in London. You fancy another trip down there?"

"Today?" Evan looked horrified.

"All right. I suppose it can wait until you've recovered. Although the way you're polishing off that egg and chips shows me there's nothing wrong with your appetite."

Evan pushed his plate away and got to his feet. "I suppose you'll be wanting a report too then? A xerox copy of last night's report won't do?"

"I just bought you egg and chips, boyo. Don't push your luck. Just be glad you're not me. I've got to explain why I mobilized NCIS, Interpol, the Foreign Office all for nothing."

"'Uneasy lies the head that wears the crown,'" Evan quipped.

"Don't tell me you're going all bloody highbrow on me just because you're marrying a Cambridge graduate." Watkins drained his own teacup and got to his feet.

Evan went to his desk and got out a pad before he realized that the report would have to be written on the computer. He was still not entirely comfortable around computers. Something inside his head always whispered that he'd press a button one day and wipe out the entire memory with one fell swoop. He sat and jotted notes to himself while plucking up the courage to cross the room and start up the machine. He looked up gratefully as the door opened and Glynis came in.

"The boy hero returns," she said, grinning. "What a coup for you, solving the whole thing single-handed."

"I just happened to be the one on the spot, that's all," Evan said uneasily.

"Don't be so modest. You found the place and you got the kid out safely. Good for you."

"And now I've got to put it all in a report." Evan made a face. "I don't suppose . . ."

"I am not the department typist, and I don't do reports," she said firmly. "You've got to learn to come to terms with that machine someday. Go on. It won't bite."

Evan moved across to the computer. Glynis stood, half watching him, half examining the in-tray.

"Oh, did you see a letter came for you?" she asked, and dropped it on the table beside him. "From the County Council. Probably telling you that you can't dig out your sewer line because it's on the site of an ancient well!" She laughed as she went to her own workstation.

Evan opened the envelope with a sinking feeling. What would he do if they had denied him permission to reconnect to the water mains or told him that he'd have to hook up to the sewer system in the valley?

His eyes skimmed down the page.

Dear Constable Evans,

In response to your request about workers who might have been involved in putting in the water mains in the Llanfair district — our records show that the following men were in our employment as labourers at the time:

Ernest James, 35 Caernarfon Road, Bangor,
Daniel Jones, Upper Garth Road, Bangor,
Tom Penri, Ty Goch, Llanfairfechan,
Richard Gwynne, Waunfawr Street, Caernarfon

Evan snatched up the sheet of paper, double-checking what he had just read. He heard Glynis yelling, "Where are you off to now?" as he rushed from the room.

CHAPTER 31

"Come on!" Sarah tugged at his bare arm, making him jump. He had been standing in deep shade under the oak tree, tense as a coiled spring, waiting for the signal to start the game, and had just decided on the perfect plan of attack. To his right he could see Henry, crouching behind a bush. He had chosen the rocky route — zigzagging up along a trail of boulders that gave almost perfect coverage all the way to the top. Evan had decided on speed. Val — the current king on top of the mountain — would be watching the boulder route, since it was most often successful. He wouldn't be watching the open area ahead of Evan. If he was fast enough — and he prided himself on his speed — he could sprint for the bush ahead, wait in perfect safety behind it; then another sprint should bring him to the big rock and striking distance of the summit.

"What?" he whispered to Sarah.

"Let's go," she whispered back.

"Go where?"

"To find the fairies."

"Not now."

"Yes, now. Come on. Nobody will miss us. Henry will be trying to win. Val's in the castle. We've got ages."

Evan looked down at her — her blue eyes pleading with him, then up at the summit of the hill. He stood poised on a knife-edge of indecision. For once he had a chance to beat Henry, and beating Henry was important to him. Even though Henry now let him play with them, he was still the skinny Welsh kid who didn't go to boarding school and knew nothing about the rest of the world. But then he also wanted to please Sarah. The way she gave him an adoring smile was worth more than winning any game.

She slipped her hand into his. "Let's go, Evan. Come on. Please."

He almost relented. His mind went through the ramifications of what might happen if they were found to be missing. He'd get shouted at for taking Sarah away. He might be forbidden to play with them again, seen to be a bad influence, not reliable. All of those were bad enough, but then he played out a scene in his mind where Sarah said, "He was taking me to show me the fairies," and he pictured Henry and Val beside themselves with laughter. "You know where the fairies live, do you, Evans? Little Evan likes to play with the fairies — do you wear a ballet skirt then? And pretty wings?"

That decided it. "Sorry, Sarah." He shook his head. "I'd get in big trouble if we were found out. Your mum wouldn't let me play with you anymore."

Sarah pouted in the way that only she could pout, her whole bottom lip jutting out defiantly. "If you won't take me, I'll just go by myself."

"Of course you won't. Don't be stupid. You'd get lost."

"No, I wouldn't."

"You're not going anywhere alone."

"You can't stop me."

At that moment came the shout from the top of the hill, signalling that the game had started. To his right he saw movement as Henry dodged to the first rock. Sarah made as if to dart away and Evan grabbed her by the arm. "No, you're coming with me, Sarah," he said, with sinking heart, as he watched Henry move ahead of him up the mountain.

* * *

It must have been the next time they played that Evan wasn't with them, and she took her chance to go up to the mountains alone. He should have told them; he realized that now. He should have warned them of her intention, but he stayed well away from anything linking him to fairies. One of the reports said that the dogs had initially tracked her up not down. So she had gone up and met someone — Richard Gwynne? Evan pictured the big, brawny man with his muscles showing through his torn undershirt.

His hands gripped the steering wheel. Calm down. It wasn't necessarily the same man. Richard Gwynne wasn't exactly a common name, but it was possible that there were several of them floating around Wales. Only the Richard Gwynne who now lived at the caravan park and made twisted metal sculptures had told him that he used to work for the council and lived with his mum on a council estate in Caernarfon until recently. And a man who lived with his mother for most of his life and now had become an antisocial misfit might certainly fit the profile of a paedophile.

Evan felt red anger surging through his brain as he drove. If Gwynne had harmed Sarah, Evan would make sure he suffered. He could picture his hands around Richard Gwynne's neck and was shocked at himself. What kind of policeman would he be if he took things personally, even if this was personal? The logical thing to do would be to turn around, call the station, and have somebody else sent to interview Richard Gwynne. But Evan wasn't in a logical mood. He had to know for himself. He had to find out what had happened to her, however bad it was.

There was a fierce wind blowing off the Irish Sea, bending the tall grass on the mountain like a brush going through long hair. When Evan stepped out of the car and came through the gap in the hedge, it caught him full in the face, peppering him with fine sand. He bent into the wind and crossed the meadow. As he passed between the vans and came out to the dunes, the sand became unbearable, blowing into his eyes and mouth and making it hard to breathe. There were whitecaps on the usually peaceful estuary beyond.

"Who is it?" Gwynne's voice yelled in response to Evan's pounding.

"Police. Open up."

The door opened a few inches. "Oh, it's only you," Richard Gwynne said. "What do you want this time?"

"To talk to you about a missing girl!" Evan had to shout to make himself heard over the hiss of the wind.

"I heard on the news she'd been found. The mother faked the kidnapping, stupid cow."

"Not that girl. Another one. Twenty-five years ago."

"Twenty-five years?" Gwynne looked amused. "Are the police so desperate for something to keep them occupied that they're going back twenty-five years?"

"We found a child's skeleton, Mr Gwynne. We think you may be able to help us identify it."

He was proud of the way he was keeping his voice calm and professional so far.

"I don't see how I could help you." Gwynne shrugged.

"You used to work for the council, didn't you? You worked connecting up remote farms to the mains water back in the late seventies?"

"That's right. I did. How did you know that?"

"You put in the pipes at a cottage above Llanfair."

"I might well have done. Can't remember now. I did so many of them that year."

"We found the child's skeleton in one of the trenches that you dug when you put in the pipes."

Richard Gwynne opened the door wider. "Just a minute. You're not hinting that I might have had something to do with putting it there?"

"You or someone working with you," Evan said.

"Listen, mate, first of all, I love kids. I'd kill anybody who harmed a little child. And secondly — we worked in teams — four of us, so even if one of us had wanted to bury a child in the trench, he'd have had three other blokes watching him. They were all good blokes, too. Family men. And we were all driven down to the council yard in the van at the end of the workday."

"That doesn't mean that one of you couldn't have come back afterward and done a little digging of his own."

"So could anyone else who had a spade," Gwynne said. "Everyone in the village would have seen us digging."

Of course this was true, Evan had to admit. Everyone in Llanfair knew everyone else's business all the time. They'd have been well aware that a trench was being dug at Rhodri Morgan's cottage. So they were back to the old question — how did Sarah or Sarah's body get over the mountains to Llanfair?

Richard Gwynne was staring at him defiantly. "You got anything else to ask me because you're letting the sand blow in," he said and started to close the door.

"Yes. Tell me about the other men on your team."

"Like I said — they were good blokes. Family men," he said. "Old Tom Penri, I remember him. Then there was a Dan. I can't remember the last one — tall, skinny young kid right out of school he was. But he wouldn't hurt a fly. Edward something, no Ernest, that was it."

"Thanks for your help, Mr Gwynne," Evan said. "We'll be following up on this, so anything you can remember at all — anyone you talked to while you were digging, anyone you saw on the mountain might be of help."

"I don't know if I can remember anything that happened that long ago. Like I said, we put in hundreds of pipes that year all over the place."

"Do your best, won't you?" Evan said. "The family has been trying to find out what happened to their child for twenty-five years. We owe it to them to get to the truth."

"It must be bloody awful for them," Gwynne said. "I'd help if I could."

He closed the door. Evan stood in the blowing sand outside with frustration and disappointment rushing through his brain. He had wanted this to come to a conclusion — he had wanted it to be Richard Gwynne so badly. Now he realized that they might never know what happened to Sarah. He'd suggest to Watkins that each of the men be brought in for questioning, and that they should run background checks on all four of them, but he hadn't much hope that the background checks would prove anything.

He returned to his car and started to drive away. Did he really believe it wasn't Richard Gwynne? Gwynne had seemed to be concerned, but then, as DI Watkins had said, lots of child molesters and serial killers seemed to be nice chaps. A small voice echoed through his brain that if he were anything of a real detective, he'd be able to get to the truth. If only they knew where the molester had found Sarah. Surely there must have been some kind of struggle, and some scraps of evidence must have been left to find? He drove through Porthmadog too fast and swung the car up the narrow curves of the Aberglaslyn Pass. He could call Dr Telesky and find out if any hairs or fibre scraps found on the skeleton didn't belong to Sarah, and he could trace the most likely route back over the mountain . . .

Stop it! He told himself. You are being absurd. We are talking about a crime that happened twenty-five years ago. Nothing will remain. No evidence. Nothing. But still he couldn't give up. As he drove through Llanfair, the children were out on the playground with Bronwen. He watched as they held hands and danced around in a circle, playing some kind of singing game as Bronwen clapped. Some of the little girls had long hair that blew out behind them as they skipped, so lightly that their feet barely made contact with the ground . . . just like Sarah. Now that the memory had been reawakened, he was never going to be able to put her out of his mind again. And if it was Richard Gwynne who'd buried her at the cottage gate, he owed it to Sarah to prove him guilty.

He pulled the car to a halt and started the steep climb up to the cottage. The crime-scene tape had been removed from the hole that had been dug, and water had seeped into the bottom. Evan squatted, staring at his reflection in the muddy water. Footprints. Gwynne must have worn boots, and the crime squad must have found footprints on the other side of the mountain. Did they take any casts? He'd go back to Superintendent Meredith and quiz him again.

He jumped a mile as he saw a face appear above his in the reflection and nearly lost his balance as he scrambled to his feet. He was surprised to see Daft Dai standing there, staring down at the hole.

"What are you doing up here, Dai?" Evan asked. "How did you get up here from Porthmadog?"

"The bus," Dai said. "The bus driver knows me. He lets me ride for nothing."

"That's good, isn't it?" Evan said. "Now if you don't mind, Dai. I'm rather busy at the moment."

"She's gone then, has she?" Dai asked. "They came and took her away?"

Evan looked at Dai's innocent, childish face. "Now how did you hear about this?"

"It was in the paper," Dai said. "I heard Mrs Presli talking with the milkman. They were saying that the same man had probably taken the two little girls, but they were wrong."

"Yes, they were," Evan said, "but how did you know?"

"Because it was me," Dai said, his face still soft and innocent, devoid of frown lines.

Evan smiled at Dai. "Come on, Dai. You know it wasn't you. You're just saying that because you like to go to the police station and have a cup of tea and a bun, aren't you?"

"No, it really was me. I buried her here."

"I'm sure you didn't, Dai." Evan was still smiling. He remembered his first encounter with Daft Dai as the locals called him. He'd claimed to have killed two men who had fallen to their deaths on Mount Snowdon. In those days, when Dai's mother was still alive, he lived with her somewhere in the area and roamed the mountains — when he wasn't locked up for a spell in a mental institution. It turned out, of course, that he had had nothing to do with the deaths.

"You've never killed anyone, have you, Dai?" Evan said kindly. "You aren't the kind of person who'd want to hurt anybody."

Dai shook his head violently. "I didn't say I killed her," Dai said, "but I was the one who buried her. She needed a proper burial, didn't she?"

Evan stopped smiling and stared at the little man. He was gazing up at Evan with his soft, childish eyes. "Why did she need a proper burial, Dai?" he asked gently.

"Everyone has to be buried properly, don't they, or they don't go to heaven."

"What did she look like — this little girl you buried, Dai?"

"Pretty," Dai said. "Pretty hair, and pretty shoes, too. She had flowers on her shoes."

"And was she wearing a skirt with flowers on it, too? A red skirt?"

"That's right. Did you know her?"

"Yes," Evan said. "I knew her. Did you know her too?"

"No. I didn't know who she was, or I'd have given her back to them. That's why I buried her myself."

Evan could hardly get the words out. "Where did you find her, Dai?"

"Up there. The other side of the mountain," Dai said. "Up above Llyn Ogwen. Do you know where that is? Over on the other side." He named the lake beside the road just above the Thomas farmhouse.

"And — and was she dead when you found her then?" Evan could hardly bring himself to say the words.

"Of course she was. Been dead for some time, I reckon."

"Would you tell me all about it?"

"Am I going to get in trouble?" Dai asked.

"I don't think so. But we could go to the police station, and you'd get a cup of tea and a bun if you tell me the whole story."

"*O'r gore*. Let's go then."

"You can tell me the story first, Dai. Then we'll go and get the bun," Evan said, trying not to show his impatience, "then you can tell it to the other policemen again when you've had your tea."

Dai nodded. "I was walking up in the hills up there, the way I always did those days. I used to live up there with my mother, you know. She's dead now. Did you know that my mother died?"

"Yes, I heard, Dai. I'm sorry," Evan said.

"I miss her. It's lonely without her, but Mrs Presli is nice to me. She lets me use her binoculars sometimes."

"I'm glad for you. Now go on with the story."

"When you get to the high part, just before you'd go to the top of Glyder Fach — do you know that hill? Right before it gets steep?"

"Yes, I know it," Evan said. "Just before you go to the top of Glyder Fach."

"It's boggy up there, isn't it?" Dai asked.

"Yes, I seem to remember it's pretty boggy."

"Well, that's where she was. It had rained a lot that year, and it wasn't just boggy — there was a proper little pond in the middle of the bog. Well, I was walking past and I looked across, look you, and I saw this hand. I couldn't believe my eyes. There was this hand coming out of the bog. For a moment I thought it was waving at me. Of course I thought it was one of the Tylwyth Teg beckoning me, so I wasn't going to have anything to do with it, cos they take you down to their kingdom forever if they catch you, don't they?"

He paused for Evan to nod in confirmation.

"Well, I didn't want to be taken down to their kingdom forever. But then I got curious because it didn't move or anything, and I wondered if I'd made a mistake and it wasn't really a hand, so I went to see. It was very boggy. I had to be careful, or I would have sunk in myself. I had a terrible job getting her out."

"I bet you did."

"And it turned out to be this little girl. She was already dead, you know. I couldn't bring her back to life. I didn't want to leave her up there, where the foxes might get her. I didn't know who she was. So I thought I'd carry her down to the nearest police station. I knew there was a police station in Llanfair. You weren't the policeman there in those days, were you?"

"No, Dai. Not in those days."

"I thought not."

"Tell me more about the little girl, Dai."

"She was heavy, you know. She didn't look as if she'd be heavy cos she was only a little thing, but she was. I was sweating like a pig by the time I got her to Llanfair. Then I remembered that I'd been in trouble with the policeman. He said I'd been looking in windows and if I did it again, I'd go to prison. So I got scared. The policeman might think that I killed her. I didn't want to go to prison. So I decided not to tell anyone. Someone had been digging holes outside this cottage, and they'd left one of their spades behind. So you know what I did? I dug the earth out again, and then I gave her a lovely burial. I picked flowers to put all around her and I laid her out nicely. Then I said all the prayers I knew and I sang 'Calon Lan'."

"And you never told anybody, not even your mother?"

Dai shook his head. "I didn't want to get in trouble. You're sure I won't get in trouble now?"

"No, Dai. You won't get in trouble," Evan said.

* * *

Later that day Evan drove to the Thomases' farm. The old man listened attentively, his face wrinkled with concentration as Evan spoke. Then he nodded politely.

"Thank you for coming to tell me, young man. We're much obliged to you. It's good to know she didn't suffer too much." He cleared his throat gruffly.

"I presume your family members have all gone home by now," Evan said. "Will you be calling them?"

"I'd rather it came from you, if you don't mind," old Tomos Thomas said. "I'd rather not talk about it if I don't have to. She was very dear to me, you see. A very special child. The light of my life and when she went . . ." He turned away abruptly. "Thank you for coming, young man. Now, if you don't mind, I've got sheep to see to."

Evan watched as he stomped away, his hands thrust deep into his pockets.

* * *

"So she got trapped in a bog and drowned," Henry Bosley-Thomas said, after Evan had phoned to give him the news. "Where was this again?"

"In the high country, on the way up to the Glyders."

"My God. What was she doing up there?"

"Perhaps she wandered off and got disoriented," Evan said.

"But she'd never have gone that far alone. Someone must have taken her up there and abandoned her. Perhaps someone threw her in the bog."

"I think it was just a horrible accident, Henry. She wandered off. She was very persistent when she wanted to be."

"Yes. Very stubborn."

"At least it must be a relief to you to know," Evan said.

"A relief? Do you know what you've just done to me?" Henry's voice was bitter. "You've condemned me to hell for life."

"But why? It wasn't your fault."

"Of course it was my bloody fault." The words resounded in Evan's ear. "I was in charge of her. I was supposed to take care of her. I cared more about winning a stupid game than looking after my sister. I've had to carry that guilt around for my whole life. I really hoped that someone had snatched her away because then I could have argued that he was bigger than me. I was just a boy. There was nothing I could have done to save her. But it was all my fault after all."

"You were a child, Henry. You thought like any child would. You can't be blamed."

"I blame me. My wife thinks I did it, you know. Because of the guilt, I suppose. She really believes in her heart that I killed Sarah. That's why she won't have kids — just in case. My wife, who is supposed to be the one person I can trust and turn to." He paused then asked. "So you don't think one of us would have had time to take her up there and push her in a bog?"

"No, I don't."

"I told you I saw Suzanne going down, didn't I?"

"Henry, Suzanne won the game, remember. And she would never have done a thing like that. Your own sister."

"You're right. This has driven us all crazy — made us think things we should never have thought. Of course Suzanne has paid, too. A ruined life. All of us have paid. Will you call her for me?"

"Suzanne?"

"Yes. Call her and tell her the news?"

"I think you should do that," Evan said. "And while you're at it, you might apologize."

"You mean because I suspected she had something to do with Sarah's disappearance?"

"That and other things, I'd imagine."

Henry sighed. "You're right. I — we all made Suzanne pay for not being Sarah."

CHAPTER 32

A blustery week mellowed into a mild, soft weekend, with cotton wool clouds and a good amount of sun. Evan had finally received a communication from the inspector of listed buildings and met him up at the cottage on Saturday afternoon.

"So what do you think?" Evan asked, as he stood beside the shell of his future cottage.

The scholarly little man continued to stare, frowning with concentration. He wore round wire glasses, which managed to look hip on rock stars and beautiful people but made him look like an aged Billy Bunter, the prep-school nerd.

"What do I think?" he echoed. "If you want to know what I think, I think it's an old ruin and not worth rebuilding."

"So you don't think it's a historical building that has to be grade two listed?"

"Good Lord, no. Probably no older than mid-eighteen-hundreds," the man said. "Who told you it should be listed?"

"Mr Pilcher, from the National Parks."

"Those blokes — pen-pushers, the lot of them. They wouldn't know a listed building if it jumped up and bit them."

Evan grinned. "So you see no reason why permission should not be given to rebuild this place."

"I'd recommend that you tear it down and start again, young man," the man said, "but you do what you like. I'm certainly not about to list every shepherd's cottage in Snowdonia."

Evan shook his hand. "Thank you very much. You've made my day."

* * *

That evening he took Bronwen to the Red Dragon for a celebration drink.

"You've been staying away, haven't you, Evan *bach*," Betsy said, looking around him to give Bronwen a lukewarm smile. "Too busy with other things, I suppose."

"I do have a job, Betsy. Now that I'm in the plainclothes branch, I don't have regular hours anymore."

"Did Miss Price tell you I paid you a visit the other night?" Betsy asked, making Evan instantly hot around the collar. "I wanted to show you my new outfit, but you weren't there. I wanted to get a man's opinion, look you. Barry says I've got good legs and a good figure, but he doesn't like me to be too revealing, do you, Barry-my-love?"

Barry looked up from his conversation at the far end of the bar.

"I'll make mincemeat of any man I find ogling you. I've made that very clear." He went back to his drink.

Betsy turned back to Evan and Bronwen. "Luckily for me, I could see that Miss Price didn't think much of the outfit, so I took it back. I like to keep him on his toes, but I don't want him to go around punching anyone."

She grinned. Evan gave Bronwen a glance and was pleased to see that she blushed. He handed her a glass of chardonnay, and they went to join the group by the fire.

"I saw you coming down the mountain with some bloke this afternoon," Evans-the-Meat said. "Not another of these forensic people, I hope."

"No, that's all finished with. We know who the little girl was, and we know how she died."

"I hope you've got the bastard," Charlie Hopkins said.

"There was no bastard. Just a tragic accident. She wandered into a bog."

"Then who buried her?"

"Daft Dai. He thought he was being helpful."

"Daft Dai. We should have thought of him?" Charlie said. "Of all the stupid things . . ."

"So who was the old chap up there today, Evan?" Evans-the-Meat insisted.

"The listed buildings inspector, taking a look at my cottage. He says it's nothing special and as far as he's concerned, I can do what I like with it, so I'm going to press Mr Pilcher to give me my planning permission on Monday."

"Mr Pilcher!" Mr Owens almost spat out the words. "Don't mention that *hen diawl*'s name to me."

"Is he still giving you grief about your barn, Mr Owens?" Evan asked.

"Giving me grief? Driving me crazy, that's what he's doing." Bill Owens glared at the assembled crowd. "He was back at my place last week, and you know what he told me? He said I could finish my new barn, but I'd have to paint it green so that it blended in well with the grass."

"Paint it green?" There was general laughter.

"What did you say, Bill? Are you going to do it?" Charlie Hopkins asked.

"I told him it was the daftest thing I'd ever heard. And what about when it snows? I asked him. Do you want me to nip out and bloody well paint it white?"

* * *

The next day Evan and Bronwen drove to Llyn Ogwen, then parked and hiked up the hill. The Thomases' farm spread out below them. The lake glittered in the morning sun. Larks sang, as they rose in the warm air.

"This is lovely," Bronwen stopped to admire the view. "I'm so glad we're doing this. It's been ages since we've had a day off to take a walk."

Evan watched her standing there relaxed and happy, wisps of ash blonde hair blowing around her face.

"I'm glad you're here with me," he said. "I felt I had to come here again, just to see for myself, and to share it with you."

They continued to climb, up a narrow gully, shaded by oak and ash trees. "This was the big oak tree," Evan said, as they came out to upland meadow. "We always left our snacks here when we played the game. And that's the hill where we played capture the castle."

Bronwen looked up at it and nodded with approval. "It does look like a fortress with all those rocks. I bet you had fun here."

Evan turned away from it and followed just the hint of a path upward, beside a little stream. Trees grew beside the water, shading them as they climbed. The clear splash and tinkle of the water as it bounced and fell over rocks were a musical accompaniment. It was hot and sweaty, sheltered from the breeze. Evan marvelled that Sarah had dared to come this far alone. Then the last of the trees died out, and the little stream meandered across a high, bleak plateau with a ring of mountains rising ahead. The first of the heather was blooming, painting the slopes purple. The path, such as it was, disappeared into an area of tufty grass, soft and springy underfoot.

"Are you sure she came up here?" Bronwen asked. "It's an awfully long way for a small child."

It became damp underfoot as the stream spread into marsh. Their feet came free with a sucking sound at each footfall. Then Evan came to a sudden halt. "Oh," he said.

"What?"

He continued to stare. Ahead of them was a small, round pond. Mist rose from its surface, drawn upward by the sun. The area around it was bright green — a green so glaringly bright that it dazzled. A lump came to Evan's throat. The fairy ring, where the grass was greener, the magic lake. Of course she would have thought she'd found the Tylwyth Teg at last, not knowing that the bright green grass was a warning sign, not an invitation, and the magic lake was a bog. If he hadn't refused her when she'd wanted to sneak away with him, if he'd been less intent on winning that stupid game, she'd never have come up here alone. He had pitied the Thomases for the guilt they had carried throughout their lives and hadn't realized until now that he shared that guilt with them. From now on he would be carrying the same burden as them wherever he went.

"Was this it?" Bronwen asked.

Evan continued to stare at the shimmering water. "I was right all along," he said, in a low voice. "She was taken by the fairies."

THE END

ACKNOWLEDGEMENTS

I have several people to thank for their help with this book.

First, my buddy Paul Henshaw of the South Wales Police, who was kind enough to answer my questions yet again and put me on to DI Chris Parsons of the South Wales Police, who filled me in on child abduction in the United Kingdom.

Dr P Willey, professor of forensic anthropology at Chico State University, graciously gave of his time and attempted to set me straight on identifying and dating a skeleton.

And as usual Clare, Jane, and John gave me their brilliant insights.

* * *

This book is dedicated to Jane Finnis, my friend of forty years (yes, we were infants when we met). She has been my songwriting partner, the other half of my cabaret duo, my fount of information on the National Parks Service, and now she joins me in my current career with the publication of her first mystery novel.

* * *

Also, a special word of dedication to Jan Telesky, who was the high bidder in a charity auction of the English Speaking Union and thus won the right to appear in this book. I hope she approves of herself and I'm only sorry I couldn't find a way to bring in her ballroom dancing prowess. You know what a poor dancer Evan is!

ALSO BY RHYS BOWEN

CONSTABLE EVAN EVANS SERIES

Book 1: EVAN ABOVE
Book 2: EVAN HELP US
Book 3: EVANLY CHOIRS
Book 4: EVAN AND ELLE
Book 5: EVAN CAN WAIT
Book 6: EVANS TO BETSY
Book 7: EVAN ONLY KNOWS
Book 8: EVAN'S GATE

Thank you for reading this book.

If you enjoyed it please leave feedback on Amazon or Goodreads, and if there is anything we missed or you have a question about, then please get in touch. We appreciate you choosing our book.

Founded in 2014 in Shoreditch, London, we at Joffe Books pride ourselves on our history of innovative publishing. We were thrilled to be shortlisted for Independent Publisher of the Year at the British Book Awards.

www.joffebooks.com

We're very grateful to eagle-eyed readers who take the time to contact us. Please send any errors you find to corrections@joffebooks.com. We'll get them fixed ASAP.

Printed in Dunstable, United Kingdom

72143133R00160